THE TOFFEE MAN AND THE KINGDOM OF ENDS

by LK QUINN

All characters, other than those clearly in the public domain, and place names, other than those well-established such as towns and cities, are fictitious and any resemblance is purely coincidental.

Published by New Generation Publishing in 2025

Copyright © LK QUINN 2025

First Edition

The author asserts the moral right under the Copyright, Designs and Patents Act 1988 to be identified as the author of this work.

All Rights reserved. No part of this publication may be reproduced, stored in a retrieval system or transmitted, in any form or by any means without the prior consent of the author, nor be otherwise circulated in any form of binding or cover other than that which it is published and without a similar condition being imposed on the subsequent purchaser.

ISBN: 978-1-83563-344-1

www.newgeneration-publishing.com

New Generation Publishing

For Anita

The **Book**Challenge
WHAT'S YOUR STORY?

This book has been supported by
The London Borough of Barking and
Dagenham Library Service - Pen to Print
Creative Writing Programme.
Pen to Print is funded by Arts Council, England
as a National Portfolio Organisation.

Pen to **Print**
WHAT'S YOUR STORY?

Connect with Pen to Print
Email: pentoprint@lbbd.gov.uk
Web: pentoprint.org

ARTS COUNCIL ENGLAND

Funded by UK Government

Barking & Dagenham

Chapter 1

The film is finished and the tall red velvet curtains are swished across the screen. We are up from our seats and we get to dance. On the stage. I stand between where the red velvet meets and wave them gently – they ripple up, up into the dark and I get dragged up into the wind of it - up into space like Apollo on the news. The dust showers into the beams of light on stage and I am racing through the planets chased by Aliens.

If I can make it to the moon, I can save the world.

But the woman with the ice cream tray pushes the curtain away from me and smiles. "Jubbly, Fab or Tub?" I say the words silently, and again, and again. I dance my arms like an engine, "Jubbly, Fab or Tub, Jubbly, Fab or Tub, Jubbly, Fab or Tub," until she laughs.

"Not today M'am," I say in a space mission voice. "I got some mean aliens on my back," and I zoom onto the stage shouting, "Jubblyfabortub," spinning through all the other kids and my bag flares out so I press it to me until I get to the other side and down the steps. Now I've escaped I feel for my gobstopper, and check nothing fell out.

I don't want ice cream anyway. I didn't get enough money back off the bottles this week. Gloria couldn't help this time. She usually finds loads of them outside the pub and along the big roads. I go along the canal and under the bridges and find some good ones, from picnics and boozers. When we cash them in, they have to be clean, so we drag the bags in the river on the way to the shop. When we're over the road, we sit behind the wall until it opens and have a laugh. When she turns the sign, we straighten up and carry the bag up to the counter between us with the clinking bottles. Mrs Smith is always sorting the papers out.

I was on my own today and when I started to explain, Mrs Smith said she knew all about the travellers moving. She said she wanted to talk straight with me, "Gloria got you wandering off into town I know. Your mum wouldn't like it April. It won't be me, but sooner or later she'll hear about it." Itchy itchy chin. "I don't suppose her lot mind," she says as she gets the crates from the back, and then speaks more kind, "I mean, Gloria being a bit older." I count the bottles into the crate. Mrs Smith gives me the money. "If you ever want to help your mum out, I could take it off her credit. Our secret." I nod. But I'm keeping today's money. Maybe Gloria's right - she says Mrs Smith gets narked because we don't spend the refund at her shop, but she wouldn't put a curse on her because Mrs Smith always says we are helping out nature in the long run. Gloria works out the money before we get there, and she's polite, but she says people are careful of the curses. We always have enough for ice cream.

Anyway, Gloria's family are leaving this afternoon because they didn't get council permission. She had to go out round the villages all week doing lucky flowers and fortunes with her mum, so they could get money to move on. Her mum says she's got the gift of the gab, but her dad says it is empty jugs make the most noise.

I liked doing stuff with a girl, it's mainly boys on the caravan site. Mum says it's because the council are more likely to give you a house if you've got a baby girl, except if you're already walking like I was, then God gave her four boys after me, so he wasn't helping either.

Gloria can't read or write even though she's older than me. She's never been to school. She said she's never even seen inside the door of a classroom, but she sings me all the songs and tells me all the stories of people though, just from remembering. And she's taught me about making anything you want out of stuff people throw away, so it don't get wasted. Like, unravelling old jumpers for knitting and weaving new things, and how to make a carpet with little bits of rag.

All the people that pay the rent are on a hardstand from the council because we got to go to school, and we get our own toilet in the block. Mum said that slab of concrete gives you rights. We don't take our van on the road. It's probably because mum can't drive, and Dad has to go to court a lot, so he's away for ages sometimes.

I won't go to town on my own from now. I need to help mum. It's annoying because I made an adventure map like the books. Even though I know the way quite easy, I made a map to get here and back, and some of the places I explored. Today though, I go round the corner and down the alleyway, over the bridge, and along the towpath which goes right past our field. I've got my pinhole camera glasses on, with my pirate patch. Pinhole glasses only really work with one eye. You have to walk carefully and think about what you want to look at. You can't go fast. It's like seeing a film of your life, only better because you are in it at the same time, and you get fizzy, and smell all the smells and feel the whole world like hundreds of bubbles popping on your skin.

When I get to the footbridge, I sit on the steps and get my gobstopper in my mouth and get my notebook out to write some ideas. The canal is an olden secret road to our field, but it's miles before and after. In the past when there wasn't cars, barges came right along to the old port to do the deliveries and take stuff away. It's closed down now. Only a little boat could be on it now. Our teacher said that when something's not cared for anymore, nature just takes its course. In the summer all the ducks and fish and rats just break through the green surface and leave dark mouths just wide enough to bite a piece of sky before they slowly close.

I like the skyroads after the rainstorms better. The potholes and ruts along the tracks and paths get filled with sky. To run along the skyroads barefoot is like being on a magic carpet, splashing through the clouds and sparkling sun above the treetops, or on a clear night like you're up in the moon and stars. When it's hot, the puddle water jumps up your legs and into your clothes and laughs with you as you smack and stamp your feet into the ground. The best way to run through skyroads is with your jellybean sandals so your feet don't hurt on the sharp stones. Or glass. I cut my foot once. I stopped still. I watched the blood twist and curl around the water like a genie from a lamp. Like red ribbons on a glory day twirling in the wind, until they disappeared. I wanted to do it again, but the cut took ages to get better. I had to walk squelching in blood like it was normal, because Mum would have got mad at me about being stupid and not wearing my sandals.

The canal is more scary though. Now, it's full of sky and islands of duckweed. Sometimes creatures squeak and squawk in the reeds, or scratch and flap, echoing in the bare branches. Then they frighten each other. They can't hide or get muffled in the leaves anymore because the trees are bare from the tree disease. Most of the leaves went brown and fell off before summer. It's like it is always nearly winter now, until they are dead. Things get more beautiful when they are about to die. Saying goodbye. I lie down on the bank and look through the trees with my glasses, so I can focus on different parts. I read a book that said the idea 'the unexamined life is not worth living', which means if you don't look carefully at life you shouldn't bother to have one. I don't understand all the words, but I am learning them. And also, I have to keep it secret, but I have the biggest load of books you ever saw, and they are not kids' books either.

Over the track from our caravan site, next to the riverbank, is the old tin Tabernacle. They use it to store the old books and newspapers until they get pulped. It's all got a high fence covered in weeds. They haven't used it since the war because too many people got lost from God. My teacher said the books won't get wasted, and they will all get made into new books, but I think nobody cares if I use them again first. Anyway, they keep bringing them, but they don't take them to get made new yet.

You wouldn't notice it unless I showed you in, or you were the van driver with the keys to the gates. Even though it's really high, it's got lots of trees by it, and it's all made of corrugated iron painted in green, and it's rusty where the paint is getting dried and broken off.

Outside the fence, there is loads of stingers up to my ribs, and they go from the track up to the high fence of green leaves. The gate is padlocked, but I found a way in round the back, off the track. I held a sack to protect me so I could jump and stamp a path through the nettles in a zig zag. Us older kids, and the house kids from up the hill, play in the old canal port buildings, but just in case I did the path zig zag so people didn't see where it went. I dug a hole under the wire fence to get through easy, and then I covered it with the sack and put it over the dirt. I can bend the fence back a bit, enough to crawl under, and then roll up the sack and tuck it by the side for coming back. I don't mind if I catch a few stings off the nettles. There's a way in the back from the river path, but I don't want no one following me. I saw a film at cinema club where a spy did it.

When it's breezy the Tabernacle sounds like a big old giant with clapping bones. The walls creak and crack and wheeze from the wind and whistle sad songs through the holes. You can see across the flat of the meadow from the riverbank and the other way to the lane and the gate into our field. It's even better when you get inside. I go through the side door, hid by the brambles, it's got a broken bolt, so I can lift it a bit and push in when I want. There are windows above the massive doors, and on the inside, there are stairs you can go up and see out like it's a castle looking over onto the woods and fields on the hills. The windows got loads of dust, so I just rubbed little bits clean to look out.

All the benches and prayer stuff are inside pushed up around the walls, and there is still coloured glass shapes in all the windows. It's not pictures like the church up the road, but inside where the sun shines through it makes rainbow arrows, firing at the books I should go and look at. I choose two colours before I go in, so I can choose in case the first colour is right at the bottom and I have to wait until another time, but I am usually at school when the sun shines the colour right down.

The stacks grow and change when they dump a new lot. I can climb the stacks of newspapers and books tied in bundles, like bricks, and on top I can make dens. Once they came when I was there, but they couldn't see me up in my cubbyhole. I make my cubbies away from the leaks, but it's nice when it rains and you hear it on the roof, and it echoes inside, and you can watch streams of water pour through the holes like shining wands running into the books, waking up the worlds. There are so many books and papers, so many words. I can't believe that there is so much writing and they will throw it all away. I found a big fat dictionary, which tells you words when you don't know them, so you can get the code. It's tiny writing, but I got my Lucky Bag glass and I keep it on a string under my jumper. I can't always understand the words that tell you about the words. I don't mind, even when you don't know them in your head, saying words, all my body knows it - feeling the air come in and out of your body - making shapes on your lips and tingles on your tongue. It is the best feeling in the world. And I am making a message for the Aliens in case we get attention now we are sending rockets.

I don't go down by the altar though, or in the vestry. I think it might be a sin to go in if you don't get invited. Anyway, I hear noises in there sometimes, but Gloria said most weird noises are just birds, or rats. I think about it too much. And even she said we shouldn't go in a church - it's probably cursed by the dead - but she don't care about God.

Time to get back. I put my gobstopper back in the bag. The sun is at the top of the trees now. Crows are filling the branches. They swoop off all together to twist and turn in the sky and bring more into the flock to land again, until the tree is shivering with them from top to bottom watching the canal for food. Rats are swimming out of the way to hide in the bank. I jump up and run across the bridge at the old lock that leads into the field just before the caravan site, so I can get across to the river and have a go on the tree swing if no one else is there. Saturday is the one day I tell one lie on purpose, which is about going to the cinema club. Mum would say no. I always say I'm going to play on the river. So it helps.

Through the trees I can see most of the travellers have already gone, there's just a couple of vans and trucks out on the track. They made a big bonfire last night, and we all had pop and cider. After us kids got sent to bed, they carried on dancing and singing songs about broken hearts and finding love. You could hear the echoes of the sounds everywhere, rolling back from the hills across the meadow, like the valleys and the stars in space were joining in. I sat on Mum and Dad's bed so I could watch out the window. I saw Dad wander off, and Gloria ran after him with a bottle of booze. She came back and sang with everyone, but dad just disappeared. He hates singing.

I expect Gloria's still here, helping her mum pack the last things. I'm not sure if she wants to say goodbye again. She said it's bad luck. We wished each other luck on a stone, and she threw it in the river. She said she likes me but it's just time to move on.

Now, I can hear angry voices. I know that one. I run along the river and climb over the stile. Oh no, I can see Mum. A police car has come. There're people coming from the houses up the hill, and off the site.

Dad is standing there, in the middle of it all, stealing a look of everyone with that stupid grin on his face, one hand leaning on a pickaxe and the other combing his quiff through with his fingers. What's going on? I run to Mum. She's just staring at Dad, snivelling really bad. I stretch my hands round her cold fist and slip my fingers into the dips between her knuckles. Her fist opens. I flip my hand into hers, and I can feel the twitch of her hand, of me warming her.

Some of Dad's mates try to take the pickaxe from him, but he yanks it back and grins, whilst he pushes them away to make space. He spits in his hands and takes the handle and swings it over his head, and back down into the pipe. There is a big crack. The crows explode from the trees, and the water reaches for them, high into the grey sky. Up and up, out and out, like a gigantic glittering Angel had come ... and everyone breathes in altogether, mouths wide open, like a whisper in a dream, 'We'd forgotten the sky was so far.' For a moment it seems like the world stops. It is still. Forever. All the air inside us. Then the Angel falls like angry rain, and everyone is soaking wet. Screaming.

The police jump over the gate. Everyone here is running to their caravans. Mum is chasing the police, who are chasing Dad, the other way. He still has the pickaxe.

I pick up Luke and Matthew and Mark drags John, and we run to the van and slam the door shut. The bed is still out, so we get over to the window and watch. It is hard to see because everyone is shouting and cheering round the other side. I go to the end window and look out and see Gloria over the fence, clapping and jumping up and down with her skirts bouncing over her shiny white boots, "Come on Andy! I'll give you a leg up the tree."

Her Dad grabs her hair and tells her to shut her gob and get in the van, and shouts at Dad, "Andy, do you want a lift?" Dad pelts across and tries to reach the truck in time, but he trips over the logs by the fire pit from last night. He rolls over and grabs the squirrel bones and throws them at the police; they're all covered in ashes.

The police get Dad, and they pull him up. He is laughing, and he winks at us like usual as they march him past the window. Mum comes storming behind, and picks up a corona bottle from the bin, and smashes the end of it on the concrete. We all press up against the window to see. It is jagged and sharp like a big knife. I've never seen Mum smashing stuff before. She has lost the fear of God. She is waving it in the air as she catches up and says they'd better leave him alone. I can't get breathing.

She isn't far from us now. I shout out to her, please God change her mind. She can't hear me. The policeman with sideburns reaches from behind her. He snatches her arm with the bottle in it, and she falls on her back. He drops beside her. Holds her arm to the ground with his knee, until she lets go. He says she'll thank him for that one day. She won't. She shouts, "Fucking pig".

He says, "Calm down and get inside, if you know what's good for you, and your kids." She spits at him and tries to pull away, as she takes a swing at his head and knocks his hat off. The twins start screaming for Mum, and Matthew bangs his fists on the window like a drum, "Pig! Pig! Pig!" and Mark joins in. It's like the song of this place, and I know it. I join in too.

The policeman just stays still, and keeps saying her name really nicely, "Mrs. Smart. Mrs. Smart. Mrs. Smart. I want you to calm down." He just keeps saying it like he really wants her to be calm. Not winding her up for a laugh like Dad. He is waiting for her to get tired of shouting, but us kids are quiet first. All of us just watching. Inside me it felt like bubbles were bursting, popping like the tick tock, and rushing through my ears. He turns and looks up at us. And I think because I am the biggest, he looks at me and smiles, and I can feel he doesn't want us to feel bad and scared. I can feel the warm of a tear come down my face. I suck my cheek and crunch it in my teeth, so I can taste the strong of the blood; like when I get gold stars on my work. And we watch until she is quiet. And then he turns and holds out his hand like a prince to help Mum get up. He is still on his knees. And the song from school is in my mind: The princess slept for a hundred years. A hundred years… and that is the song of love for my mum now. She takes his hand and looks around like she had just woken up at last, and she realises, as she pulls her frilly nightdress over her knickers. And I wish I could roll back the day and make it different.

She doesn't turn around as she comes back in. She punches the wall of the van before she comes up the steps. It shakes, and Luke jumps and cries. She says she is sick and tired of trying to do the right thing, and Dad will probably go to prison now because he broke his parole. The policeman opens the gate, and I watch them get Dad in the car, and they do a report on the radio before they drive off. I do a sneaky smile, and I make a funny face at Luke, and he stops crying. When Matthew takes the boys back out to play, I make her a cup of tea. I tell her she is better when Dad's in prison. I was thinking it might make her feel nice, but she said she'll break my neck if she hears any more talk like that; Dad was actually nicking clothes off the lines last night for us kids. She said, "Them people got filthy minds. Disgusting talk."

Well so what, Dad likes Gloria better than Mum. He's always teasing her and laughing at her stupid jokes. She told me he gives her secret booze, and they have some fun, because she's thirteen. I'm only ten, and I can't take my drink yet. We used to go and sit on the bank of the river round the back of the old tin Tabernacle when it was warm, under the tree, and away from the stink of the canal. One time, she gave me some of her mum's booze, and she said my face was a picture. But she said I'll grow into it when I get tits. She can drink anything. She's got tits coming already. She showed me. They're not that big yet, just purple lumps, but she said they always get big white ones in her family. Then she asked me to nick some of Mum's sherry next time, because Dad said that Hope had some decent stuff; Gloria thinks Mum is posh because she grew up in a house.

Gloria was all excited the next time when I got it for her; we climbed up the bank, and she laid on the grass, glugging the bottle half empty. I just laughed when she offered me a swig. I didn't want it; I'd put my piss into a panda pop bottle and mixed it with sugar and some old medicine. Gloria couldn't even tell the difference.

Chapter 2

We're on our own now. Sometimes we see people through the skeleton trees walking along the paths of the river or canal, but only the birds come in our field. I made the deal with Mrs Smith at the paper shop that if I took the bottles to her, she would slip in a packet of fags for the returns. It hasn't stopped mum cadging fags off people she doesn't know when she goes up on the road and keeping an eye out for dog ends to make rollies.

Our caravan site got in the newspaper, and mum said that's why Dad got more attention in court. They sent him right off to prison. Mum said we're not to talk about it with anyone because he might get out on parole. But at least some good come of it, because the council have sent everyone to a house now. We have to wait until there's one big enough for us, because mum had the most kids, and I have to have a room to myself. It's the law. They said we could go to a hostel while we wait for something, but mum said no, that would be it. They would break us up.

The council took the empty caravans away the week after people got moved, and the whole field is ours. Mum's glad they cleared it because we might get hippies and squatters in. The others left loads of boxes and bags of stuff for us. Mum made the council take most of it, because it was junk, but she said I could keep some clothes and old sheets and blankets to make dens with, and I sneaked some for my cubby.

I used all the fallen branches from the trees for poles. We used wires and safety pins to put old dresses and shirts together for sails. I sneaked some things for the cubby in my church. It's harder to keep out of Mum's sight now everyone's gone. If she finds out about me going in the old tin Tabernacle, I know she won't let me do it anymore in case we get trouble from the council. She definitely wouldn't let me take any books out of there because she don't want more trouble. When I read one at home, I pretend it's from school. But the teacher won't even look at my face and said, it's best if I don't take books home. I think I would get nerves about it too. Anyway, I think my Tabernacle books are more interesting. There aren't so many pictures, but there are maps. And, I found a giant map of the moon. It might be lost from a spy who was hiding there, because it has all the secret paths on it and words like a moon language, but I have found a book from long ago that tells you what they say.

Me and Matthew made tents and sails on the empty hardstands. We used the old barrels, bikes and prams to stand the branches into, and now it's palaces and ships. We are pirates on the moon sea protecting our van ship left on the shore of trees, and returning to our treasure chest, in disguise as a broken car along the end splatted with bird poo. Everyone has a ship, and I made some signs so they can choose which one. They are places I copied from the moon map, and I tell them about the idea of it. Matthew wants to be the Oceanus Procellarum because it is the biggest, and it is storms, so Mark is going to be Mare Imbrium which is the big Sea of Rain next to him. I'm going to be all the ones from underneath up to the top, Tranquillatis, Serenatis, to where Mum is in Lacus Spei, because that is the Lake of Hope, at the top of the moon, and we are following her up and over the hill to the mystery of the far side. Luke and John will just come in my lands most of the time. They can't remember the names anyway, and even Mum likes being in our seas the best. I need a secret name for the old tin Tabernacle, but I can't think of it yet.

The council sent an advice woman. Mum said she'll be looking for excuses to put us in a hostel, which is like a prison for families, so we had to show our best side and clear everything up. She didn't come in the door, but we had to move the steps along to the windows so she could get up and look in, and she said she could see it was a bit cramped. She didn't count we got the whole toilet block just next to us. Mum said to keep quiet about that. They'd count it as luxury. It's easier to dry the washing now we got the whole lot. We got lines inside every one of them, and we can close the door because the gap at the top lets the wind in but it's dry. I asked Mrs Smith for the old wooden crates to put over the toilet seats, so we could hide our ship sails, and even coats and shoes.

The shower room at the end of the block is really freezing now though. Mum puts the paraffin heater in for a while, and then two-bob for the electric when we go in, so we get a long time of really hot water. Mum plays tag with us all in the steam clouds and I like it because we sing and it echoes on the walls, making up words of our own that almost sound the same, but they are not. We use the whisk to make the biggest load of bubbles in the sink, and we put them on our heads and balance it, and then we run across to the van and the one who keeps it on to last is the winner and it's their turn to share the chocolate buttons when we get rubbed down and dressed. And we play, all pink and warm, and mum gets tea from the chip van, which stops on the top road by the shop every week. And then we pull mum's bed down from the wall and put the radio on to get Luke and John to sleep, and then we put the table down and make the bed for me, Matthew and Mark. We top and tail, and I look up through the skylight into the stars, listening to the owls and frogs, and the boys revving cars over my feet. It tickles, and I want to laugh, but I keep dead still. I want it to stay like this forever.

In the early morning light, I watch the rain sliding over the window, and the music as it patters quick and slow around the walls and over the roof of the van as the wind blows this way and that and whistles through the wheels underneath. The mould is spreading across the ceiling, like black stars on the yellow paint, they're coming down the wall, and I join them dot to dot and find the pictures as the light comes. The sky is like the bed of Princess and the Pea, the clouds pile up like lumpy mattresses, leaking sheets of purple and red that hang down between, and the golden pea of the sun between will come to wake us. I need a wee, so I pull Mum's cardigan on over my pyjamas, and I go out to the block. I keep the toilet door open and watch the valley mist rolling and rising around the field. It's over my knees. Nobody is awake, and I wonder what the valley looks like from above. I duck under the wire onto the towpath and cross the bridge to run up the bank so I can see it before the sun comes and burns it off.

And clouds are panting from my mouth as I look down. And light is coming, but not much. But soon. The birds are waking. When I get a recorder from school, I will learn their song. It's our own world. I don't want a bedroom of my own, even if they do send me to prison one day. My Tabernacle rises like a palace from the mist. When I get released on parole, maybe I could take the pram, and just go and collect bottles from all around and into town, and we could pay the council for it. And we could mend the holes and make shelves for the books. And I close my eyes to make it real.

When I open them. There is a burst of red sparks and a flick of flame from the end. And first I think it could be how a wish happens. And then, I see a stream of smoke coming from near the vestry at the back. Then I'm scared. What if I made some something happen. Not a wish. But some rats' teeth sparking on the matches I got ... or something. Something! What if all my books burn and there is a fire – and we get sent to the hostel - and I can't remember if I did anything that would make a fire – and what if all the books and my moon map is burning and the bottles I am storing for Mrs Smith this week – and I left my special glasses in the bag. I start to run. I trip on the root of a tree down the bank. My elbow hits a stone. My face crashes into my arm. But I get up and run, banging my legs because I can't see them. It doesn't hurt until I climb under the fence and stop to listen when I open the tabernacle door. I feel sick.

It is dark and quiet, but I feel loud inside. No flames or smell of smoke. The dark makes everything bigger, but as I stand still some light of the sky shows the window over the big door and my eyes get used to it, and there is nobody there. Unless they are hiding. My legs are shaky with hurt as I walk to the pile of books, so I am hidden too. I hear a cough and a thump. But it is not in here. It's in the vestry. Maybe it's God. Or Aliens? But then I feel a sea of brave. A quiet sea, of warm waves. I stop thinking about it. I stand up straight and the calm takes me to the door. It doesn't sound like robbers, or like it is more than one person. The sound of humming. Cheerful hum. It's a man. Radio music, voices. Like a car. Dialling over the stations. Rolling over the sounds so they are long squawks.

And I knock. My heart is jumping. The radio stops. It is quiet now. I knock again, 'Hello." No one answers. I feel more scared now. They heard me. It's too late to run.

"Wait!" a voice like Zorro. Thunder like horses across the floor. And the door opens. No mask. Just glasses, "I wasn't ... just had to move the cupboard", and I can see the wood stove burning, and I can't help it; I am laughing. He looks round like he's lost, and then at me, "Hi there. Eli. A cup of tea? A Coke? Talk?" I never had a coke to myself before. I nod. And he moves a chair to the stove, but I wait by the door. "Are you in the films?" He laughs and shakes his head. His hair is long as mine. He turns round to close the books on the desk, and folds a big map to make it small. Like he was guilty. Like he minds what I might think about it.

"You sound like a cowboy. Or spaceman."

"Ah? Oh! No. Of course. Just American." Sshhh… as he pulls back the cap on the bottle and hands me the coke.

"How did you get to here? Are you a spy?" I drink my coke and I feel like a detective.

"Long story. Family. You? Live in the van?" I nod.

"I saw the smoke, and ... This is my place." But he steps past me, and he is looking up across to the wall at my moon map. It still wasn't proper daytime yet, so he goes right up to it and put his glasses up. And then he gets really excited.

"Incredible! Do you know what this is?" And he started to feel the paper and look up close. "The Wilkins' Map of the moon. Not original, but a good xerox. Armstrong studies this." He turns to me, "He's the Astronaut that's going to land on the moon. How did you get this?" But he's not listening. He's running his finger through the seas, and he is saying their names. I say them with him, and he turns to nod at me as we say each one. I feel proud. Like I'm getting ticks at school. He waves his hand under Mare Tranquillitatis , "Ah - You see these craters?" I don't say anything. "These are the Kant series. The Kingdom of Ends," and he sighs, and looks up to find the words, and they come slowly, "Act so as to treat humanity, whether in your own person or in that of another, at all times also as an end, and not **only** as a means." It sounds important and kind, and it echoes in the roof.

"What does that mean?"

"Mmm – we have a duty to think about problems and respect and help each other become… ourselves."

"How can we not be ourself?" and he says it is a good question. "Is it like a story in a book? My teacher said all the stories have beginnings, middles and ends?"

"Well, yes – it's Immanuel Kant. My Dad would have said he earnt his place on the moon. There is a book." And he turns to look at me and laughs, "Maybe not just yet. Hey, I'm so sorry. I mean - breaking into your place." And he held out his hand, "Eli. And you are?" Mum said to walk away when a stranger wants to take your hand, but I don't want to leave. His hand is stuck in front of him, and I feel bad, so I turn to look at the map closer.

"It's just here. Just empty. For storing old books when they get to their end. It's like a Kingdom of Ends." And I don't say my name. I'm thinking I'm going to look for Immanuel Kant when it's light. And that's it. This is The Kingdom of Ends.

"Your family own this?"

And I want to say yes. This is our valley. All the way along where you can see. And we are storing this because we've finished it now. We needed new books. And they just let me have this so I can be on my own when I want. And I think about how it could be true. And he might believe me. But I get a feeling.

"No." I tell him this is my secret place. My mum doesn't know I come here. That we are waiting for a house. But I don't want to go. Because no one comes here except me. So it's like my house. Except for now, he's here. And he says, sounds like I could be a good caretaker. He's not telling anyone. And maybe he'll fix a few holes in the roof to preserve the books. To contribute. He's got to get lodgings soon though. It's getting too cold for washing in the river. And I get an idea.

If I tell Mum that he is staying here fixing some things, but the council don't know. And I could ask her if he could have a toilet on the block and use our showers if he gives mum some fags, because she is always running out. He is cleaning his glasses and checking they are working properly now the light is coming up. And then I am telling him everything, without stopping, about Dad in prison, and the council and the hostels. And that we don't fit in with people in the houses, and I don't want to leave our field and the birds, or this church. And I want to be a detective in space. And he laughs. He says he will think of a way to talk to my mum and see what he can do. It's a good plan. I'd make a good detective because I make a good case. He says he didn't like new things either, but like someone said about going to the moon, we do it because it's hard - and doing new things is how we learn.

And it's really light now. I notice I made a mess of the arms of mum's cardigan. It's got mud skids, and bits of grass. I try and brush it off. "I got to go. Can you sort it out with Mum today?" And he said he needs to do a few things, and think it through, but as soon as he can, he will.

When I get back all the boys are in mum's bed, so I put the table up and pulled the curtain across, to do reading and keep my fingers crossed on both sides between turning pages.

It takes two days. Mum goes to the newsagents to get some bread and milk. She's really excited when she gets back, and she sends the boys out to their camps with sugary jam doughnuts. And she says we can sit on the steps with ours. She's got news. She'd sat on the bridge for a fag, and there's a man comes over, a yank, living here in that old church over the road and they got talking. Bit of a hippy, but he's a laugh, and a bit of a handyman. Now, she's invited him over to have a cup of tea later. She said he could use a toilet in the block, and a shower when he needed one, and he was going to help out a bit. And she put her hands on my shoulders, and then she says she'd been turning a blind eye, but she noticed the fags I nicked when I went up the shop for her. She knew I meant well, and she was grateful. She didn't want to hear any more about it. We've got to change our ways. It might make it more complicated if I tell her about the money from the bottles. I'll just save it.

I want to tell Mum so much what I learn from the books in the Tabernacle, that it's the Kingdom of Ends, and all the stories, but I know that she will get cross even if Eli tells her that I'm really good. When we get a house, she said she will be excited that we'll get on our feet again, but I don't know if I will like a house. She said I lived in one for a while with her mum and dad when I was a baby. She said I'd like it much better. But I like the pictures of wind and wet. I like finding faces in the clouds and the grass as the wind moves them around. The mildews blooming shapes like flowers that spread across the meadow from their seeds each year – and the stories we make. This summer there were more poppies than daisies. She told me they're from when she gets dressed up with red lipstick and goes to the shops, she runs across the meadow free as a bird painting all the white daisies with kisses - so when I walked through on my own, I curled my hands over their heads in the long grass and get all the kisses back for me. And one day when I'm big I will get lipstick and do it for her. And we will do cartwheels along the valley, daring each other along the river's edge like me and Gloria did. We can come back here one day.

When Eli comes over, he just says he's seen me around the place. So, I get to hear him do it again. It's even better. Eli does Science things, and he works with lots of people that are working out flying to the moon. He said he's got some books about planets if I'd like them, so I could learn all the facts about them. Mum said it was right up my street. I pretended I read some of it at school, and it explained how the rocket will work in zero gravity when they go to the moon next summer. Although there isn't any weather or gravity in space, there is a little bit on the moon and that will help it stay there, because it will pull it in like string. He said gravity is invisible, but we've got it everywhere, or everything would fall off the earth. In between, the rocket won't have to deal with gravity, nothing pulling it back, so they don't need much petrol once they get going. And there isn't very much on the moon, so they got work to do. Gravity is important, and I looked it up in the dictionary before: crime has some gravity, clever people have gravity and things that happen can have gravity or be grave; I told him. He said I had too much gravity and go and play - and that was good for science too.

Eli came from America to meet his mum when his dad died. She hasn't seen him since he was a baby, so they didn't know each other very well, and she's got a new life for God now. Mum said God will dump her. He laughed really loud. He said it's okay, he just wants to know about his ancestors. Mum said after that he was a good bloke, a bit of a clever clogs, but he made her laugh too.

The rats have come in The Kingdom of Ends from the riverside now, so they can get a good place for winter. It rained a lot before the cold came, and when it did the shallow water across the meadow got frozen – and the grass that stuck out was all frosted. Then when the snow came last year, it was beautiful, but you couldn't hear a single squeak outside except from some birds. In here rats scratch around.

And I didn't used to like them. But Eli told me that rats are clever, and they look after each other. I like it that they are making nests, like us. When the books go rotten, I tear the good pages into pieces so I can make it easy for them getting it to their places where they live. Eli found loads of boxes of letters and numbers for the hymn boards in the vestry. And I'm going to put some on a string and make a proper sign to go inside across the top of the big door, so it's a proper place, and people know where they are.

It snowed one night. I woke up when it was just morning, as the sun was stretching down from the hills, and I crept out. All my ships were covered in white, and all the shapes looked like the moon had landed and sunk into the valley, covered in the long shadows of the trees. It glittered in the net of shadows like pirate treasure flying from the sea. I couldn't hear anything but the water of the river as it cut a dark line through the white valley. It's like we are the only people that are alive on the whole world. I made the names of all of us from footprints: April, Matthew, Mark, Luke, John and then Hope, instead of Mum, because it's like she's one of us. I stamped a big heart around all the names. If you're the one to make the first footprints in new snow you get a wish. When I looked up, Mum was in the kitchen window having a fag and smiling at me. Mum said she couldn't believe it when she looked out of the window, and there I was, chuffing along like a steam train. She came out and said, "Will you look at my girl". She rubbed my hands between hers, one at a time. My wish came true. And I saw Eli, watching us through the fence, quiet and alone. I took big steps to where there was a space in the heart, and spelled out Eli. And I waved both hands. He tiptoed to see. He pointed at himself, and I nodded. He put his hand on chest and bowed. And I made a wish for him and his mum too.

Chapter 3

The calls of returning crows across the valley broke Eli's thoughts and he headed for the vestry. Once inside, he watched each pillar of breath hang and fall in the cold air, like distant galaxies, as he pulled the map of 'The Sea of Tranquillity' from his backpack, gently unfolding and smoothing its creases over the small desk. His mother had refused his most prized gift. It was the Moon, he'd explained, excitedly, and (he'd almost called her Mom) he was part of the astronomical team at NASA that made it possible to chart every chasm and slope. "The sins of man - breaking open Gods mystery," she replied and turned away. It hurt him, and he'd felt they were strangers again.

Now, the light was fading, and the corrugated walls shuddered as the squalls rolled through the valley. From the door, he watched the birds rising and swooping, calling each other to roost. He remembered as a small boy, standing on the shoreline in the early morning, proudly watching his father's low altitude flight manoeuvres.

Time to warm the place up. He pulled a flint and striker from his pocket. His father had presented them to him on a camping trip. He recalled watching him striking the steel to the flint, before setting a nest of grass alight. One of many treasured rites of passage his father had dutifully taken him through. He hadn't expected to set fires in England; but it was always to hand. He thought how his father would be nodding with approval as he sparked up the wood stove, and once that wisp of smoke was drawn into the upward draft, he closed the door.

Sitting back at the window, he saw the caravan on the far side of the field. April was playing chase with her brothers, their dark heads flitting and bobbing, slowly consumed in the dusk as their shrieks and laughter were carried on the wind. And he felt the tug of his boyhood, dry seasons in the Everglades, running back to the camp through the sawgrass prairie, whooping and hollering, always keen to raise some sparks of joy in his father's life.

The fire in the wood stove was blazing now. He caught his reflection in the mirror, his hair shoulder length, and he'd given into a beard. In the reflection, he saw his father as a young man, and he wondered if his mother saw that. Twenty-four years after she had seen them both off, his father boarding with all the other GIs and their English brides. His Dad said he'd thought she might reconsider, in time. He'd waited for the call, but it never came. He'd never had more than the small envelope she'd slipped into his pocket, necessary administration with an address to contact her, were it ever necessary. Though he'd grieved to his death, his father had decided that necessity never came. But when Eli had found the envelope amongst his father's possessions after his death, he had felt free to recognise his own need.

When he'd arrived in London his mother had long gone from the rectory address. She had left a forwarding address, which was finally presented by an elderly Chaplain after he'd fumbled through a cabinet of papers while making bumbling enquiries about the connection. She was the other side of the country now he'd said, as if to discourage him, although he accepted that she had been a friend of a relative, who had moved to the US as a GI bride after the war. It was as close to the truth as Eli felt he could go.

He'd planned to stay in London with his father's military friends, but now it had become more complicated, and he would need more money than he had accounted for. After considering forgetting the whole thing, staying put, and enjoying himself, he finally decided to see it through. He sold his leather suitcase and two of his three suits and bought a backpack and a map. England was smaller than the state of Florida, and in less than half a day he'd hitched a ride to the West Country, within a few miles from her home.

Eli decided as the road followed the river, he would walk towards her and find somewhere nearby to stay. He fell in love as the blaze of the autumn trees and the passage of the cold blue sky reflected in the slow-moving water. This was the England he had seen in books and magazines. He could almost hear the choral refrains of green and pleasant lands. A memory of the romance that he embodied for his father.

When he reached a derelict canal port, he could see he was passing south of the address and thought of getting up to the road to find lodgings. A fence across the path, from the end of a disused church, led him alongside the building. The first door to the riverside was locked, and dusty windows reflected the sunset and obscured the view inside, but as he pushed past the tangle of nettles and bindweed around the back to the other side, he found a door that opened into the nave. The light was fading, and it smelt a little damp and musty. It was piled high with stacks of bound papers and books. He could make a platform for sleeping. This could do for a night, until he found something better. And, almost immediately, he did. He opened a door to the side of a platform that led into a vestry. The furniture - a desk, chair, armchair - were thick with dust. There was a wardrobe stuffed with coats and cloaks that would be the perfect base for sleeping. In the corner was a log burner with a nest of ash, now solid, but a stack of logs surrounded it. He ran his fingers through the desk drawers of handwritten notes and found a set of keys at the back of one. It worked the door direct onto the path he came in on, and another for the inside door. But he decided if he moved the shelves across the inside door, he and fellow intruders would not be troubled by each other.

Across the track that ran along the other side, he'd seen a single yellow van in the corner of a field, but the view was cut off for the most part. Other than that, the place was isolated. The river glittered as it cut along the meadow bank outside, and an iron pipe that crossed it lent itself to a pathway. It was not unlike home; the birds, rising, falling, and curling to the invisible currents and thermals, alongside the browning clumps of reeds, tufts of grass, thistles and the stubble of fall that spread across the meadow on the other side. Home, but for the cold mist that was already setting into his bones. This was perfect. By the time he met with his mother he'd made himself at home.

He'd noticed letters and notes with her name on the church noticeboard and pinned his own amongst them. He'd explained that he'd wait in the back right-hand pew after every lunchtime service the following week. He had no expectations. If she did not approach him by the end of the week, he would not return. But he prepared; he'd decided to wear his remaining suit each day. He wasn't as heavy as he'd been before, in its loose creases and folds, as he sat in the pew, he felt the whole world had outgrown him.

She came on the second day and sat beside him. "I hope I am able to help," she said, with a brief sideways glance before she fixed her eyes on the pulpit, "I must tend the graves after the service. We can talk there."

There was no emotion, no fuss. Eli himself was now shrouded in doubt, clutching his shirt sleeves, brushing the welts of his shoes on the kneeling mat. "Of course, I'll be right with you," he said instinctively, realising his relief to be obeying orders.

He came to realise, over time, that this was her way. Her pastoral care was respectful but briskly integrated into her routine orbit. But her respect could feel threatening, as if the slightest disappointment could bring catastrophe, like a misaligned screw in the body of the rocket. Despite his requests she insisted on calling him Elijah, his name, the one intentional thing she had given him she said. Her only point of familiarity.

In the graveyard they had arranged to meet at an ancient spring along the valley, then a path that led them off the beaten track. He'd tripped through fallen branches and brambles and crunched through sunlit clearings and finally sat on fallen trees to eat the sandwiches she brought. And it became a ritual.

As she unpacked the food, she was always silent. He felt her eyes upon him, observing his gaze, his breath, how he stood. He was careful that she should feel he did not notice, but he felt it. They ate their picnic formally, in silence. Then she would pat and fold the waxed paper. It was time to talk. He was surprised at her lack of curiosity about his father, and his own interests. But she would listen as he talked about their lives.

He flinched when Eunice gave the reason that she had 'abandoned him'. She'd quickly come to see that he, and his father, were not her calling. She had done the right thing, she insisted. She could not have provided any more than shame. She did not want him to live under that shadow. Nothing good would ever have come of it. God had his plan.

Eli felt her loneliness, sharp and cutting like the sawgrass prairie. He felt closer to the part of her that held the promise of love and a future his father had spoken of, that had brought about his existence, and brought him here. He observed that she didn't refer to the Reverend as her brother, but she was deeply committed to his work. And it more often seemed to be his plan, rather than any God's.

After a few weeks, he realised he might need to find somewhere more secure, more permanent if he was to remain. Eunice had not asked about where he was staying, and he didn't want to press the matter. But the river grew colder and more turbulent as it swelled with rainfall, and he needed a more civilised washroom. And there had been the worry that he would be discovered. So, he was grateful one morning when he'd woken cold and damp, to set the fire, and had been discovered by April, and her family.

He found himself to be a happy subject in The Kingdom of Ends, as April earnestly referred to as their secret. For he discovered he had been living in the annexe of her very own library, unknown to her mother. The kids were not allowed in the church, and that was final. He found himself calling over most days, and fish and chips round the campfires he made for them became a regular and entertaining event.

There were days he felt guilty at maintaining April's lie, but as he watched and listened from the vestry, or when he was on the roof, repositioning slipped tiles, or outside tightening the bolts to close the gaps in the corrugated walls, she would be stood among a shifting landscape of bundled papers reading her selected texts. The stilted stumbled phrasing, as she phonetically sounded out words and phrases – meant that sometimes the meaning was unclear, but at times it revealed itself despite her lack of literal understanding or judgement. It was her faith. He remembered different ways of understanding.

When he found Kant's 'Critique of Pure Reason' among the piles, she wanted to read it aloud. These repeated declarations were delivered with great earnestness on behalf of mankind to invisible and well-meaning aliens, who arrived and departed in invisible rockets at short notice. He was not alone.

Her repetition of a whole paragraph seemed to work around her clear excitement of phrases that she explored for their cadence and rhythm, "It is the Land of Truth, surrounded by a wide and stormy ocean, the true home of illusion, where many a fog bank and ice, that soon melts away, tempt us to believe in new lands, while constantly deceiving the adventurous mariner with vain hopes, and involving him in adventures which he can never leave, yet never bring to an end." And then the open sweep of her arms as she jumped down the stacks to the repetition of "The Kingdom of Ends", a phrase that he was so happy to have introduced. What he came to feel was that she drew the essence of love itself from the order of the sounds for their own sake, their own shape. There was magic in the engineering of the invisible. And he was reminded that Kant himself had said, 'All our knowledge begins with the senses… proceeds to understanding … and reason.' And he delighted in listening.

He watched as with each departure, and return to her home, she patiently tilted buckled prams and bikes to a working wheel and dragged them onto the empty hardstands from around the field. Rather than a tangled pile, she instinctively found a place for each one so that it should have some integrity and be considered right, related to that old print of the Wilkins map of the moon. It was so reduced from its original size that most of the names were not legible. He tried to help her out, of course, but as she pointed out, so long as she knew where they were, did it matter if the names were different. There were lots of words for the same thing in the dictionary, and she had discovered Wilkins' 'The True Book About the Stars' in the latest delivery to her Kingdom.

Eli looked across the meadow to the river, laying his head back against the medieval stone that marked the strip of fertile land allocated to a farming family. The carved signature was no longer decipherable, as with the other stones aligned at intervals along the boundary. He liked the anonymity. It gave him access. A possibility of belonging. He imagined the families, watching from the hills as the river came roaring through the valley, bursting its banks flooding the plain, and they praying to their Gods of land, sea and sky for the warm rains and spring sunshine to awaken the seeds they scattered in the sodden earth.

And there was the moon, pale in the late afternoon sky, a foreshadow of the full moon to come. He saw it all differently now, these past weeks he'd stepped into the romance of a childhood, planting his own memories into the ages of the world; longings of a time that was never there for him, but had given him meaning and purpose.

The moon had always been a place of wonder for him. He had been steeped in the moon and its myths, the stories that had laid the foundations for thought, on which, for all its modernity and progression, humanity still looked up and hoped to see itself, feel itself, saw mother come to embrace and watch over their sleep. Mother or no mother, that yearning still gave him comfort.

As a child the moon was beautiful, and he could see it now, remembering some paradise of clouds and seas, and winding roads across mountainous passes, from bay to bay, through lakes and marshes - all inhabited by the hopes and dreams of mankind - maybe the paradise that their Gods had promised.

When the first pictures had arrived, it was clear that it was barren and indifferent. Rills and craters surrounded the seas that were no more than vast wastelands pulverised by meteorites and volcanic eruptions, smoothed to a mirrored shine in the hot solar winds, merely serving to reflect what we most wanted, or needed, to see. It was the truth. Wasn't that the beauty he craved? Gravity was weak and exhausted, holding little to it. But in April he saw the sense of wonder that he missed and needed.

Eli also enjoyed Hope's company. For all her bad fortunes she was still noble and sensitive. Like a white-tailed deer, on the edge of human settlement. Her large brown eyes alert, stamping her feet to alert her young who'd learnt to keep their heads down in the undergrowth until they were called to follow. Her sense of humour seemed to compel her to hold herself responsible for all the works of others, and particularly her absent husband Andy. And strangely, there was something of his own mother about her. What his mother might have been in another life, and his fate had his mother not left him with his father.

It was only natural then that once Eunice had so roundly turned from his gift of the map that he should give this to April, who he knew would treasure both it and the moment of giving with all her heart, so he could forgive any careless destiny it might suffer in the future. That miraculous map that held the images of transmissions as the observational crafts sought targets of opportunity for the perfect landing ground.

He was not wrong. April had loved it and was able to transpose the paths that Wilkins had identified as Armstrong before her, and her own Kingdom of Ends to the craters beyond the shores of 'The sea of Tranquillity'. As much as he was tempted to guide her fingers to the exact handling of the map, to keep the sharp creases, as with anything precious his father had told him, if it is not properly used with love, then it had better never have been given, or known to exist.

He explained the process to her, of how the maps were read and shared – and soon numbered coordinates appeared on the hymn board, marking the pathway - always beginning with Kant's craters, nearest to the shore, and working through the other names. He made up some cards with the letters N, W, S & E. And so, the adventures of the pirates and their ships across the hardstands of the field became games, where the stories of the God, the characters, philosopher, or scientist depending on the named destination, were acted out. And she would test him by recalling the heroes with reference to their coordinates.

One morning he woke up to pull back the drapes at first light, he saw that it had snowed. The rising sun threw sharp shadows of the trees far down the smoothed white slopes into the valley, until they climbed the drifts. He scrambled to dress and had to push the warped and weathered door against a bank of snow to step outside. But for the black cut of the river, the valley was a smooth white. The muffled silence was only heightened by the sound of the river rushing through, and the snow in the branches splitting and slipping to the ground. He smiled at his childish impulse to be the first to leave footsteps and claim his wish. But he saw he'd been beaten to it. Across the field, April was cautiously closing their caravan door and turned to press her feet down each step with a careful joy. He watched as she stepped into the sheet of snow, screwing her eyes and reaching her clenched hands with longing. Casting their long shadows beyond, the hardstand constructions took the form of angelic forms outstretched in the light.

And he was moved to see her take giant springing steps to the side of her van; then smaller ones as she began to spell out words in the snow: April, Matthew, Mark, Luke, John and then finally, Hope. And all mothers are Hope. Then she appeared, and sat on the caravan steps, smoking a cigarette. And April walked towards her, 'Ta Dah', chuffing her breath to imitate. Hope reached out, clapping April's hands in hers, giving each a brisk rub, until April fell forward laughing and hugged her mother. As she clung to her in the silence, he understood that her wish had come true. And he realised his own wish too, when she turned and saw him, and added his name to her family heart.

When April had turned to wave, he felt as she had said, this was their world, their family. Their world, their family … he belonged.

On his last night of Christmas Eve, he bought the last Christmas tree from the newsagents, and all the tinsel and angel hair they had left, and a sack of presents for the next day. Before the boys had gone to bed, he'd found himself sat at the table, as they waited eagerly for him to finish mashing the potato scooped from their skins scooping potato with cheese; their upturned faces delighting in the smell. In the warmth of the gaslight, while the sausages grilled, April, with the flourish of a magician, revealed that this table also turned into a bed. And look, another bed pulled down from the wall, over the 'playground'. Look. It always amazed him that the space was larger than it looked from his window. The worn and patched linoleum, and the rust-stained studs on the seamlines of the van itself had not matched the vision of nobility he'd had. He wondered how it managed to hold them all, alone open to the winds in the middle of that field. As Hamlet's, 'I could be bound in a nutshell and count myself the king of infinite space...'

He returned to the vestry to pick up his bag in the early hours of Christmas day. The trees fell back and disappeared into their own shadows, all drunk and maudlin on starlight and the moon. He'd sat and watched the wind as it flocked the falling snow, weaving the trees and branches catching the tails of its swirling murmuration, revealing its invisible pathways through the air. And as he walked away, he felt himself disappear from her, from them. The liberty of neglect was something they shared, a familiar release.

When he left to hitch a ride that afternoon it was getting dark again. He felt the grinding rumble of the swollen door against the floor, as he pulled it closed behind him. The laughter as heard them return from their Christmas dinner to the van echoed in the empty valley as he walked through the deserted canal port, and up onto the empty road.

Chapter 4

On Christmas Eve it was Eli's last night. He made a fire outside, and Mum said I could sit out with them and stay up after I read the boys a story. And when I came out Eli had a surprise. He'd bought a Christmas tree in a bucket, and it had tinsel and angel hair and it sparkled in the firelight. He'd asked mum if I could stay outside after the middle of the night, because there was a special practice rocket that was going to orbit the moon, and we could listen to it on the radio.

It was like a party because him and mum made big fags so they could share them, and we all made toast in the flames of the fire. I never seen Mum so happy. I dug a stone out the grass with my fingers and squeezed it with a wish, and I gave it to Eli so when he got home, he could give it to the astronauts to take next time, when they get on the moon.

Mum and Eli were laughing and talking, and I listened while I laid on the snow in my anorak and watched as their sounds went rising up into in the sky. It was nice, because Mum asked me what I was thinking. I said the sky looks bigger now the field is empty, and the more you look the more stars you can see. And so, they both copied me, and they said it was true. Eli said the world was changing fast. The Revolution had started. He said that kids like me were the future of the world, so I had to be the best I could be. I got butterflies. It felt like it was real. I said I was imagining a tower made out of the sound of our words, and they laughed, and Mum said she could see my beautiful castles in the air. Even though I want to look at Eli and Mum much as I can, I'm glad we were staring up to the sky, and I've got tears in my ears. This is the last day of Eli.

Mum didn't wait up for the message from the moon, because Mrs Smith at the paper shop had invited us for Christmas Day. Me and Eli listened to the radio and watched the moon while we waited. And I thought about the Aliens all getting their ships close to listen. The astronauts read the bible about the beginning of the world: 'In the beginning God created the heaven and the earth. And the earth was without form, and void; and darkness was upon the face of the deep...' . And I never thought about that before, about the beginning and the end of things. And I said to Eli, I didn't want it to be the end. He said even if you never meet a person again, when you are friends, you are connected. He squeezed my shoulder and said it's quantum entanglement. You'll work it out Detective Smart.

Maybe he will visit England again one day. Or I might surprise him and go to America and get a job there, and I can be a detective on the moon. When Eli said goodbye, I watched him walk across the field until he disappeared into the dark. And that is how the end happens.

I found the bible in the books and memorised the Genesis, in memory of the moon, and Eli, the day after New Year's Day. I am in the Tabernacle when I hear the locks go on the big doors. It's so quick that I run up the stairs to get behind the tabard that hangs from the balcony rail. I can't see them, but I can hear them tutting and moving things around. 'Rats and riff-raff will always find a way in! Well, at least it's nice to think that all this rubbish can be pulped and reused.' Just in case, I take my favourite books and save them in a crate in the toilet block.

In the New Year, Mum got the deposit back for the gas bottle, and bought a new dress in the sales for when the man from the final decision office came. It was red, and covered with big black and white flowers, with a black bow under her bosoms to make them look nice. She melted the frozen flannel between her hands and wiped our faces and brushed our hair with partings. We sat in a row on the bed, with our coats on while they talked. We drank panda pops and ate baked potatoes in newspaper wrapper to keep our hands warm, so he could see that we couldn't have a normal life, even if she tried. She said it did the job. He said it might have been in our best interest that there weren't any more houses in the town that were big enough, they had a nice place in a village above the valley that was nearly ready. We would get a fresh start. We moved the week after.

We walked five miles along the main road and two miles up the hill, with the pram and the pushchair. Mum said it would save the taxi money the welfare gave us. Me, Mum and Matthew took it in turns to push the old pram with her record player and records with clothes stuffed round, and the pushchair with the twins. Mum said there wasn't room for my books, but I made a bag out of a jumper for my space books and hung them round my neck. It was easy along the valley, even though it was a long way, but the hill was really steep, and it got darker and colder as we went up. Mum said she didn't realise it would take so long. The woods were black and empty, except for the snowy branches like skeletons when the moon came out from the clouds, and the screeches and cracks shot into your belly and down into your knees. We pushed faster and tried not to slip on the icy patches. I was shaking sometimes, but Mum laughed and said it would warm us up.

Mum had the keys wrapped up in her letter from the council and directions to our new place. It was freezing when we got to the house, and the light switches didn't work. We were going to have light switches like at school. She lit a match and we found two boxes of candles on the draining board, and there was a big plastic box of cheese sandwiches with a flask of tea. Mum found a card from the Electric man, and it said they will come again tomorrow to turn it on because we were out. And there was a letter to 'Mrs Smart', with writing like she was a Queen, and keys inside. Mum said it was from the Reverend who is like the boss in a village. She read it out, "Dear Mrs. Smart, We welcome you to your new home. Please enjoy the fare we have provided. I hope I do not offend, but I have taken the liberty of putting in and making up the beds. I have set up the grate to light a fire and take off the chill. I will call in tomorrow to identify the family needs and help settle you in. I also return the spare keys that were left with us by the council officer, so that we could prepare for your arrival." Mum pulled the keys out of the envelope and looked at them lying in her hand like she couldn't believe they were there, and then she smiled as she squeezed them tight. "Both sets," she said, "when you got both sets, you know it's yours." And then she fixed a candle in a cup, and we all followed her. We were so tired that the only noise was the sound of our feet.

With a house, just because there is a wall it is not the end of it, and then the outside - there are doors and stairs leading out and up, like a stack of different shape caravans all joined up. The boys have a bedroom, which is a massive room in the roof of the whole house. Mum said it is an attic. Underneath, I've got a bedroom and Mum has a bedroom. And there is a corridor. It's a bit like the van down the stairs, because the kitchen and the living room are one big room, but it's as big as ten vans without walls. The walls are so thick that they have a shelf big enough for us all to kneel on and look at the stars. Mum comes over and moves Luke and John to her lap. And everyone is looking out with sleepy, shining eyes, until Mum said we might die of cold and be statues.

Mum lit the fire, and we sit round it while we eat the sandwiches and drink the tea. Mum said the boys can go to bed with their clothes on, and even though they've got a bed each, they share one. Mum said they'll get used to having their own when it gets warmer. I've got to sleep in a room on my own, but the window is high up the wall, and I can't see out. I can't hear the wind or the birds and animals on the outside, but the house is full of creaks and cracks and scratches – like someone is on the way, but nobody comes. Mum says I can stay up with her, and sing hymns with her, because there's nothing else to do, but then she falls asleep on the floor. I get the blankets from my room and cover us up. It's a bit scary having a fire open indoors. The light of the candles and the fire jump and chase the shadows around the white and yellow walls, and we're in a bubble, and it's warm, and my mum is breathing quietly and slowly; then quick and deep like something was stuck then jumped out. When I stroke her hair off her face, she breathes slow again.

We haven't got curtains yet, so the sun is bright and creamy through the frosty windows when we wake up. We look round the garden, and in the sheds, but the long grass is still stiff and white so we're soon back inside. We run up and down, hiding and calling, shouting and laughing at our new sounds. Just as Mum is sending me and Matthew out to find the shops, the Reverend Fisher, arrives. He doesn't look like the boss of anything. He just has normal clean clothes like a teacher. He doesn't concentrate on the person he is speaking to, even Mum, and when he's finished talking he leaves his mouth open and strokes the hair on his chin, so you don't know if he's finished yet. So that's why Mum was getting mixed up. He didn't realise that we wouldn't have many things with us. But, he said never mind, he had brought hot chocolate in a flask, and lemon cake that his sister had made, and some basics, to keep us going. He told Mum that they had collected some furniture in the community, and other things we might need, which he would bring later. When we finished the cake, he said him and Mum better check the list. He took a packet of pencils from his jacket and he said I could have the rest to share out. Mum said keep them to yourself, don't give them out, they'll draw everywhere.

By the time it got dark again, we had electric lights, a table and chairs, a cooker, a sofa, a radio, towels, tablecloths, saucepans, plates and knives and forks. Mum said some of it was a bit old fashioned and worn out. I liked those things the best, the little marks and tears was like it could be we had always lived this life. We had pictures on the walls; just people doing normal things like walking along paths of trees, and eating at the table, and having a picnic, except they all had long dresses and suits with tall hats, like in the past.

The fire is going, and Mum is singing in the kitchen while she makes the tea, and she said that she's remembered more than she thought she would about living in a house, and she will like doing cooking now she's got the room, and we got the mains gas. I miss the sleepy warm hiss of the gas lights, and the shadows, but Mum says the gas mantles were a fiddle. She said she likes all the mod cons. I scrunch up and close my eyes as I listen to the rattle of saucepans as they boil on the cooker and the suck of soap as mum washes her hands.

We're going to the church jumble sale tomorrow, and Reverend Fisher said we were invited to thank the Lord for all his gifts on Sunday. I can't wait to meet the people. Mum said it was more of a favour to God, but they gave us all these things as presents, and it's a good sign they want us to stay.

It was still cold and icy outside, so Mum didn't follow the map Reverend Fisher left us. Mum said she definitely wasn't going down that lane with her heels. We went round the long way. We didn't get to the jumble sale until it was nearly at the end, and Reverend Fisher said most of the stalls were packing up. But he showed us to his sister, Miss Fisher, who was tidying up the kids' clothes with another lady. She was folding all the collars and rolling all the belts, so they stayed neat in the clothes when she put them in the sacks. Miss Fisher was too busy to look at us, but her mouth was in a smile. I think they were a bit cross that we were late, but they did get the things out to hold them up on us and check the sizes.

Mum sat down on a bench and stared away from us, even when I walked over for her to see the polka dot dress that Miss Fisher said was right for me. It's got white pockets on the front, and it's dark blue with white dots, with a white belt to make a bow at the back. It's like new. Mum got up, stabbing her heels across the wooden floor making dents, like she meant it, until she got to the door. She turned and did a pretend laugh, and said people round here had more money than sense, chucking stuff like this out. She lit up a

37

fag and walked out down the steps. Miss Fisher raised her eyebrows, and asked Reverend Fisher if this is what we should expect and pushed my dress into the bag without rolling the belt. Reverend Fisher shook his head and touched her arm, and said to put all the bags together, and he would drive us home. Miss Fisher sighed and looked away, and she looked sad. So, I told her that her cake was the best cake I ever had in my life, and it was nice of her to think about us having cake. She looked at me like she'd forgotten about it, but she did say it was very gracious of me to say that. Gracious is a holy thing to be. I know it from Mum's hymns. We'll have to get used to using lots of new words now we live in a proper world.

We all got new winter coats too; proper grey Macintoshes with belts, but I'm still saving my red anorak. Mum's coat was grey too, but soft wool with a big collar she can pull up past her ears. We took off the dry-cleaning tickets. They're not really new, but they smell better than new, like someone made them nice for us. We're wearing them to church today. The ice has melted away now, but it's cold, so Mum said we could all walk down the lane, because the church was next door to the church hall. There's lots of holes and bumps in the path, and mum got unsteady on her feet and fell into an arch in the wall and got saved by a rusty door. Mum said she's not going down that way again.

Kids had to go into the jumble sale place, and the stalls were put together with chairs, and it was Sunday School. I said I was a bit worried that mum had to go into church on her own, because she wasn't used to the people, but Miss Fisher said we would all join the adults later. Miss Fisher was the Sunday School teacher, and we were going to make friends and learn about the bible. I said I was keeping my coat on in case, and so the boys did too. When we were at the tables, everyone had to go round introducing themselves, because we were new to the village. She said my brothers' names were called to the holy trinity. She said a nice way of learning something about each other would be if the older ones told our favourite bible story. Me and

Matthew were going last, and I couldn't think if I knew one, and I thought about the baby Jesus, and then Matthew said it first, the whole nativity play. Miss Fisher looked at me, waiting for my turn.

"In the beginning God created the heaven and the earth. And the earth was without form, and void; and darkness was upon the face of the deep…" And I was just going to say the first few lines, but every time I got a breath it was quiet, so I said it fast right to the end, "…and the gathering together of the waters called the Seas: and God saw that it was good." And then I let the quiet happen, because I didn't know anymore.

"Extraordinary! How… Oh my goodness. The time!" and Miss Fisher jumped up and went to listen at the door that went into the church. We all had to line up and file in with our heads bowed.

The door leads all the kids to the benches at the front. I could hear the piano playing as we walked quietly over the brown carpet. Reverend Fisher says, bow our heads in prayer, so we keep our heads down. I look behind me to find mum, and she's just at the end a few benches away; and her eyes are closed, clenching the back of the seat in front, but she is smiling.

I look up all around. And the white walls, and the hymn board, and all the numbers are for places on the moon I don't know. There are bunches of flowers on the altar, and on special stands, and in the window with Jesus. It's Jesus in a garden, and words on a ribbon round his feet, that says 'Suffer The Little Children'. There are some kids holding his hands in the garden, and they look happy. There are big red roses with green thorns painted on the glass, and the bunches of flowers in pots on each side of the picture on little shelves – and some plants on the windowsill that spill down the wall. It's like the picture is coming alive into the world of love. And the smell is beautiful, and the air tastes like caramac squares. And I think of my old tin Tabernacle, lonely and cold now, creaking in the winter wind and ice.

And in the quiet I hear someone grizzling, and it is me. I can't stop.

Nobody waits around for too long once they get past the Fishers, but our family is last out. They shake Mum's hand and tell her what wonderful children she has. Mum laughs quite loud, like she thinks they might be joking, and Miss Fisher tells Reverend Fisher that I had recited word for word the story of Creation. He ruffles my hair, "No wonder. The word moves us all," he says.

And we all try and stand still as they talk, even Luke and John. Mum said she was sorry about yesterday to Miss Fisher, and that she just wasn't feeling well. She's just started a new prescription from the Doctor. Reverend Fisher said he'd heard about the advancements in medication, and she would be right as rain in no time. Miss Fisher went and got Mum a hymn book and a bible and said it was the best medicine, and she should read a little every day, then she was really cheerful to us kids and said that for the next few weeks we are doing show and tell, so we'll all get to know everyone like family.

We're walking a long way round home, because Reverend Fisher said there was a park down the road on the other side of the green. It's the first time we've seen this side. We fall in time with Mum's steps and echo between the high old walls, like an army in our grey coats, all neat. There's a big sign on the wall of the house before the green: 'Harold and Harold; Restoration and Repairs of Clocks, Watches and Barometers.' And my feet start stamping to the beat of the words as I say them, and the boys start stamping too. And as we march past, I see there is an old man who is oiling the hinges on a gate, when I shout Hi, he looks up and gives us a nod and turns back to his work.

We race across the green and over to the park. And we all go on swings, roundabouts, and the see-saw. We see how many of us can get on the other end from mum to make the see saw balance: the best one is mum and the twins, and me and Matthew and Mark. I ask mum what a Barometer is.

She said her mum had one. It measures the pressure in the atmosphere.

Chapter 5

We didn't go to church the next week. It started snowing that night. It snowed so much for the next few weeks that the school was closed. From the attic windows we could see across the village as everything got covered in white, and big drifts built up around the walls and fences. And I felt sad because it made me think about the old tin Tabernacle. And all the books and all the memories were broken to tiny pieces. And the Tabernacle floated to the sky and turned upside down and all the tiny white pieces were falling from the sky. And I felt scared that when the warm came it would all melt away into the dirt.

When it stops and the sky is blue the winds come and blow it from the trees, like dandelion clocks. And maybe all the pieces of writing and memories will be like seeds, and just make surprises everywhere.

Mum just reads her hymn book and the bible from Miss Fisher. She said she read it already, and she's just reminding herself, so we don't disturb her. Every room is the same creamy white colour, but in the attic, there are black beams across so we have put all the beds together to make a giant bed, and hanged some sheets so we are on a giant ship that we can play on, and still all sleep together sometimes. Mum said we can while it's cold like this.

Now I've got my own room I want to stick my map of the moon from Eli on the wall, but Mum said we have to wait to get it sorted properly. But for now, I've pegged it to clothes hangers and bent the hooks to put on the windowsill ledge, because it's quite high up and there's lots of room on the wall. And I faced my bed to it, so the sky is right above it, with the stars or the snow or just black. And I hanged my polka dot dress next to it, and that looks like stars in space.

We went outside to make snowmen, and made them taller and fatter every day, patting down the fresh snow into ice. It's warmer up here on the hill than it was down in the valley, and the sun gets in our garden all day, but the snowmen don't melt. Mum was worried we didn't have enough in the cupboard to keep going, but without even asking, Reverend Fisher brought a box of tins and packets of food in a big box from their stores at their house in case we can't get to the shops. And even if we could, Miss Gomer, the shop lady, told him the deliveries couldn't get up the hill. I got the box off Mum, so I've got like a drawer on the floor to put my private things in. I can hear Mum and Reverend Fisher were downstairs talking about God and praying to thank him for the food.

It's icy in our garden because we run around it every day, so we pushed the soft stuff from the edges to make a skid slope for the trays. There are some good things about living in a house, but it's harder to go out. You have to have a reason, and I miss having a toilet block to store things. And anyway, I don't know many places we can go and just play where grown ups can't get cross about it. There are some ditches around the fields, and there's a tree in the bank with a hollowed out trunk like a cave, but it's just enough for one. The park is big, and it's got swings and stuff, but there aren't any places like the Tabernacle or the docks. There are houses all round us here, and people are watching us, and mum said we've got to try and be normal.

One day when it was getting light, after I went to the toilet, I stood out in the porch and I was remembering the valley. The snow was falling again, and the wind was blowing. I closed my eyes, and I whispered everything I could remember as the snow fell from the sky and melted in my hands. I remembered when it was warm, and the wind was cooling my wet arms. Mum is turning the crank and rinsing the washing between the rollers, and I am pulling it through the other side into the basket; holding it away from the water that is squeezed out. I look down into the tin bath as the water falls from the ringer, and I watch Mum's reflection ripple and sparkle. And when I open my eyes, the snow is clean with no footsteps, and I get my shoes and coat on over my pyjamas and go out to do my first footsteps wish. And when I get to the gate, all the road has no footmarks, or car tyres, and no one is there. I just keep going. And I'll make a wish for every house I pass. And there isn't even any lights in the windows, so it will go into their sleep, so they can dream their wish. And, I'll still get loads for me.

I march along the frosty snow in the silence, but I can hear the crunch and a squeaky thump. I am a moon explorer. And as I turn into the lane, I think I'll just go the way we went up to the park. When I look to the bottom lane it looks like a long keyhole. The tree branches are full of snow and fall over to lean on each other and make an arch. The lane is still full with snow. But someone has cleared a deep path with a shovel, and it's scattered with ashes of wood and coals. The walls of snow are nearly up to my waist. I take big steps like a giant. When I get past halfway down, I see the door in the wall, sunk back in the snow, like in the cinema. I pull the latch, but it's stuck. I kick the snow away to find toe holds in the wall and climb to the top.

It's a tiny field. The wall goes down the lane, and round the bottom end. But there's a caravan near the gate, like a big fat round one on wheels so big you can see the tops above the snow. Like a history one. But there is the shape of a wall, or hedges surrounding it. It's old and maybe people don't know about it anymore and I could make a den. My feet have got freezing now. Time to stamp my feet warm and make wishes. I try to get down the other side, but I slip and fall between branches and thump onto my back. Squawking birds fly from the big hedges, and I watch them make a fuss as I lie on my back until they go back.

There's no footsteps, so I walk a thin line to the middle, and then I make a spiral out. There are steps up to the caravan, so I go and stand up on them to look. My footstep shapes looks like a Toyland lollypop. My pyjamas are sticking to my legs my socks are squelching in my shoes, but I didn't feel the cold anymore. I hear a knock and I turn round. A face was in the window of the door. An old lady face, staring at me. I was so scared I slipped off, but my hands grabbed a step and I landed straight up. I ran to the gate. Mum will kill me if someone tells her. There was a big log against it, and my heart was beating fast as I rolled it back a bit, out the way enough to open and squeeze through the gate. I ran skidding on the ice, and saved by the ashes down the lane. Thick drifts of snow were blocking the road at the bottom, and it was icy underneath. I waited to see if anybody was coming. When I get to the bottom of the green by the old man's house, I can hear shouting and crying. Not crying but hurt. I think it's a grown up. A man. I stand still. I can't hear the words. Just the sad. Like mum. I make a wish for him. And then I walk quick as I can up the side of the green, back home.

Matthew was downstairs when I got back, and said he'd tell mum I'd been out. I said I'd just been on the skid slope.

I go into my room. It's really freezing so I put on as many clothes as I can and get under the blankets. The frosty window sparkles now in the sun, even as it melts away. I look at the moon maps Eli gave me, and I remember all the places in the caravan field that fitted the moon places. And I was thinking about it, that we have the moon here too. That you can see the moon everywhere, and wherever you are, the moon places fit to the places around you. So if I make a map of the places on this hill I know already, and then I can add new ones when I find them. And then, I can work it out. And I can join the pieces if it gets big. I get started with the places with our house and the way to the church.

It stopped snowing, but it stayed cold. The whole village had to have a snow plough, and salt and grit go round everywhere so we could all get back to life. Mum was desperate to get out, so we all went to the shop together. The shop is next to the church. Reverend Fisher had bought some furry boots for mum to wear, so we all walked down the lane. Mum said they were fuddy duddy clobber, and she was only going to wear them when she had to.

There's a big queue of people in the shop, so we just fit in, right at the back. Even mum said it too cold to wait outside. But it's nice to look at it properly as we shuffle towards the front. The polished glass shelves are full of shiny tins, even the ones at the back and down the middle, and they are all reflecting up and down, and into the mirrors down the wall. It's so shiny it's like a palace. Underneath the shelves are all the vegetables and fruit, and it says 'Please don't touch. Ask for assistance.' And people are asking, because we have to stand in a line so that the shop lady can get to them. Her eyes look giant behind her glasses, like she can see everything all at once. She says 'excuse me' every time, even when people move out the way. She's very tall and thin, so she has to stoop a bit when she puts the gloves on to pick things up and takes them to get weighed by her desk. You can hear her getting them balanced and checking with people if it's OK if it's a bit over or a bit under.

When we get to the front, Mum starts talking to her about the Giro, and she said we choose thruppence each on sweets, because we haven't had any since it was snowing. I'm saving mine. Because I am the tallest, I passed down the sweets off the rack and I saw the shop lady's cubby hole for the phone, by the side of the door to the back. It had a big photograph above it. I think it was like her when she was little, sat on the shoulders of a big boy, and three other big boys in front leaning forwards with big grins, and their hands on their knees. And on the other side of the door, a drawing of a pretty little girl having a picnic under a tree. It kind of looks like the shop lady. I'm not sure.

"Is that you when you were a kid?" Mum gives me a look and turns to the shop lady.

"April! Mind your own business!" and then she quickly turns to the shop lady, "Sorry Miss Gomer. She's full of questions this one. Miss Nosey Parker."

"Sorry Miss Gomer."

"No need to apologise. It is me. I want them to be remembered." And she walks over to the picture. She runs her finger along the three boys leaning forward. "All three of these boys went to war and never returned. It's our duty to remember them." Mum looks embarrassed. Looks at the tins. So, I ask another question.

"What about the one at the back with you? Did he come back?" And her head goes back. She peers down at me from nearly up in the ceiling.

"Yes. He did." And she goes back to the counter to finish serving Mum.

An old lady comes from the other side of the middle counter. "Went a bit queer," and she says to Mum, "Gave up the church. No wonder he's taunted by the devil in the night."

Miss Gomer turns to her, "We've all got things that keep us awake at night!"

"As Maybe. But it's not my conscience!"

"We weren't in the trenches," and the old lady falls silent. "Nice to meet you Mrs Smart. We'll see you soon. Now, how can I help you, Miss Carter?" We follow Mum out the door. I can tell from the way she talked to that Miss Carter, Miss Gomer doesn't like people to say mean things. If that man came back, she might still be his friend.

When we get outside, Mum says to keep away from people like that. Don't give her anything to talk about. But, there's no smoke with fire. Don't get involved with any of it. The best thing we could do was follow the guidance of the Fishers. I asked mum if we could walk up the park because I was making a map of the village. She said she wasn't going right round there again, but me, Matthew and Mark could go if we wanted, so long as we went straight there, and didn't hang around for too long. Matthew and Mark wanted to go back with Mum because they were hungry, so she said I could go on my own.

I walk down the bottom of the green. When I pass the clock repair gate that old man is in the garden again. He's just digging and pulling things up. There's a daffodil under a tree, and loads more that haven't got open yet, but you can see the yellow folded inside. I stand and watch until he turns round. He nods and touches his head like a little salute and turns back to his work.

There's a bench up on the green, so I keep going up and sit down to draw this bit. You can see more of the places from here, even the roof of the church. There's a little message on a metal plate on the bench, 'Lest we forget Joseph, Peter and John Nesbit. Who gave their lives for us, so we might be free.' And I think this must be for the memory of those three boys in Miss Gomer's picture. I feel sad thinking of them, and their faces being dead now. And if they are like when the foxes or the other animals die, and all the insects come to eat them. And I'm drawing a picture about it when I hear a motorbike stop just behind me. And when I turn round it's a policeman.

"Hello there young lady!" And he pulls his helmet off. As he comes over to the bench, I remember his face. It's that policeman that tried to make mum get out of trouble at the caravans. It's hard to look up as he gets close. He sits beside me. "I was hoping I'd be able to get a quiet word away with you?" I can't get up now. "I hear you paid Clara a visit. The caravan?" And I tell him I didn't know. I was just looking around. I'm making a map. I'm just looking for dens. And I didn't want him to tell Mum if I had to go to prison.

He laughed and said, not to worry. It was just a caution. Clara was just a bit surprised to see a stranger in her garden. He knew from church we'd moved here, and he'd seen us. He thought it might be me. He could see it was all a bit different up here in the village. Not so much freedom. He thought making a map was a good idea. He wondered about the three skeletons on the green with the animal heads. I told him it was just about three brothers that died, and I was thinking about what happened to them. I never saw a person that died. He said he was glad to hear it. I was too young to worry about all that. Now, he and Clara both agreed there wasn't going to be any mention of this to anyone else. We could all look to the future.

* * *

I'm smoothing down my dress just like I saw Miss Fisher do, right down from my waistband, and then from my bow down over my bum, tucking my dress down to my knees. I practised all week in my bedroom, but I dripped milk down me this morning. The polka dots cover 'a multitude of sins' Mum said, 'It doesn't show.' And anyway, it's my space dress.

I've got my map rolled up under my arm. I'm one of the show and tell kids this week, and we can say some words about our favourite thing and thank God for the gifts we have in life. My best thing is my map, but I like this dress too, and I want her to see that I am very thankful. My mum shrank my cardigan because she's still getting used to having a boiler, so I unravelled it and made a new hair braid, a necklace and bracelets. My socks have gone grey, so I'm sitting on them, and watching the others, but I'm thinking about my practice to introduce the map of the moon; and all the important work that is being done by Eli. People will know I am serious when they know I have a friend in America who is helping with the moon landings.

When it's my turn I unfold the map and put it against the back of two chairs, and I make it sound mysterious. I say that everyone has seen this place, but no one has ever walked on it. Yet. And I see if anyone can guess where it is. And people shout out places from all over the world that we do in school, and I say, No! And then I tell them it's The Moon. And everyone gets interested when I tell them all the things I learned about the Lunar Seas, and all the things that Eli told me. And I show them the place where astronauts are going to land and they all get round the map, and because they're all clean for church I say they can touch it if they want. Miss Fisher has been asking questions from all the other kids show and tell, but she doesn't ask me anything. She's not even looking any more. She's rubbing the back of her neck, pretending she's got a headache. She doesn't even tell me it was interesting. She doesn't say well done, like she did to the others.

When we are coming out of church with Mum, Miss Fisher says she would like a quiet word with us. She just spoke to mum. She wouldn't look at me. She said that The Moon was not an appropriate show and tell in a place of worship, and she wondered if Mum thought it was sensible for me to be learning about such things at my age. Mum said it was difficult to stop me, but she would try, and I could tell she wanted to please Miss Fisher. She wanted to get things right. Miss Fisher advised her to look through my books, and consider what was necessary for a healthy young mind. Books could have a bad as well as good influence. I tried to not say anything, but I couldn't say nothing. And I said my friend Eli had helped me choose all my books and he knew about which were the best ones for me. Miss Fisher went all blotchy, and said she thought it would be best if I listened to my mother. And then she took my mum's hand between hers, and said she would see her in the week, and smiled at her.

When we got home, Mum had a drink of sherry to help her nerves. She said it's hard to make your way with these people. She wouldn't stop me reading books, but I had to keep my gob shut and stop showing off. She was working bloody hard to make everything alright for when Dad came home. The Fisher's had helped us a lot, and there were important people in the village that would take notice of them. Reverend Fisher is even trying to sort out a job for Dad. Mum was getting help from the doctor now, and she's trying to get better. It helped to have them on her side. I needed to make more of an effort to fit in. And I want to make it all right for mum, and I want to fit in as well. I just do my schoolwork and make my map. I don't give them nothing to talk about me.

* * *

Dad has been home for a month now. Jasper from our church spoke at the prison meeting, and he was sent back home from prison on parole. Mum said they've made the law better now and they are helping to look after families when they make an effort to change. So, we all did a good job. The welfare got a television for our house, so we can get together and watch cowboy films and the wrestling together, and Dad can learn about scores to win the Pools. The telly is for Dad really, but when he got his driving job he has to stay away sometimes. Mum lets me stay up and watch telly with her. She's been drinking more since Dad is back because it helps her relax when he winds her up, but she said she's got into the habit of it. When she falls asleep, I don't wake her up and I switch over to watch about getting ready to be on the moon. She won't let me watch it when she is awake because Miss Fisher has warned all the parents that they mustn't let their kids do it. Mum said she's right, books is one thing and seeing it is another.

On the night before the rocket was going to land on the moon the telly meter ran out and Mum said she wasn't going to put in any more money until it was all over. When she went to bed I came back down again and put a shilling in the slot. They were already there. It's very dark and empty where they are. Not a single tree or animal, or anything. I kept the sound down and watched the pictures until it ran out. When I went to bed I climbed up to the windowsill and out the window and sat on the roof by the chimney. It's a bit closer but still too far away to see them, and I imagine them jumping along. And they have to tie string to their belt. If you fall off the moon space goes a long way, and they might not find you, so you have to make sure it's a big knot.

Chapter 6

When Andy had dropped the trailer off at the yard, he drove the cab home. He'd started to leave it outside the house parked up on the bank. There was plenty of room to get by, but the neighbours flapped and said, 'it was monstrous against the skyline'. He smirked as he imagined them when they came out to water their rose gardens and trim the climbers over the dry-stone walling. He'd had to bite his tongue. After that, he'd arranged with the pub landlord to stick it in a corner of the car park outside. Pretty decent of him, Andy had thought, considering he barely knew him. But then Hope had moved into the village with the kids when he'd been inside, and she had a knack for pulling in gratuitous favours. He toyed with the idea of popping into the pub for a quick one as he parked up, but decided against it, he needed some good kip. He could barely keep his eyes open. He'd grabbed a few hours on the ferry, but it was too choppy to settle for long.

As he came up to the crossroads, he reached for a fag from his pocket, and realised he'd left them in the cab. Shit! He used to be able to rely on Hope for fags, but she'd rarely had any herself now. Send April out for them. Right now, he fancied a tinned steak and kidney pie, chips, and mushy peas. Hope knew to have that in the house, especially when she knew he was due back. His mouth was watering already. Comfort. And Hope was bound to be gagging for it. She was always pawing him since he'd been out. She wasn't what she had been, but got to do your duty, he thought, keep the bloody peace and get some sleep. The sun warmed his face, and if it carried on like this tomorrow, he'd take the boys out for a drive in the cab. He was in such a good mood that he nodded at the old bint who'd been watching him as she snipped at her hedge. He put on a strut as he felt her eyes bore his back, eyeing his holdall with suspicion.

It was good to see the front gate; he'd been away for just over a week. There was no denying it, it was good to be in a house. He could see the kids in the garden, and the yelps as they caught sight of him and started screeching up the path. He closed the gate, set down his suitcase and presented his open arms. "Dad!" The boys grabbed his legs, "Can I get on your shoulders?" shouted Luke. Andy backed up to the wall so he could climb onto him easily, while Matthew checked out his pockets and handed the sweets around. Andy liked the cheek of him. He noticed that Hope was losing some ground with him since he'd been back. She'd got too stuck in her ways.

It was good to see them being proper boys. Matthew and Mark dragged his bag down the path behind him, "April's been bossing us again Dad, after you said she can't," Matthew announced.

"John's not well. Mum's crying," added Mark.

Andy braced himself as he ducked through the front door. Hope never stopped crying, just the slightest thing would get her going. Bloody work shy that was the problem! She needed a job. It would give her something else to think about. His Mum had always said, "Women like her don't know the meaning of real work. You'll rue the day you set eyes on her. You'll be the one paying for that kid of hers."

April looked up from where she sat on the Sofa with John's head in her lap, stroking his sleeping face. Hope was nowhere to be seen, "Where's your mum?" he asked, glancing round the lounge and along through the kitchen.

"She's in bed. Mum's been waiting for you to get back. Granddad's dead. She got an emergency telegram!" Andy looked at April. The smudged streaks down her cheeks. She stared at him as her eyes brimmed again, her lips pressed into a thin line, trying to hold them back. She didn't get that from Hope, as much as she bloody worshipped her mother. She was always willing to pick up where Hope left off with shopping, cleaning, bathing the kids; she made herself useful, and she didn't talk much. She did like to wander off by herself though. She was getting to that age now. He didn't want anyone spoiling her.

Matthew dragged the bag into the house, and Luke slid down from his shoulders shouting, "Presents!" Matthew sat on it and told them they had to wait for Dad. John woke up in the noise and jumped over into his lap as Andy collapsed back into the armchair. April went to the kitchen to make tea.

A rush of tiredness came over Andy. You couldn't get away from anybody here, he thought. Unless you made a point of it, or went for a piss, either of which was guaranteed to bring on a round of questions from Hope. Bigger than the van, but he felt more open to scrutiny at a distance.

"Andy," came the wail of Hope's voice. He rolled his eyes. "Andy!" short and demanding. The sound of thunder on the ceiling as something was dragged down the landing to the top of the stairs. After the knock of heels on the bare wood, Hope appeared at the foot of the stairs in the open door. "I've got to fuckin go darling. Has she told you?" Andy said nothing. "April! Didn't you tell him? Make some tea for us – there's a love. Do you want a sandwich for now? I could send her out for some fish and chips before I go." Hope went over and sat on the arm of the chair and flung her arms around Andy's neck and pulled herself back to try and catch his eye.

"Where the fuck do you think you're going? I just got back," said Andy, deliberately avoiding her look. Hope stiffened.

"Don't start now! I've got to get to Mum's tonight. The funeral's tomorrow! I said I'd be there by teatime. I'm going to be late as it is. You know what she's like."

"Yeah – and what the fuck about me? What about the kids?" The kids fell silent and look uncomfortably at each other. John started to cry in Andy's lap, burying his face into his jacket. Andy stared into the distance, "I'll drive you tomorrow," he spoke slowly "I need to sleep."

"Nobody said you couldn't fucking sleep you bastard. April's here! My dad is fucking dead!" Hope had stood up at the side of the chair, glaring down with contempt. Her mouth twitched and grimaced; he knew she'd been drinking. "I'll tell you what we get out of it if you really want to know. We get some money for a car. Mum wants to buy us a car so I can go up and visit more often. And she's going to take me shopping for the kids' shoes for school. Yeah, that's right. Thought it might shut you up! Who do you think sorted us out while you were away? We owe her something you know," her voice began to tremble. When she was defiant, she could never keep it up for long. She'd break in a minute. And she burst into tears, "I can't take any more," she went upstairs to her usual refrain, "I'm going to get my pills, I'm taking the bloody lot."

The boys stared at each other. "Dad? Can we take presents outside?" pleaded Luke. Andy walked over to the kitchen table and slung his bag on top and emptied it out. He handed out boxes of sweets, and the plastic guns he'd bought. The boys disappeared, back into the garden

Andy looked up to the ceiling to the sound of muffled sobs, "Forget the tea, I'm gonna sort your Mum out and get some kip."

"Dad," April faltered, "She is really upset, you know, about Granddad. And I am. But I've been helping. She had to go to bed. She's got a curse as well." Andy shook his head, that's all he needed to hear. He took a note from his wallet and held it out to April, "Take the boys and get some fish and chips for tea when it opens. I'm going to help your Mum get ready and get some sleep."

Andy could barely keep his eyes open as Hope was in the final throes of packing. There was no point arguing with her. She had already arranged a lift to the train station with one of the neighbours. He watched as she pulled a couple of dresses from the back of the wardrobe that she kept for visiting her parents. The last thing he remembered was the smell of Shoe White as she sulkily dabbed and painted her stilettos. No fucking. No Pie.

When he woke it was dusk. He could hear April's voice silencing the boys as they made their way up to the attic bedroom, stifling their excitement, as April told them Dad was asleep. If they weren't well behaved Dad would be too tired to take them for a drive in the cab tomorrow, she told them. Good girl he thought and decided to stay on the bed until they'd settled down. His bag was at the door. She'd even lugged it upstairs. He pulled out the cheap bottles of Scotch he'd bought. He fancied a drink. He sat back on the bed, drinking from the bottle.

The house had fallen silent, and it was dark. He heard the stairs creak as April crept down, closed the door, and switched the television on. He was awake now and was feeling pleasantly drunk. He leant out of the window into the night breeze. He needed a bath. He'd pour himself a proper glass of whiskey and lie back in the bath.

He went down the stairs – through the crack in the door he could see April lying on the sofa with her legs leaning up against the back, watching TV. She jumped as the latch clicked and he walked into the room. Her wide-eyed sudden focus on him as she span round and sat upright, burnt through his drunken haze; like waking to bright daylight.

"I'm just watching a film. Can I stay up 'til the end?" he liked it that she asked. Her hands were pressed onto the seat under her knees as she looked up at him. Sweet kid. He pretended to be surly, "You can if you make me a coffee later. I need a bath."

She smiled and slumped back with an affectionate sigh that took him by surprise, "Thanks Dad! Do you want some toast as well?" He hadn't eaten all day. Yes, he would like some toast.

Andy lay back in the shallow bath and took another glug of whiskey. He wished Hope was there; they'd have a laugh. She would have knocked back this whiskey like water. She was great when she was drunk. She didn't give a shit. When they first met, she was dancing on the tables in a coffee bar, flashing her knickers. She was living with her parents. Religious types, but wanted to do the right thing by her, and her little bastard. Boring she said. They had a bit of cash, but they didn't like to spend it. They didn't want to do anything rash. She wanted to live.

They moved into his Mum's place. They'd had a ball. She got a part-time job in the record shop, and he fixed cars, cash in hand. Cars were all he knew. He was the youngest of her boys, and they were all gone now. Mum looked after the kid, although his Mum liked a good drink too, they'd all got on. But, it was fucking trouble, having a little girl around the house. He'd grown up with brothers. When Hope fell for their first kid, he got what he wanted, a boy, and they kept coming. You'd think it would have made her happy, but oh no. He wasn't good enough for her Mum and Dad and they wouldn't help out, so he got into 'handling' second-hand cars for a living. He'd done time before, but he was footloose and fancy-free then, he'd been able to go with the flow when he got out. But with her, when he'd come out there'd been another mouth to feed, and she was even more bloody miserable. His mum threw them out after Matthew, and they'd ended up in the van. He'd got to like it. Life was more relaxed He still liked his little breaks at her Majesty's pleasure though. It cleared the decks.

This time though; she'd really got them sorted out. She got the house, she'd tapped up support from the church and got him parole and a driving job, and now the old bastard was dead it looked like they might get a car. Maybe even a bit of dosh. She might bloody cheer up.

The water was getting cold now, not that he could really feel it anymore. He grabbed the bath towel and wrapped it round his waist. April looked round as he walked across the lounge and put the whiskey bottle on the coffee table next to his armchair, "You look like an Egyptian king," said April.

"Don't mind if I do," Andy replied, drawing himself up in a regal pose, "I'm ready for my coffee and toast." He gave a double clap and sat down laughing in his armchair.

April relaxed, "You're drunk aren't you, Dad?"

"Nothing wrong with getting a bit drunk in your own home. Now where's that fuckin' coffee? Eh?"

"I got it all ready when the film finished," said April proudly.

When she came back from the kitchen, she was tightly holding a tray. It had a steaming cup of coffee; sugar in a bowl; buttered toast piled up on the plate with a clean knife lying beside it, and two pots; one of marmite and one of jam. Her face was beaming as she placed it on the table next to the whiskey, "It is done my Lord." She said as she stood back for approval.

"You know – you're a great kid. I swear I don't know where you get these fancy ideas from."

"I read it in a book … and we do about the past at school – in the old world people used to have their tea on a tray in the garden."

"Fucking 'ell! Bit late for that – it's dark. But I bet Kings had their tea on a tray anytime, anywhere they bloody liked. Thank you kindly, little Madam! Why don't you get yourself some, and join me?"

"Can I?"

"Yes, you bloody well can! Right, I need a clean shirt." He crept upstairs. He didn't want to wake the boys. When he got back April was buttering her toast. Andy turned to tighten the towel round his waist and walked back to the armchair, "Now, let's have that toast." He took a large swig of coffee, and filled it up again from the whiskey bottle, and gulped it down. The warmth of it made him shudder, "Oh, that's the business. Wanna try some?"

April's head dropped forward and she stared in surprise, "Really!" she said.

"Yeah, go on, a little bit ain't gonna hurt you. Me mum used to give it to us when we were babies. I'm still here, aren't I? Helps you sleep." April held out her mug, Andy reached over with the bottle and splashed some in, "Go on then! Knock it back!" April spluttered at the first mouthful, then tried to look like a grown up. Andy laughed at her, "You should see the faces you're pulling."

Once he'd taken the first bite Andy ate greedily, he crammed the toast into his mouth, and chewed until it was gone. He laid back in the armchair. He felt satisfied. Comfortable. Home took on a rosy glow, and he breathed in silence.

"Thanks for that. You're good company." They sat in silence. Andy poured himself another whiskey. "Another?" April nodded, as she held out her cup her eyes were bright and glazed. "You know, this is the first time we've been on our own together. Get to know each other a bit. Have a bit of fun."

Andy fell back again. "How are you feeling?" he slurred theatrically.

"A bit dizzy… but nice… Do you think Mum's OK?" she said quietly.

"Oh, come on, don't get maudlin … nothing worse than a maudlin drunk." For a moment he felt a pang of guilt. "Come here, give us a cuddle." April stood up, and stumbled forwards into his lap.

He held her close as she started to cry, "I want Mum," he felt the drops of her warm tears fall onto his chest. He held her tighter. "Do you want to sleep with me tonight?"

"Yes." She snuffled. He felt warmth pulsing through his body.

"You know what that means don't you?" April remained silent. "It means that you're the mummy tonight."

He almost dropped her down on the bed. She had fallen asleep and was a dead weight now. He shifted her limbs to make her comfortable. The sky was clear, and the moonlight flooded through the large windows across her legs. He could hear the rustle of the trees in the warm night breeze through the open window, and the occasional bark of a dog. Funny, he thought, how you could appreciate something as simple as an open window and a quiet night once you've done a bit of time. He sat on the sill and looked out; lit a cigarette and blew smoke rings into the night.

"That looks like magic Dad." He turned to look. She was lying there, on her side, watching him. Not looking at him, but following disappearing smoke rings, "I wish I could do that."

"You can do anything you want. You know that don't you? Just a bit of fun."

"Am I as much fun as Gloria? She said you had a good laugh" April said, as she sat up on the bed to see the moon from the window.

Andy raised his eyebrows, "Mmm, she tell you that did she," and he walked over and pushed her back down as he fell by her side, "I don't know yet do I."

Chapter 7

Your mum was away last night. She'll be back soon. You made the breakfast. You liked making breakfast. You made toast, and you made cornflakes and milk, and Dad gave you money to go and get juice and coffee. He said it's like France. You made it nice. You made all the boys sit up properly and not make a mess.

Everyone complains when you make rules, but rules are very important. Your teacher said that. She told you that the world would be broken if you don't have rules. You can see that. She said rules help you think about things, so you can solve problems. She said it takes a genius to break the rules. That's how we make progress. When you grow up you might be a genius.

You like to make rules about the spoons. You like them to be shiny. You should put the cornflakes in the bowl, and people should only put the milk on when they are sat down at the table. Ready to eat. You can't keep getting up and down from the table. No running around, or they will get soggy. You can't always explain this to young kids, but they must try. You have to remind them. You do it again.

Today is going to be very warm and sunny. It said on the radio. It's going to be a hot summer. That's good because you've got a long holiday. You'll be at home. You can go for walks. You can help Mum. It can be hard work keeping things tidy in all the rooms.

They want to play. You don't listen. You count the cornflakes in the picture on the box. You count the furniture.

The armchair on the door side belongs to your Mum. Unless she wants to lie on the settee. She sits in Dad's chair when he's away. She sits anywhere she likes. Her record player is in the window seat. Behind her main chair. She used to work in a record shop. She loves her records. She knows them all by heart, and you do too. You like it when she sings them. When she makes up her own words, she makes you laugh. You copy her. Sometimes, she tickles you when you sing. A test to see if you still can. Sing when you laugh. She is very careful and very strict about her records. They mustn't get scratched. Nobody. And you mean nobody, is allowed to touch Mum's record player. Or her records.

When it's sunny, you like the door to be open. It makes you feel clean and happy. You have opened it today. But the boys want to go out to play. Their cornflakes are getting soggy. They aren't concentrating. They tell Dad they want to take their toast outside. He winks at Matthew. Well they can. You need to scrape it first. You burnt it. Sometimes, toast is hard to make. You have to keep an eye on it. Concentrate. You can't leave it under the grill for too long. It's irresponsible to let them take their toast outside. You are meant to be in charge. You understand. You like to do it yourself. You know what they mean. If they have a drink first. But running in and out of a house with orange juice and toast gets messy. Someone has to clean it up when it gets spilt.

You tried to kiss them before they went out to play. You read it in a book. Kissing children makes them behave. It don't though. The trouble is boys don't always like to get kissed. Boys are different from girls. They don't like reading. They don't like school. They don't care about shiny spoons. Mum said that they don't get different when they grow up.

Your dad says that it is a good thing that you are clean and tidy round the house. He shouts at Mum about the mess. Says she's a mess. It makes her sad. She always gets sad when Dad is with us, even in our new life. She says it's easy for you. You're not at home all day. One day you'll know. You do some cleaning as much as you can. You surprise her sometimes. She doesn't notice. Doesn't say she does. She notices if you don't. After breakfast you will polish all the knives and forks and spoons, so that they are very shiny. She will notice then when she gets back. It will shine like treasure.

That is why your brothers prefer your mum making breakfast. She really doesn't mind. Only if you bother her. Or say you don't want anything, or something else. She gets upset. You might get a slap round the head. Once she's decided you will get a slap round the head, no matter how long you stay out of her way, you get what's coming to you.

Your dad is not your real dad. He told you. Mum told you first. You didn't let slip. He told you things that you should only tell grownups. He said you are very grown up for your age. A little woman. He told you that you are much nicer than your mum. You wish he didn't. It's scary. You think your mum would be really upset about that. So you have to be really careful not to tell her. He doesn't see the good things about her. She's nicer when he's not there.

Mum isn't happy. Granddad was ill. Now he's dead. She's gone to his funeral. She won't even see him one last time. Neither will you. Mum told you he thought she made a bad choice about keeping you. He said you should have brought joy to someone that wanted a baby. Instead, you brought misery through the door.

Granddad didn't like Dad from the first day he set eyes on him. Mum says if she knew then, what she knows now. You make your own bed, and you have to lie on it. It's not funny. She doesn't make the beds very much. What if you're not in your own bed. It's a joke she said. Just a saying. You know it's silly to think about that. You know it's complicated. If you ask about complicated stuff they say, 'you're just a kid'. You remember to say the right thing. Not what you think. Everyone gets upset, and it gets really bad. You just bring more misery. It's not worth it. And you mean misery. Even Dad said that.

Everything was so different from before. It's ever since Dad's been back. Moving here was like a pretending dream. You used to go and see him in prison, with Mum. The welfare said Mum could stop taking you bigger kids because of school. She just took the twins. So they didn't forget him. You were glad about that. Well sort of. You did want to go with her. Prisons are scary. The walls are high. So people can't get out. They have to be trapped. It makes everyone angry to be in there. You can hear the keys locking the iron gates. People crying when it was time to go. You were glad you could all go home. Mum making you dinner. Play Ludo before bed. When the boys were asleep. You could stay up. You and Mum. Looking at catalogues. Making plans. Mum with a small golden Sherry. Just a little one.

Before visiting time, sometimes, Mum went to the pub first. To calm her nerves. Once she shouted at the prison guard. He said she didn't have a ticket to get in. He was nice. Gave her a cup of tea. Gave you some squash. He explained about the rules. Dad forgot to tell them about your visit. He said he would bend the rules. Called the guard man. Hey, let Dad have our visit. Dad laughed at Mum making a fuss, and said she was drunk. You stood behind and held her.

You don't talk to anybody about the prison. Mum said you have to put the past behind you. It will be different now we don't get Giros. Mr. Fisher did a reference. Got Dad a job driving lorries. He drives to the boat. Crosses the sea. He told you some French words. You say Bonjour. Ca va? Ca va bien Monsieur! Je suis April. Ooh la la. You told your teacher. She said impressive. It will help to prepare you for big school.

You can use shiny spoons like spy mirrors. You've found a way to sneak. Watching Dad in the other corner. You've got your back to him. You're pretending to inspect the spoons whilst you shine them with the tea towel. It's like he's in a crystal ball in the future. Twisted in space. He's reading the paper in his chair. He said life's a joke. There's nothing worth listening to. Except yesterday. You know he listens to everything you say. He watches everything you do. It's better when he is across the sea. He says the village is full of fucking sissies and snobs. You be careful. Don't you get like that. It's not easy to get it right. Mum said he had to get used to the new life. You know what he means. It's different to the van, to the valley. We can't go back. It's gone now. He wasn't with us when we first lived here. People still have to get to know about him.

Dad fucked you last night. He said he did. He asked you if you loved him, and you said yes. You thought he would tell you off if you said no. But he hurt you anyway. He nearly choked you. You want to tell Mum when she comes home. She'll tell him not to. She wanted you to tell her if you started. If you bleed and your fanny hurts. It happens to girls. Well it is. You feel a bit sick. You don't know how to say it. He said if you tell, he'd go to the prison again. Mum will be back on the Social. You had a bit of fun. You'd break her heart. If she knew what you'd done. He's right. She was dreaming of us all getting on our feet. Living a normal life at last. You would bring misery again. We will be in a bad mess. You woke up early. Went to wash. You stopped bleeding. It was only a bit. Not that bad. Fanny blood is sticky. Tastes salty.

The sun shines on the spoon. It makes a strong reflection. Strong and bright. It can reach the other side of the room. You can move it to make it point on what you want. You can make it dance. It looks like magic. It's not. It's science. You can do science. Your teacher shows you. It all depends, but your mum gets interested when you explain it to her. But, it all depends really.

This is a very important year for mankind. You don't want anything to spoil it. Man has landed on the moon and science made it happen. Well, people did science and made it happen. And Eli. And you wonder when your stone will get to the moon. You put a wish in it. You would like to go to the moon. You want to be a detective. Your teacher said that you are very good at solving problems. That's science. Like Eli. There will be problems on the moon that need solving. There are lots of interesting problems in the whole universe. You can solve problems if you think about them. You would like to be the first girl on the moon: April Smart,

Moon Detective Agency. You wish your mum had called you another name like Lucy or Jane. No one else is called April that you know. She said it was the right name because you were born in April. That doesn't make it the right name. Lots of people are born in April. What if there were only twelve names in the world. She said she just couldn't think. It was right at the time and that's that. It's just up to your parents. Her name is Hope, and she says it doesn't suit her either. You think it does.

You want your mum to come home. You just want her to come home. You could sing for a bit, and then you could go out to play. You promise God, you won't tell her today. Today would be a bad day to tell her you are feeling sick, and you've been bleeding. She's just had a funeral. You could write a prayer about it. You could do that. You can tell her another day.

You're wiping the table, and Dad is watching you. You can't think of what to say. You don't want to look at him. You don't want him to ask you anything. You want the table to be shiny.

"Oi, you better fucking tidy up in here as well … your fucking mother'll be back soon, probably be in a right fucking mood after the funeral. Look at me when I'm talking to you … You'd better knock that fucking stupid look off your face - you'll end up like her if you're not careful. I don't know why she made such a fucking song and dance about it - he hasn't even bloody spoken to her for years."

You don't like it. Now, when he says fucking. You know what it means. You get the things to clean the telly end. You want it to be nice for Mum. When you're cleaning the carpet you push the carpet sweeper towards him like a sword. You don't feel scared. You wore your trousers today. He said that he's not your real Dad, so it's like you're his secret girlfriend. You will never have a boyfriend like him.

He asked you to make a cup of tea. He's only joking. He tried to pull your hand. You pulled it back. You walked away to put the kettle on. You want to keep busy until Mum gets home. You read your book. Write your prayer at the table. You hide it in your true book of stars. You make covers for your books out of the left-over wallpaper. You keep it quiet.

And. You can hear Mum. You can hear her. The boys are shouting and running up the path to the gate. The twins run in to tell Dad. You want to shout and run too. But you think. You better put the kettle on again, so the tea is fresh for her.

They all come squashing through the door. You feel like laughing, crying. Mum has lots of bags, and Matthew and Mark. They drop them inside the door. A fence between you. Gran has sent lots of sweets and toys for us kids. You try to smile at my mum. She is cuddling John, and he is putting his hands over her face. She can't see you. She sits in her chair. You try to stop the boys from emptying the bags. Matthew kicks you and Mark is laughing. They grab some sweets, really sly, and run outside. Luke sits by Mum.

"Oi, make your mum a cup of tea then you dopey cow," Dad says, like he's telling a joke.

"Yeah, come on love, I've had a long day." It's like she doesn't even want to look at you, even when you take the tea. She doesn't even notice when you go upstairs. You stab a hole in the wall. Through the plaster, with a spoon. You post your prayer inside. You push the bookcase hard against it. No one can see it.

They're talking about the will when you go out the front door. Mum says it will be more than enough for a new car. You can hear Matthew and Mark round the corner of the house, counting out sweets. You've got your planet book from Eli. You sit on the wall outside the gate. On the crossroads.

You like sitting on the crossroads. It can be busy. People meet. Most of the time they don't come. You sit on the wall. Under the hum of the pylon. It's easy to climb up. Put a leg on either side. A pile of stones, with a smooth rounded top. You can rest your book on the wall, or hold it up. Today you smell. You know you do. Smell of Dad. You smell of burning tyres and whiskey, old petrol and manky milk, of cigarettes and pilchards, of shit sweets and spray polish, and it feels like what you're made of. It makes you feel sick. There is wind over the crossroads. Blows the smell away. Your legs were feeling weak, hurting where they join your body, but they feel strong around the wall. It makes you cry. You can't help it. You are crying quite a lot actually. You hold your book up to your face like a posh lady on a quiet horse and read. You have to work it out.

Chapter 8

Miss Gomer's shop sells Bazooka Joe's, like the ones that Eli liked. He said he had them since he was a kid. He got lots of science stuff from saving wrappers when he was a kid. They are from America, and when I've collected enough wrappers I can get a telescope, binoculars and a camera for looking and recording things. And, as well, chewing is good for my eyes. Like right now, I'm sitting on the bench on The Green, and I can see across the roofs to the trees along the hills up from the valley. Even the ones that are very far away, miles away. I can't actually see the detail of the leaves, they are like green clouds. But, if you chew like a cowboy, and squint your eyes, it helps you concentrate on the details. If I had a telescope, I could look really up close though, at the long grass round the edge, up the walls, and see every leaf and all the green hills and trees and the clouds. At all the stains of gold lichens. From here I can see that they are dropped all over the rooftops and the walls all the way down the hills to the valley roads. After it's rained, they really show up. It is like the stars are breaking up, melting and dripped down in the night when the clouds aren't there to soak them up. Well maybe not even the stars, but something. The space rocket had to let big chunks go into space, and they were on fire. The man on telly said we don't know the consequences on the stars yet. Like my mum doesn't know the truth about Dad and me yet. She'll might say that I've got to sort it out for myself. Or get flippin' angry.

When Dad's home I go out for as long as I can so he can't see me much. He's given me a wink and a shilling three times now, when Mum sends me to the shops. Perhaps he's sorry now.

If I sit here on the bench, nobody can see me from the other side of the hedge when they go by, and nobody looks up the slope from the road past at the bottom. Anyway, I sat all afternoon once and nobody noticed. It's nice there because I take some crackers and the birds come and take the crumbs that fall off. And I touch the sign of not forgetting the Nesbits, so they can be here and watch with me. I wonder why the clock man doesn't come and sit here. I didn't want to ask him about the Nesbits. Mum said she's heard to steer clear of him, he's trouble, but I stood by his gate and talked to him before when he is gardening, and he just talked to me about what he was doing in the garden. He wasn't out today.

I was reading and then watching the window of his place the whole time, and I didn't see anyone moving. Anyway, I might as well go in the gate. I might as well! I could call in on my way to somewhere past there. He's right next to the bottom of the green, so I could go up that way to the lane after.

He's got a tiny spy window that looks up to the green. From the green his house looks like a grey boat because of the slope of the road up the wall. Or it could be like a whale, and the window is the eye. Like Jonah. A small eye. It's really small, and it's the only window on the whole wall of his house that looks out. He still doesn't look out though.

I saw the woman next door watching me from her upstairs. She's got lots of windows. It's not an old place like his. They're nosey. One of her kids is in our class. He thinks he's really posh because his dad's a builder, and they've got signs everywhere round the village saying their name. Everyone knows Mr Crane ... and Mr. Crane knows everybody. Oh, Mr Crane is a very big pain! I'll tell Mum that song, that'll make her laugh.

His old gate makes a creaking noise. The wood is cracking and splitting. I never done it before, but I open the latch and stand on the bottom rung, it swings slowly right round wide open, back to the wall. It sounds like clock man when he was having a think about my question –

Mmmmmmmm ... slow and creaky. He didn't mind when I asked questions. Not from the gate when he's in the garden. I like standing on the gate, talking to him. Now he knows me, I think he won't mind if I come in now.

He told me that three generations were born and died in this house, and he'll be the fourth and last. I wonder if his mum used to stand on the gate like this when she was a kid mmmmmmmm... He said she had green fingers, and she could make anything grow. And that's true. When I turn round and look at the garden there are plants of every shape and size and colour. Like you see in a storybook about palaces and princesses, or books about in heaven at Sunday school. Every day that I come here there are different plants: tall red, blue and yellow flowers, small white flowers, big red daisies and small white daisies in the grass. I like the big flowers, that when I look close up are made up of lots of tiny flowers. There are flowers that climb to the roof, and froth over the walls. Like milk in a saucepan.

It smells nice here, and the wind is gentle because it's closed in from walls except over the valley. It's like when they have the ballroom when the princess gets married. The plants are too polite to speak. The leaves flutter like fans, and they just bow nicely in the sun. Pleased and peaceful people, who are glad to see each other. The clock man makes me feel like that because he thinks about what he says to plants. And to me. He said plants have good manners and take their turn most of the time. But we have to help them about getting overcrowded, we can't be lazy or greedy for them. He says that not all plants get on together and see each other off. Sometimes, they don't get on with the land, and then they curl up and die and their seeds go somewhere better. Some plants you can just put anywhere. He likes to save the sensitive ones and puts them in special pots that have just the right dirt in them. I didn't know things could die without the right dirt.

When I knock on the door, I hear a chair scrape against the floor when he gets up. Perhaps he's having a sleep. He hasn't recovered from his cough since the winter. He said it was a bad winter, too much snow and rain and not enough frosts to kill the bugs off. In the porch he keeps all his medicines. He has dried out all the old plants, smelly herbs and flowers, and hangs them in the porch. They look really nice, even though they are dead and brown. I wouldn't like his medicine though it's full of spider webs and flies. Maybe that is why he doesn't get better.

When he answers, I can hear all the clocks ticking. I can see them all down the wall with their pendulums swinging. It looks like there is another dance, and on the shelf along the top, all the other clocks are sat waiting to be asked.

He is too big for his door, so he has to stoop down. His white hair is sticking out around his head, like the sun and it's a bit yellow. I think he forgets to stand up straight again sometimes, like he's always ready to get in his house again. He's got a big brown coat with pockets down to his knees. He said it's to protect his clothes, but that is his clothes if he never takes it off. He wears lots of shirts and jumpers, and all the different collars all get jumbled around his neck.

I think he wears special gloves with the fingers cut off for doing the clocks and takes them off for gardening. His blue eyes are big and watery like he is crying, but when I asked him before he said no, he's not upset, he's just old.
"Hello April. What you up to?"

"Well … I can't be long, but I just thought I would come and say Hello … and to ask you about that thing we said."

"Ah! What thing was that then?"

"What you said last week…about…you might learn me garden stuff in the holidays. I don't mind doing it for nuffin, and I could make it nice with you. Learn about things in the right place, and I won't get on your nerves or anything."

It's alright to ask him. I stepped back a little bit out of the porch so he could come out. I crouched down and started pulling up the weeds in the path. He laughed, and his breath was wheezing in and out of him. I pulled all the ones around the porch out. "See, it's harder to do now … if you don't feel well."

He looked around, and I think he was thinking of his Mum, because he said, "Don't your mum want you doing her garden?"

"Well, she said she will later on, but the council haven't digged it for years, so it's too hard – and the little uns'll only mess it up anyway." I don't think my mum will ever want to have a garden. If she ever gets rich, she said she'd have a swimming pool and a load of concrete so people could dance and have a bar. The council cut the grass last week. "She only wants the grass cutting for now. It gets rid of the dandelions, – and us kids makes it worse blowing the clocks to tell the time … So can I?"

He is walking along the borders and he's not looking at me. It's not a good sign when grown-ups go quiet. It usually means no. I don't want to pester him. "Well, I can't see that it'll do any harm if …"

I jumped in before he got a chance, "Yes, yes, yes, YES! Oh, really can I?"

"Alright!" I tried to calm down and stop being so excited,

"Mind you, I don't want you running down in and out of here every five minutes. Maybe once a week or so! And - I'm not making no arrangements. If no one answers the door – no one does. And - I don't want to hear no gossip about anyone's business, and I don't want no one hearing about mine." I didn't interrupt.

It was like we had already started doing work. I wanted to ask about all the different kinds of dirt. Perhaps he would let me plant some of my favourite things from pictures, "We could make roses round the door bit and …"

"Hey! Don't you forget whose garden it is. My mother spent all her life making this garden. I like things the way they are – just needs a bit of care that's all. Don't want no young ones telling me what's what."

"Sorry. Well, you could learn me what things have to be done – an' then sometimes I could do it by myself if you're busy … or fed up with people." He laughed. "Well, I get fed up with people sometimes, and I go round the Barley Fields or read. So, I know what it's like if you do get like that."

One of the nice things about the clock man is that you can look him right in the eye and he doesn't get angry. He looks back at you in a kind way, like it's important to tell the truth. He raised his head back and looked at me like he was a detective, "Hmm…" and went into the cottage. He came out with two black toffees in his hand. He said he makes toffee before. It's special medicine toffee that makes him feel better. He held one out to me. I knew it was magic as I looked at it sat in the curl of his hand. "Can I come next week then?"

"Well, like I said if..."

"Thanks," I said, "See you." I took the toffee and ran.

When I walked across The Green I chewed the toffee. It does taste a bit like medicine, but I know it is magic. It made me think about everything I was going to learn. It made me think about interesting things so that I didn't feel sad anymore. He's not the clock man, he's The Toffee Man.

When I got in Mum was drinking, sat in her chair, listening to records. I knew she was in a bad mood. I don't want to ask her where Dad is. "What took you so long?" She sounded really mean. I didn't know if I should tell her. But then there would be too many things to try and remember not to say.

"I've been to see the clockman."

"What the old bloke on the Green? There's talk at the shop. He's not right in the head. A wrong 'un."

"He …" I tried to think of something different. She would only say I had to do our garden if I wanted to do gardens. "He … might have needed some shopping … he's a bit old. And he's not very well."

"That's not our business. Someone else can help him. I've got enough to deal with. He's trouble! I told you before, and I mean it. Stay away."

I felt angry when she said that. It's not fair, but you can't talk to Mum when she's been drinking. Since Dad's been back, she just shouts and says nasty things. She always says sorry after, if she's been really horrible. She's got special tablets that will make her sad go away. The doctor told her she wasn't supposed to drink, or she would get a bad reaction from it. And she doesn't take any notice. The best thing is to get out of her way for now. "Mum. Can I go down the Barley Fields?"

"No you can't! You can take the boys up to the park! Get them out from under my bloody feet."

I feel like telling her about Dad. That he thinks I'm nicer than she is. But I don't, the magic of the Toffees stops me.

Chapter 9

Miss Katy Gomer watched April coming down the lane from the shop window. She had been polishing the tins in the entrance display rack, paying attention to the rims that were dulled from handling by customers. She was admiring the silver crescents of the tins gleaming in the late afternoon sun and looked across to see the late afternoon sun shining through the trees. As the sun splashed and danced along the road, April emerged from the lane and sat against the wall on the grassy bank and began to read a book she took from a shopping bag. It was heartening to see any child with such habits, but particularly this one. Since the arrival of her father, it was more often April that came to the shop now, but she had heard that Hope's visits to the off licence were more frequent.

Miss Gomer was wary of familiarity with either Hope or April, bracing herself against appeals for credit. When she had asked Fred for advice on the matter in his role as village policeman, he had a advised a polite sign addressing all customers. She had felt that would be vulgar and offend her regulars. Her mother had never had to display such a sign in the decades since she had established the shop, even in the war years. Her mother's authority was built on intimacy and discretion; skills she had assumed when she was a maid for local gentry in her youth. Her father was a senior clerk at the factory where many of the villagers had worked too. Between them they had been privy to all the lives of people in this village and knew more than any one person knew of their precarious, or immutable bonds, and what informed them. The table talk that revelled in the weaving together of the tales and imaginings left Katy with a horror of sharing the smallest secret. Putting up a sign would underline her growing sense of the loss of authority.

Fred said we should be showing them the way. They didn't know any different. Different communities. Give them time. When Clara had reported the trespass at the station, he'd had a conversation with April. It was a simple mistake. April had apologised to Clara. Miss Gomer knew that to be true. Certainly, now, whenever she came to the shop, she invariably collected a few things for Clara. What she did know for certain is that the father had a criminal habit, and there were rumours that these habits had led to imprisonment on more than one occasion. Fred said he was known to the police, but a petty criminal. The modern way was to be more supportive, and now the family had a home, he had a job, it was felt things would change.

Rev Fisher had asked Jasper to help. Fred had spent a lot of time with Jasper, who had made local headlines as a lawyer in support of recent justice system reform; the Smart family exemplified that mission. All this left Katy feeling that they should be alert whilst they were learning new ways, correction was a duty too.

By the time the bell over the door rang, and April walked into the shop, Katy had worked her way along the shelves with the duster and was back behind the counter. She was agreeable towards her but remained silent. The child did seem a little more subdued than usual as the shopping on the list was checked off and paid for; she would usually take any opportunity to engage. She waited for a second as she handed April the change, for the usual request of penny bubble gum with the remaining pennies, but none came.

When April suddenly produced two half crowns and asked for stamps, Katy referred her to the post office booth at the side of the counter. Her demeanour changed, as she fidgeted her feet and avoided her gaze as she held up the money to the screen, mumbling a request for two sets of the Concorde stamps on display, asking if it was a space rocket. Katy felt a stab of inadequacy. She liked to think that she could respond to most questions the village cared to throw up. Everything was changing fast. It was difficult to understand the purpose of it all. She seemed to receive notifications every week: new postage, new money, new allowances – all involving entirely new processes. She was quite relieved when the phone rang, and she was able to turn her thoughts to taking a grocery order for preparation.

She scribbled down the list, keeping her eye on April, as she brushed her hands along the shelves as she dawdled to the door. Suddenly April disappeared, and just as abruptly stood up again, clearly in the process of stuffing something into her pocket, making a jubilant skip to the door. Katy covered the receiver, startled by the sharpness of her own voice, "Can you come back here a moment please?" April turned but stood still at the door. "Don't you go anywhere! I'm watching you in the mirror." That child's face was full of guilt. She was obliged to confront it. "Sorry Mr Pynchon, I have a customer. Can I call you back in five minutes when I've checked the stock? OK. Yes. Thank you." She took an audible intake of breath as she put down the phone.

April took a few steps back to the counter, "I haven't done anything." April lifted her head in defiance as she spoke and looked her straight in the eye. She saw immediately that this was a familiar defence. Katy took a breath and tried to think how she was going to do this. April persisted, "I haven't got anything. Look!" She offered the bag of shopping. Katy beckoned her to come closer.

"I don't like to be put in this position April. Can you empty your pockets please? Here on the counter. Please." April walked slowly right up to the counter. Her face was bright red. She was breathing fast. Staring alternately back through to the shop front and then focussing on Katy's large, bony fingers. Looking at them the way Katy did herself, and she felt her own breath quicken, the blood rushing to her own face.

"It's just private things Miss Gomer. I haven't got anything. Honest! I'm just saving some things …" Katy watched tears welling, and tears pricked her own eyes, and she dare not blink in case they should escape. She could hear the blood coursing round her head, as she spoke again.

"I asked in a perfectly civilised manner if you could put the contents of your pockets on the counter. Please don't be rude!"

"I just needed a club ring … for my club … I got it now. I …"

"Are you trying to blame others for your own bad deeds?" April's mouth fell open. Miss Gomer attempted to soften her tone, alarmed by the desperation in April's face. "Give me the ring April. Someone will have lost it. We'll say no more about it. You'll have to go elsewhere from now on." Katy didn't want to say that. What were you supposed to do with these children? At the very least one expected a degree of honesty when they were caught red-handed. It didn't matter what Fred said. She was doing this child a service. She had been right. It wasn't a pleasant duty, but it had to be done. One shouldn't have to deal with these things. It should the parent's duty. She would speak with Hope.

A hopeful plea broke her thoughts, "Finders keepers Miss Gomer? It was on the floor."

Really. It was just too much. "Just because something is on the floor it doesn't mean you can steal it. It is stealing April. Give me the ring or I shall call PC Pilcrow right now." And April emptied her pockets onto the counter. There were, as April nervously explained, some 'magic' pebbles, Indian feathers from the tribes in the Barley Fields: a small pencil from her colouring box, and several sheets of paper which were clumsily stitched to make a stick man comic, and a thick roll of Bazooka Joe comics with an elastic band around them, with one separate Bazooka Joe wrapper still open. She was momentarily moved and transported to the world revealed through April's pockets, but persisted in her mission, and held out her hand, "And the ring? Now please! I'll be speaking to your mother of course."

April held up the open wrapper, blurting her excuses, "But ... I have to send for it first - I can get more - rings, and other stuff - but it's more than a hundred - and I want the telescope first - but it's worth it... I just found this one on the floor." Katy grabbed the wrapper impatiently. A bubble gum wrapper. She stared down into the corner there was an offer of an 'Initial Ring' for the letter 'A' in return for a quantity of wrappers. Katy felt her shoulders hunch as she watched April fall silent and crumple, and when she looked back up to face her the tears had streaked her face. "I'm sorry I nicked it Miss Gomer. I just thought nobody wanted it, that's all. I didn't mean to steal nothing. I never do that. I thought you'd put it in the bin. I didn't know you wanted them."

Then, April started to cry, very noisily. This was no ordinary cry. A howl which made what seemed like a long-awaited escape from deep inside her, and then a gut-wrenching sob. "Mu... mu – mum - I – want - Mum." Katy squirmed, not so much from embarrassment as recognition. She watched as April clutched and collapsed into the counter, as if she might find some comfort there. Katy reached out a tentative hand and finally placed it on the child's head, finally caressing her with her thumb, until she calmed. Katy thought about what could be done. What she had done.

"Wait there a minute!" Katy abruptly turned on her heels and went to the back of the shop, through the gentle clatter of coloured strips. She took down a box of bubble-gum from the storeroom and scooped out handfuls of the bubble-gum into a large paper bag.

When she came back, April was more composed, "Please. Don't tell Mum."

Katy held out the bag, "This is for you."

April cautiously opened the bag, and saw the contents, "Bloody hell – loads of them! Sorry... for swearing Miss."

"That's as maybe," she said quickly, "But, I should be sorry April ... and I am." she said stiffly. "I apologise. It was ... very wrong of me. I should have offered you an opportunity to explain. I'm sorry." And Katy put her hand forward, "Can we shake on it?"

And when April put her hand forward, they shook hands; her hand felt so small in her grip as April chattered, "I could get two rings. We could have a magic circle. What's your first name?"

"Katherine," said Katy stiffly, but surprising herself with a childish hope of atonement, "but you can call me Katy," using the opportunity to extract her hand from April's.

"I'll get one with a K for you. They stretch to any size."

"Well, that would be lovely April, but you get the telescope first. Show me when you do."

As April walked out of the shop, she saw she held the bag to her heart. Katy walked to the window to watch her as she skipped along and into the lane, holding herself to keep the warmth she felt inside. She would call Mr Pynchon and finish that order.

* * *

When Katy closed the shop at the end of the day it was a short walk home, but a world away. Once she had locked the gate to the garden wall behind her, she unbuttoned her blue funnel neck housecoat, hung it on the rack as she passed, and sprang up the staircase to the balcony.

The first-floor balcony looked straight out across the garden, over the drop of the valley across the canopy of the valley trees. Set back in the recess of the house, which had originally been two until her parents had bought the empty house next door. They had built a conservatory in the newly formed courtyard. The two houses mirrored each other, so when they had merged the two hallways and replaced the windows on the landing with French doors, it was very grand. It belied the modest rooms on either side.

It provided stars, clouds, sunshine, and sometimes an endless blue, depending on the time of year. All year round, early in the morning, and at the end of the day, she would sit on the bench, as they had done, and watch the dark winter branches become hazed with a mist of buds, blossoming into a vibrant youthful green that rustled with joy in the summer breeze, and rattled its autumn treasure at the haunting calls of winter.

When she was a child, Katherine had been given the Nesbit's old ground floor, with a bathroom, kitchen, parlour, which had the result of providing her with self-contained accommodation. She rarely saw her parents at home; perhaps in passing when they were entertaining, and later, more often when she assisted her mother with preparations for their soirees. Her parents saved their affections for each other. Sunday was family day. After the service, as the congregation paraded from the church, her father would lay his hands on her shoulders peck her cheek, while her mother stood back, flushed, and smoothing her scarf or patting down her coat.

She had spent her early childhood on the right of the house, and later, when it was acquired, the left. Just after her father had returned at the end of the war, they had eventually bought the house next door when Mr and Mrs Nesbit had abruptly left. They had received three telegrams within a month, confirming the loss of their three sons.

When the first telegram had arrived, she remembered arriving breathlessly from school, excited to share some victory she could no longer remember, to find Mrs Nesbit being consoled by her mother in their kitchen. Between strangled howls, Mrs Nesbit requested that Katharine go to the piano and play 'The Day Thou Gavest Lord Has Ended'. 'With vigour', her mother had mouthed across Mrs Nesbit's slumped shoulder. As she walked to the piano, through the broken sentences she realised that Joe had been killed.

Katharine had become accustomed to the requisite 'vigour' in Chapel during the war years, and she, despite her youth, had come to appreciate it as an unlikely source of balm, but still, she flinched as she walked to the small parlour. She selected the sheet music from the shelf a matter of custom, although she would not need it.

Without further instruction, she had played it a second time, and then waited with her hands in her lap while she considered the options. She had not heard them as they moved from the kitchen to the parlour, requesting a third rendition as they came, which they could all sing together. They had suddenly silenced by the sight of her sat upright, staring at the sheet music with tears of defeat in her eyes. Mrs Nesbit sprang forward, and kissed her on the head, "Oh, my dear, I should have thought, of course, you were so fond of Joe." And Katharine nodded, and played, and they sang.

Of course, she had been very fond of Joe. She treasured the sketches he had done of her when she was a child. She would come to the full realisation of her own inexplicable grief in the years to come. But no, the tears were not on account of Joe back then. It seemed rather petty actually; she was jealous. Jealous to have seen the tenderness with which her mother had stroked Mrs Nesbit's face, and her words: there is no loss like that of a firstborn son. There had been a fluidity in the comforts that her mother was able to give, as Mrs Nesbit had collapsed into her arms, and sobbed against her chest. Into the embroidered floral tabard she had made for her mother, and it displaced Katharine's resolve to confront her own needs.

The second telegram came the following week, cruelly testing the Nesbit's faith in God. Katharine was not asked to play when Mrs Nesbit came to share the news, but they did appear in Chapel the following Sunday, and the Reverend made visits. When the third telegram came Katharine was not to play at home at all, and the Nesbit's never went to Chapel again. The Reverend humbly knocked on their door, daily, but it was never answered. That Katherine had played Mrs Nesbit's hymn request three times on that first occasion haunted her, and tangled with her own tales, superstitions, and dreams, pulling and knotting, until the heart of her was held securely out of reach, merely an observer.

After school she would go home with the Nesbit boys. Joe was in the top class studying for exams, so he was in charge. Sometimes the younger two would tire of playing with her, so she would go for a walk with Joe, or they would find somewhere to sit in the lanes and fields. He would draw trees, and the hills and clouds, and sometimes she would sit still so he could draw her. But always, their walks began or ended with a visit to Harold.

Harold was nearly the same age as Joe, but he had left school to be an apprentice to his father, making and mending clocks. They worked at their house, but whenever Joe tapped at the window, Harold would come outside to sit with us in the garden. Katharine remembered the garden was incredibly beautiful; it was full of flamboyant and perfumed flowers. It was Harold's mother who had sold her the shop, in which she had also sold flowers. People had stopped being able to afford such luxuries, so they stayed in her garden, but she would send Harold to deliver flowers as a gift when there was an occasion. Everyone said Harold was shy, but Joe told her that his parents had died, and Harold was adopted when he was very young, and that made him thoughtful. Harold was often affectionately referred to as the 'chosen son', and he in turn, had chosen to love them and the life they had afforded him.

And over the years, as she looked back, she had seen that love had flowed like a babbling brook. And she had blossomed in the presence of love, and she imagined it might be for her. She'd spent many later afternoons in her early summers, listening to them discuss the passing light and how it fell on grass, on stones, on flowers, on faces and Harold listening out for, and explaining, any irregular notes in the striking of the church clocks that echoed around the valley, until they summoned them back home. And she watched their hands slip across each other as they exchanged some parting gift of a book, or object to be read or drawn, and caught the moment of hesitation in Joe's hand as they turned from the gate and walked home. She had become jealous of Harold, for his parents, for Joe. She didn't know what jealousy could become. How it could etch itself on every word, every look, and even a well-placed silence.

When Joe and Harold were called to service, Joe gave her his study books on drawing. She treasured them, privately, and developed the habit of their careful study on awakening, longing for his return. When he did not, and she had resolved that she would leave with other girls from the village and take up an opportunity for University, her parents would not support her. Her mother said it was God's will. God had chosen this path for them all. Katharine was to accept the Grace of God, and consider her path privately, with Him, as she was to do herself. God's Grace was not to be discussed with anyone else, or between them. Not ever.

In their later years her parents socialising was restricted to church activities outside the house, and now they were gone only she had ever inhabited this platform. For the first few years the view of the fall and rise of the valley was framed by the red brick walls but gradually the wisteria that her mother had planted at the back of the house, in memory of the boys, crept round, and with her care, created an arbour. At the end of everyday Katharine sat in her father's suit, looking out at the view, as the hues of the seasons came and went, embraced by her dead mother, as she never had in life, and smoking a pipe, as her father had done. Her parents bought her everything. Other children fashioned apple crates into dolls houses - hers was finely carved and painted by craftsmen. She felt her imagination was stolen from her, piece by piece, with every beautiful thing they bought her over the years. All that belonged to her were the manifestations of her fears.

Her nightmares didn't come in the dark, at night, as they used to. They came when the sun was up and backlit the trees in the garden and gave relief for the receding hills beyond. The birds did not make any ominous squawks or chattering sounds, flocks depart, no flapping of wings, or ruffle of feathers, or fall silent. Nothing of, or to, note.

Joe appeared at the open door as he always did. All neat and Sunday in his white shirt. He placed his foot behind the leg of the nearby chair and dragged it forward and placed his sketchpad to the side. Without taking his eyes off her, he sat down and leaned forward to rest his elbows on his knees and his head into the palms of his hands. His dark hair fell forward. He smiled briefly, then his mouth twisted, he gurgled and coughed and cupped his hands to his mouth. But the bowl he made overflowed with blood. It ran to the floor in thick glittering crimson ribbons. And she wished she had never gone to comfort Harold when he had returned. She'd heard too much.

And she cried because she knew that God would not stand for such feelings. Joe was in hell, and Harold would surely join him there one day.

Chapter 10

I'm just kneeling by the window while the kettle boils for washing up. Mum's washing and I'm drying. It's raining a lot today. I can see the trees at the bottom of the garden waving in the wind, behind the rain, which is bouncing off the ledge. It's raining hard. But it doesn't come in. When we lived in the caravan the water used to come in. It leaked through the crumbly rubber window seals. Mum used to stuff the old nappies round the edges of the frame so it didn't come pouring down the walls. You could see the stains where people didn't think about that before. We've got stone windows here, and we don't have to do that now. We've even got our own bathroom inside, where we put the clotheshorse and hang the washing when it rains.

When we lived in the caravan, we could hear everything outside. When the kids went to bed, the grown-ups would meet up outside and make a fire and have some cider. They talked about the council, and the Giros, and getting a house, and I liked listening to it, looking up through the window in the ceiling at the stars. Sometimes, when I woke up in the night; the wind and rain, the leaves and the birds scuffing around on the roof, it sounded like the prison murderers had come, and they were trying to push us into the canal. When Dad was away, he told us he would send them round if I didn't do as Mum told me. But Mum said to take no notice of him; he was a fucking joker. We couldn't blow away because the tow bar was chained to a big metal ring in the hardstand, and there were concrete blocks gripping the wheels.

Sometimes I used to think it would be nice if we did spin up into the sky and get surprised when we woke up on a beach in the sun. Everyone could eat a big dinner of potatoes and marshmallows round the campfire, and ride white horses to the train station and meet our friends from the train. When they saw us, they would run smiling from the train clouds to say hello and give us presents. That's what happened in a book I read.

Mum doesn't let us turn the lights on in the day, because of wasting money on the electric. It is quite dark though, even though it's daytime. It's too cloudy and there's not enough room to breathe. The rain is taking all the space. That's why you can't breathe so easily in the rain. And the gravity happens, which makes it harder to stand up straight. It doesn't rain on the moon, because they don't have gravity, or clouds.

The kettle has whistled, and Mum's pouring the water in the bowl. Then the tea towel lands on my head. She's only playing when she does stuff like that. Usually... suddenly she is behind me and puts her arms around my neck. "I don't know what I'd do without you." She squeezes me. I grab her hands. I like it when it's just us. She pulls her hands away, and rubs the tea towel hard into my head, and nearly pushes it through my shoulders. "C'mon, let's get on with it then." I pull the towel off my head and walk over. I'm waiting for ages. I watch the rain again until I hear the clinking of stuff on the draining board.

I can see the steam rising off the water, and Mum's hands are bright red. She hasn't put any washing up liquid in, but she's chucking all the stuff in the bowl and wiping it, like it doesn't matter. It's still steaming when she puts it on the side. There are still bits of food stuck on the plates.

I wanted to talk to Mum about Dad, but I don't think it's a good time. Not yet. She's gone really quiet. She's dropped the cup she was washing. It's crashed and broken in the bowl. She's fallen forward, and her hands are either side of the bowl in the sink. Mum's hair is hanging into the washing up. She is crying into the bowl, and her back is shaking up and down.

Everything is quiet. For a minute the sun shines like a sword from between the clouds, and everything is gold and sparkling: the grass, the trees and the washing up. I want Mum to look and see. I put my arms around her. I don't know what to do. I should have told her to put more cold water in, and some washing up liquid. I say, "It'll be alright Mum." I give her a hug, but she doesn't move. Instead, she stares down at the washing up with her hair over her face. She's trying to stop crying, and her voice sounds funny from the sink. "Will it? That's what I'm always bloody saying – and it never bloody is alright." She tried to copy my voice, like I was stupid to say it.

"Why did I think everything would be any fucking different when we moved 'ere…" She stands up and takes a dirty saucepan from the side and bashes it into the washing up. The hot water splashes out to the sides, down her clothes and on the floor. She's really upset. I think she might bash me, so I pretended I had to move to the table. That was a good thing to do, because she turns round to look at me, like she's angry, and then frightened, and puts the saucepan down.

She breathes in really deeply, like she's at the Doctor's, and comes to sit down at the table. Her face is really sweaty and blotchy, and her eye make-up is streaking her face in black lines, like when the telly goes wrong. I want to laugh. A bit. "I suppose I better have some of me pills – go and get 'em would you. They're in the drawer. Under the little table."

I don't like being in this room. It's come back into my mind now. I feel really sick. I find the little bottle. When I kneel down to get it, the smell by my face makes me think about everything too much. And I remember I had some of the whiskey. I find the pills. The bottle has got Mum's name on, 'Hope Smart'. Dad's trousers are in the corner. I run out of the room, straight into Matthew, who's coming down from the attic. "Come and see what we've made!" He's excited and I want to go, but Mum's waiting, and I've got to talk to her. Got to tell her. She'll feel better when she's had her tablets. "I will in a bit. You lot mustn't come down! Me and mum are tidying up ... I'll come and play after."

89

"Oh! You're always ages." He grabs my arm, "C'mon – just have a look!" He looks at me, and it feels like he knows. His eyes are like Dad's. Suddenly I'm crying. He let's go and runs back up to the attic, "You weirdo."

I dry my eyes and take a deep breath. Like Mum. "I'll come up after." I shout, as I run down the stairs.

I reach the bottom of the stairs and stop. Mum doesn't notice. She has wiped her face. She gets her face powder out of her bag and pats it round her eyes and on her cheeks. She is shaking. Her red hands look funny against her creamy white face, like she is wearing a mask. I walk over really quietly so I don't disturb her. When I get close, she looks up suddenly and dabs me on the nose, and laughs. "Here! Do you want me to do you? Sit here!" I walk round and sit in the chair next to her. She empties all the face things out of her bag on the table: lipstick, eye shadows, mascara, and a black pencil. While she is sorting the stuff I go and get her some water to take with her pills.

"What do they do to you Mum?"

She shakes two tablets out of the bottle into her hand and gulps them back with the water. She screws the lid on and stares at me, like I'd better be careful. "It makes it better for everyone, that's what they fucking do!" I must have looked scared, because then she said. "Sorry darlin'. Don't be scared." She bites her lip. She laughs. "Tell you what - sit down here. You're gonna get the works." She pulls all my hair up and twists it, and I feel the hairgrips slide in against my head. She wipes my face all over with the flannel really gently. She squeezes some face stuff in her hand. "Close your eyes."

I can feel her fingers quickly stroking me, all over my face, and then her thumbs round my eyes. I can hear the rain, slap and sshhh…ssshhh against the window… and the tick of the clock at the end of the room, on the mantelpiece. I can feel my Mum seeing that I am beautiful. I'm doing backstroke through the stars. I feel like the moon shining quietly in space. I imagine I am in the rocket that took a week to get to the moon. I am dancing inside, looking out of the window as I travel through the twinkle stars. I can hear the songs of her records in my head. I feel like she can hear them too, like she's moving her thumbs in time to the music. She stops.

"Now what colours do you want Madam?" I don't want to open my eyes.

"Like you." The eye shadow will be blue like the sky and have black lines like Egyptians. My lips will be red like a film star in a phone box.

She's dabbed the blue on my eyes and putting the black pencil on my eyelids. "You don't wanna be like me love. I'm no good to anyone. Waste of space. Still, when I put me face on and take me pills, they can't tell the difference."

"What do they do really? The pills."

"I don't know. They make it all possible... for all it's worth. The doctor thinks it's a good idea for now. Just whilst I get back on my feet. Now - open your mouth! Don't bare your teeth. Cover your teeth with your lips. Like this!" I open my eyes to look.

I stand on the chair, and we look in the mirror together. Bloody hell! Look at you. All dolled up. You're gonna have to watch yourself." She hooks the hair in front of my ears with her fingers, and pulls it down.

"I look nice don't I Mum?" I smile into the mirror at her. She keeps staring at my reflection, but it's like she can't see me anymore. Tears are running down her cheeks and messing up her face again. But she's not moving. Not moving at all. Just staring. It's like all her feelings are broken and still. Her voice sounds slow. "I will get better love. I will get better… I should have gone to see him more before he died. He just wanted what was right for me – and I've made a right fucking mess of things. But it's getting better…isn't it?" She turned and looked at me.

It's really important, being the oldest. You have to help out. Say good things. Maybe I'll be able to talk about it another time. Maybe Dad won't do it again. Perhaps it's just because of the funeral and Mum wasn't here that it happened, because everyone is sad about things. We all have to try.

"I need to go and have a lie down darlin'. I'm feeling a bit dozy. The doctor said it makes you dozy before it gets better."

"I'm going to finish the washing-up."

"Good girl." And she goes up the stairs, and I listen to the creaks on the ceiling to follow her steps.

I put Mum's shoes on, and I walk up to the kitchen with my hands on my hips like Mum when she's happy, and I look back in the mirror, and I look like my Mum, but small like a telescope through the big end. I roll up my dress so it's short, and I cup my hands on my chest like I've got big tits now. I haven't; it's just my nipples are swelling up.

"Well, hey good looking. What you got cookin'?" His voice makes me jump. I turn and Dad is holding the front door open with his hand on the keys. He comes in and closes it and gives me a wink with his keys swinging in his hand. I get out of mum's shoes and go to the sink. "Mum's just upstairs getting something," I said. And I wet the tea towel and wipe my face. And he sits in his chair, and I feel him watching me. I pretend I have to go to the larder, so I can hide behind the door and roll my dress back down.

Chapter 11

Now it's nearly summer, all the leaves thick on the hedges and trees, and they've grown. It's easy to keep private in The Toffee Man's garden because you can't see into it, the bushes are right up over the wall. So, once I go up the path we are hidden.

He has a logbook that keeps a record of everything even the weeds. I have to put each weed in a different tray, and they get washed. We separate the flowers, and the leaves. But that is because he eats them. And he bakes the roots of dandelions. I said they are just weeds, we got loads. The Toffee Man told me there's no such thing as a weed, it's just a plant in the wrong place, and every plant is useful, even stingers. He makes Stinger soup. He puts his gloves on and pulls them up around the wall where he's let them grow. I've been doing lots of weeding, and The Toffee Man has been showing me which flowers to keep.

A bit of sun is warming our feet sticking out from the shade of the porch. I can hear the sound of other kids playing, echoing round the valley, and someone practising a piano and it all fell into a song, and sometimes the wind takes the sound away and then brings it back through the bushes or a little echo round the walls, but the sounds that stayed with me is the busy pencil, and the creak of his chair as he reached out to check my work if I asked him. And I held the different stems and leaves of the plants up close to hear the different snaps they make.

Then I hear the neighbour on the other side of the wall speaking to her husband. Her voice hovered over us as she talked about my mum and how she dresses like a tart, and likes a drink, and her kids can't be trusted. He was listening too. I felt my face get hot, and I wanted to stand up and say something, say I was doing the garden. But I can't. It'll ruin everything. He might not let me come again if I cause trouble. I think he might say that anyway. They're talking about how Mum doesn't go to church anymore now. That's her true colours. But The Toffee Man doesn't say anything about it, he just said I was doing well, and I was getting the knack for breaking the plants at just the right place. Just to remember not to be rough, every bit had to separated carefully; snipped or pulled and placed in their separate bowls for washing and eating.

I think I should ask Reverend Fisher if we can put The Toffee Man on the list for the harvest basket, but really privately. But then I know I can't. He will tell Mum, and Miss Fisher, and they don't like him so they will just say no.

He gave me a red Clover head and told me to see if I could pull all the petals from their beds in the stem without ripping them. You have to do it so carefully, and you can hear them, tiny pops as they leave, but then I could see all the ends, white and delicate. "Now," he said, "You're in for a treat. Squeeze and suck the petals through your front teeth." I did. It was the bestest taste of sweetness. Like when you lick the dust from a Christmas bonbon from your fingers. "Nectar," he said, "Hand me the rest, and I'll make some tea."

The people next door had gone inside too, and it was quiet. I pulled myself up and sat in his chair. I sat back and looked across the garden and over the rooves down the hill into the valley. The outlines are sharp under the sun. The light slips between them like vanilla custard on chocolate crunch at school.

I hear the chink of mugs, and The Toffee Man brings out the clover tea, and a big square of toffee. He cuts it into very small squares. He said we need to let it be and it'll do us good. Don't bite. Let it melt in your mouth.

It's hard not to chew toffee. To let it be. It's like it's going to heal everything inside of me. And I feel like I belong here with all the tastes and smells, and I feel how fragile the plants are, but how strong they are too - even when they are pulled apart and even when they are dead, they have magic. People go in the ground when they are dead, but plants die when you take them out of it.

* * *

Mum hasn't stopped me reading. We had to make covers for some schoolbooks, so I have made some for my space book, and write something different on the front. I left it plain at first, but people asked me what I was reading so I had to put something on it, so they didn't. The Toffee Man's right, people are always asking about things. And they make you feel like you should tell, but you have to be careful about saying anything. Katy Gomer is my friend, but when I said about The Toffee Man's house by the green one day, before I had a chance to say he was my friend as well, she said I shouldn't have anything to do with him. She just can't tell me why. It's about him and God. I don't talk to her about the moon because she might think it's bad, like Miss Fisher does.

We never see The Toffee Man at church. I don't think he's very happy to go and be with people that tell him what he needs to do about life. I think he would like Sunday school better; he likes just listening to stories and talking about what they mean. Although Miss Fisher doesn't ever like me asking questions or answering. Even though she keeps looking at me like she wants an answer, she doesn't.

It was late when I left, and we can hear the insects now it is cool in the garden and the birds come. You get different birds in a village. On the caravan site the crows made the loudest noise, and I could work out their conversations. These little birds chatter with whistles and little songs. Their bodies are tiny, and they can flutter around a bit more.

I run up to the crossroads and get my breath as the church bell rings five times.

Mum sits in the chair with her hands gripping onto the arms. It makes her legs stronger when she kicks out at us. She is watching TV, and we are playing a game.

We have to run around the chair, and then she waits and sticks her leg out to surprise us – and we don't know which one of us will get tripped up. She only does it when it is me, Matthew or Mark. It's because we are older. When we fall over everyone else points and laughs. Luke and John don't realise that Mum won't do it to them. It makes them laugh about escaping every time.

I try and work out when it's coming. I can see my mum's hand grip on the chair, and I know she's going to do it. I roll over and make bad pain noises and pretend I've really hurt myself to make the others laugh. I want to make my mum laugh too. She just sits there still, staring past me to the telly until I get up and carry on. It's like time stops in her world, while she goes to another place. Like she's in the Wishing Chair. I think of the Clover petals and suck it through my teeth.

Chapter 12

Luke and John are shouting because Mum is swiping their hands and faces round with a flannel. Mark and Matthew had to do themselves, like me, and just stand still by the door until it's time to go. Mum's mouth is all sucked in. She's sick to death of it. We all had a bath last night, but they've been out playing cars on the path. Mark made a garage with an apple crate, and then he got fed up and set light to it. He kicked it off the concrete, and the grass caught fire. Now everyone smells of smoke and we have to go to Sunday school in the next ten minutes or we might be late. Miss Fisher doesn't let people in if they're late, not until the bible story is finished, and that's the best bit.

When we walk down the lane, I hold their hands tight, because they try to pull away and make me let go. Matthew and Mark are kicking a stone all the way from outside our gate to the church, and now their shoes and socks are getting dirty. I just want them to walk nicely for the last bit. We can hear the insects and the air is blowing in our clothes and making us smell nice, so that's good.

Everyone is waiting outside the church talking, like usual, waiting until the piano starts. It's funny because you get to see all the grown-ups really smart. The Caravan Lady is there in a blue dress. Miss Gomer is wearing big crosses in her ears like she does every Sunday. She never speaks to people when she's not in the shop, even me – even now we are friends. She wears the same crinkly black suit every week, and clutches her black handbag tightly to her stomach, so her big hands are like fists with white frosty knuckles. She looks down at her handbag like the devil is inside it. Even though the shop is right next door to the church, she doesn't even look in the window of it on Sundays.

Everybody else is talking and admiring each other's best clothes. There are lots of old people that need help to get down the steps. Most of the kids have got coats on. We haven't. Mum said it's stupid to wear coats when it's not that cold, because we won't feel the benefit when it's winter, so we left them at home. The twins keep trying to pull away from me, but I'm not letting them go. They're stretching my arms apart, and then I pull them back to meet in the middle. They do it again. It's making us all laugh.

Matthew and Mark are being good and waiting. It's not like normal, but last week Miss Fisher told them off and said that any children that didn't behave respectfully 'Before, during and after Sunday School, would not be entitled to cake with their squash after prayers'. They are making an effort like she said. When the organ starts playing everyone goes quiet and starts walking in. You can hear the birds, and all the crunch of feet on the gravel. I like the smell of polish in the church. I like the flowers... and how shiny and peaceful it is.

Mum hasn't come to church with us since the doctor said she needed some peace and quiet on her own, and she said she got a chance to make the dinner for when we got back. Mr. Fisher said that was all right, and they would keep any eye on us. But I had to promise Miss Fisher that I would take responsibility. Mr. Fisher always asks us questions about our lessons at school. I don't know why because he doesn't listen to what you say, he just nods and looks around at other people, but I keep saying what it was like anyway.

In Sunday school we have the story of the Good Samaritan. It is a story about a man who is not afraid of the robbers when he sees someone different to him who has been hurt. He stops to help him and wipe the blood, and he gives him his clean clothes, because he is a kind man. After the story we had to do living bible talk, which is like when the story is your life. Sally, who is in my class at school, said she would do that if she was in the woods galloping with her horse, and she saw a wounded man by a tree or something. That was nice of her to say that because she is really shy at school. She doesn't talk to anyone, not just me. Miss Fisher said that you shouldn't stop and help strangers unless you were a grown up. I said that sometimes people just got drunk and fell over, and you should just let them sleep it off. That's what my mum said, because that used to happen sometimes on the caravan site. She said there's no helping some people. Miss Fisher just stared at me hard, and everybody was quiet. Then Matthew said it was true as well, and that made everybody laugh.

Miss Fisher looked up to heaven, and said Well then, we had to pray for everyone who got drunk and God would help them get a better life. I asked her why God didn't help the robbers learn a better life, so they didn't beat up the man. She said it was God was giving us a chance to prove our character, and he loved us all. So I said, It's not fair for the man who was left to die so the Good Samaritan could do a test for God, if some people might not care about passing the test. She said it was not up to us to question the ways of God. Everybody had to think about that quietly for a minute until we calmed down. I wanted to say she said that we could talk about the bible like it was our life, but we could hear the organ start playing the leaving music for the grown-ups in the church. Miss Fisher said it was time for our squash. I still got some cake, although Miss Fisher warned me about being difficult, and to think about things before I said them. I do. I wanted to tell her, but I ate the cake instead.

When Mr. Fisher does his Sermon today he is telling us about how important it is to look after our families, and we must honour them, especially our mums and dads. God chooses our families so that we can learn about love and patience, and sometimes that is hard work. He said we can choose our friends to be like us. The Toffee Man is my friend, but my mum doesn't like him. And what if your dad is not your real dad? Does God choose your not real dad? I could get refused to go into Heaven.

At the end of Church, Reverend Fisher said all the children had to gather back in the Sunday School room, and he came in and put his hands in the air and waited until everyone was quiet. He said we had a special mission. He said to everyone a reminder about the church garden fete that he and his sister, Miss Fisher, were having at the Rectory. He said that they should think about any items that they could contribute. It would be appreciated. He gave us all a list of the stalls for our parents. They wanted to get volunteers for helping too. I don't think Mum could do that. But there was a telephone number to call if she could. I put it in my pocket for her.

When we got outside all the parents were waiting for their kids. Sally's Mum and Dad were waiting by the wall, and Sally ran over with her list. Then her mum, Liz, said she's had a box full of books in the boot, but they are all Enid Blyton, and they probably wouldn't be the sort of thing that people would want to buy at the fete. It was a shame though because they were all originals. She doesn't know what to do with them anymore. And then the Reverend Fisher looked at me and said, "You like these stories don't you April?" And I feel a bit embarrassed, but I do. It's my favourite books.

"I've read lots of them already, and the Caravan Family." I didn't know what else to say. Luke and John were climbing on the wall, and I started to move towards them. Liz kept speaking to me.

"Well, there are over a hundred in the box. I'm sure there are lots that you haven't read – the complete sets of all the mystery books. Sally's read them all, haven't you Sally? So - we don't need them – and I'd love them to go to someone who'd appreciate them." I can't believe it! I can't help myself turning round again. Every single book! I can read them for the rest of my life.

"There," said the Mr. Fisher, "That's another mystery solved. What to do with the books? Liz, Jasper - your work is done." They stood around me, with folded arms, smiling until I remembered to say thank you. I felt bad.

I said I couldn't carry the box all the way home, even with Matthew, because I had the twins, but Sally's mum said she could give us all a lift home if Matthew sat in the boot with the books. Sally's dad, Jasper, said he would walk home so there was enough room. Matthew said that Mum will be pissed off with me getting more books because I was reading all the time. Mr. Fisher coughed, and said he thought she would be very pleased.

It was nice being in Liz's car driving through the village, and people can see us, but I think Matthew might be right about mum. I feel a bit nervous when we park outside the gate. When we walked in the door Mum was cutting the onions to go on the toad in the hole. Dad was reading the paper. The boys had all run in front of us. I was with Sally and then her Mum had caught up with us with the box really soon, so we were all there before I could think what to do about it.

My mum's gone quiet, and my dad pretends not to notice and carries on reading. He was checking the Littlewood's football. I pulled out a chair so that Sally's Mum could put the box down, and pressed down the flaps so I could think of what to say next. "Hello. I'm Liz, Sally's Mum. It's Hope isn't it?" and she stuck out her hand. "I hope you don't mind. I've just brought these books round for April. Sally has finished them, and Reverend Fisher thought you wouldn't mind if April had them." It was funny to hear her voice in our house. It stood out. Different voices make you notice different things, and everything seemed cold and bare. Dad coughed behind the paper. My mum stared down and chopped the onions into tiny, tiny squares, rocking the knife over and over. Her eyes started watering. And we were all looking at her waiting for her to speak. Even the boys.

Mum couldn't look at her properly. The boys were standing around the table. We don't usually have other people in the house, except the doctor. Then Liz said, "That's a really nice dish with a joint of beef," and Mum just nodded. We can't have beef joints yet. When mum gets a job we can, that's what she said before. When Mum goes to the butcher's she pretends we've got a dog so we can get some bones and make soup.

Mum tried to stop staring so much and wiped her hands on her cardigan. "Would you like a drink – Liz?"

"Oh – well …"

Then Sally said, "Can I help April take the books to her bedroom?"

Then Liz said, "Yes, of course. A glass of water would be lovely Mrs Smart."

But my Mum has already got the sherry off the sideboard and opened the little glass cupboard to get the special glasses out. "It's Hope. You can call me Hope." Sally and I take each end of the box and move towards the stairs. "Out in the garden until dinnertime you lot. And Matthew, make sure the gate is closed." Mum looks across at me quickly as I pull my end of the box up the stairs; I can tell she doesn't want me to be long. As I go round the corner up the stairs, I can see my dad is pulling a face behind the paper. At least he's reading News of the World, and perhaps Sally's mum will realise that we are interested about the world. Mum is pouring herself another glass of sherry already. I better not be long, but she is being more friendly. Liz is telling her about the village fete. We are beginning to make friends with them. Maybe Sally will let me see her horse.

When we get into my room Sally looks around. I've got lino with flowers on the floor now, but I've only got my bed and the chest of drawers for the furniture, and all my magic stones are on the top. Sally said I'll need a bookcase now. But then I had an idea; we could put them on the drawers and put the stones along the top of the windowsill. I could see the shape of them when I looked out at the window at night. It would look like I was on the moon. Sally made them into little piles like mountains.

Then we lay on the bed and looked up at them against the blue sky. Sally said it looked like real mountains on Earth, because she has been to a place where they have real mountains. Her Aunty has got a house there, where they go on holiday sometimes. She said she would bring me some real mountain stones next time she went.

We started taking out the books. She told me which ones were her favourites. I really like George because she is like me. I would like to be a boy, and a detective. She said she is glad she is not a boy, because then she would have to go away to school like her brothers. I said I didn't think of that.

She is helping me put them in the right order, and then we have an idea about putting the box on its side to make a bookcase on the drawers. I got my pens out and we made some patterns and labels that we stuck on so I would know which group to put them back in. The lid of the box was useful for doors – and we had one each to draw a picture on. I made a picture of the garden from the window, and Sally drew a picture of her horse in the sunshine. I thought she was clever because she made it look like he was waiting at the stable to get into my books.

Then she asked me, "Did your dad really go to prison?" I went red and I know she saw, but she wasn't horrible. She carried on drawing, "My Dad said It doesn't matter about someone's past. He is a Lawyer. He said it's hard to make a fresh start. He thinks your dad is brave to live here. Anyway, I think you're nice. I'm glad that Mum didn't just throw the books in the dump. I'm glad you've got them." I felt so happy that I stroked her arm without even thinking about it, and it was smooth and warm, not like my goosebumps. She looked at me and moved round to carry on drawing on the other side of the box, and I watched the light move across her eyes, and her lashes made a shadow on the tip of her cheek.

When we get downstairs, Dad isn't there. The paper is neatly creased and plonked by the side of his chair. He does that when he's had enough. I wonder if he said anything. My mum's telling Liz about her life. I know she's a bit drunk. The Toad-in-the-Hole is still on the table. Sally's mum turns round when she hears us and says, "Ah Sally – it's time we were off darling – Daddy will be wondering where we are." I can tell she wants to go. My mum is staring and smiling at Sally, but she is looking straight past her. "Did you girls have a nice time? Thank Hope for having us, Sally. April must come round to us sometime."

Sally says, "Thank you Mrs Smart."

When they've gone, I ask Mum if everything was alright. She gets up and walks to the stairs, "Yeah, everything's fine. She's got her head up her fuckin arse. I put her straight on a few things." I thought she might fall over, but she took her shoes off and went upstairs. I heard her fall on the bed. I put the onions on the pie and put it in the oven. I'm not sure what temperature it's supposed to be. I put the sherry back in the cupboard. My mum's glass was empty and there was lipstick all round the top. Sally's mum's glass was clean except for the sherry that was still inside.

Chapter 13

Mum went to Uncle Derek's and Auntie Janice's this morning. Dad took her in the car with all the boys. They're going to have a day out. Janice and Derek haven't got any kids, so they like taking us out sometimes. Derek is Dad's big brother, and he is taller than him. We don't see him much. Mum is going there for a rest. The doctor said that she is going downhill fast now, and Dad has to look after us before she ends up in hospital. She couldn't believe it when he actually spoke to Derek, and they arranged for her to stay with them for a few days while Dad brings the boys home.

She gave me a hug. She seemed like she was really happy. She doesn't like it when I hug her for too long. I did today while I kissed her goodbye. She pushed me away and looked at me, and I thought she would be cross with me for a minute. But, she got five bob out of her purse and gave it to me so I could get some fish and chips, as a treat for cleaning, and tidying the place up a bit before Dad got back. I had to do it before I got my head stuck in a book.

She did her lipstick and a quick dab of her compact in the mirror. Before she walked out the door she did a dab on my nose and clicked it shut; all quick like a trick. I can smell it now. It's making me think of mum. When I was cleaning up, I found the piece of toilet paper that mum used to get off the extra lipstick. You can see the whole shape of her mouth and all the creases in her lips, like a map of her words, or I can see faces, like when you look at clouds in the sky. I stuck it in my notebook on the back cover. Now I can kiss her when she is away.

I did all my jobs, and made fish paste sandwiches, so I could save my money, and I ate them in the porch while I sat and read my book.

* * *

Patches of white hair grow along his big fingers, and they get covered with black bits and seeds from plants. He pulls the little cuttings really gently. He nods his head, and I'm leaning right up close, "I can't see anything," I say, "Are they dead? Can we put them in the sun?"

"Nooo … They'll dry out. Look – take hold of this, and give it a gentle tug, like I told you before … but very very gentle now. You're not weeding." And I did. And I thought it must just slip out the way that I had just pushed them in, but I could feel, they didn't want to come out now. I felt proud. "Their roots have spread and taken hold in the soil – that's what it is. You've done your bit with those little green fingers of yours, now nature will do her magic. I think most of these are going to thrive – I'll put some out, and those we don't need can go in the compost!"

There were so many of the life I made, and it would be sad if they had to get buried in the compost, even if they would feed the others when they were growing. The Toffee Man said life is never wasted, but I said I had a good idea. We could make all the pots nice, and I could put them on the garden stall for the Fete and then people could buy them and have our flowers, and it would make loads of money for the poor Christians. The Toffee Man said that was a good idea. And I felt quite glad that I had an idea like that. It was like when you get all ticks on your work at school.

When he was making the tea, I stood by the door and was watching around his kitchen, at all the clocks, and listened to the ticking, like clicking fingers and clapping that we do at school when miss tries to get us all to do the beat, and we get it at different times. And there are lots of pictures on the wall; and I can see from the ones close to me that it is the Barley Fields, and the lane, and there was a girl sitting on the green before the bench was there. And he said I could come in.

It was very tidy, and I don't think he is a dirty old man. All the clocks got louder, slowly marching, or running, like lots of people doing things their own way. Not listening to each other, but like a funny song of them together, that they didn't know. And that is the way that sound waves work in the world. The mug warms my hands as I drink my tea at the table. The Fishers will realise that our family are helpful, and we are kind to poor people as well. The Toffee Man said that I can have all the spare plants; he won't put them on the wall for people to take, or in the compost.

On his table lots of shiny bits of the clocks and tools were put in the right places, all around the space where he worked at mending them, like we do with the knives and forks at the dinner table at school, all neat for each kid. The paint was old and creamy on the walls, but you could still see the shape of the stones. There was picture at the side of the fireplace, by the stool, so he could look at it I reckon. It was two soldiers. It looked like the Toffee Man. Like it was his son. But he didn't get a wife. I wanted to ask him, 'Is that your son?' Then I knew it was him. Like the picture of Mum when she was a kid. He got old. I wonder what I will look like when I get old. I hope I look like Mum.

The kettle whistled on his stove just as he came to the door with a little plate that had some toffee on it, "Build up your strength for working." I like his toffee, because I do feel stronger when I eat it now. It smells different to shop toffee. "How do you make the toffee?"

"An old war time recipe passed on from my mum." He told me in the days of the war when they didn't have much sugar, she found a recipe to make toffee. It was her secret. All the kids in the village were glad of it. She sent him some to the war place, and they were glad of it too. I said it tasted like a magic spell. He tapped his nose, and said it was, and he laughed, and I saw his long teeth.

"Is that you? In that picture?" He said yes, without even looking, and he poured the tea in the cups. "Is that your brother?" He gave me my tea and looked over at the picture.

And he stared for a minute, nice and quiet, like he had to remember if it was or not.

"He wasn't my brother. I was the only one."

"Is he far? He could help us." He sighed a little smile, but his eyes were sad.

"Young lady. You're a great one for talking. Now – drink up, and let's get some work done." I was glad he said that, because I remembered his face, in the picture at Miss Gomer's shop. He was one of the Nesbit's from the bench. And I knew I mustn't say about it.

* * *

I made sure I got home in time, before Dad and the boys got back. I finished all the toffee I got for the work while I watched a science programme, and a man said the next Great War would be on the moon. I just think that would be bad because the moon is a very quiet place, and we would have to look at it every night thinking of all the people getting killed.

Dad carried the twins through the door and straight up to bed. He had one in each arm, and they were asleep on his shoulders. He shouted that Matthew and Mark had to go and brush their teeth and come up straight away, because he had spent enough money on them today, and they promised to be good. Matthew dumped a big bear that Uncle Derek had won at the fair and said that Aunty Janice had made them a big tea, because she felt sorry for Dad because Mum got drunk and fell over in the kitchen, and she had to go to bed for God's sake. But there was a bag with some big cakes that she had made for us while Mum was away.

I wanted to eat some cake, but I didn't know which to do: if I should go to bed before Dad came down or sit on the settee. When Matthew and Mark went to bed I went to the toilet, and I turned the light off and looked out of the top part of the window until I could see most of the stars.

When I went back in Dad was sat on the settee, eating cake, and there was some cake on a plate for me, on the arm of the seat beside him. "I thought you'd got lost," he said. I wish I could.

"Dad. I'm not hungry. I'm tired now."

"That's not very friendly, is it? We are friends, aren't we?" I don't know what to do. I can't say we're not friends, because he is looking crooked. And being nice as well, and I would like to eat the cake as well. Then he said, "There's a good Western on now. I thought we could watch that. It's no fun on your own." And I don't mind that.

Dad kept looking at me. To see if I liked the film. I did. And I ate the cake. Then when the cowboys chased the Indians through the mountain pass, Dad got up. He asked me if I wanted a drink, because he was. I said I wanted some lemonade. He came back with the whiskey and two glasses. He said the lemonade was all gone. I could have a whiskey with him.

It was dark except for the telly, and the Indians were having a meeting round the campfire and counting the scalps. Dad said just knock it back in one. It was hot and it felt like it was burning my mind off. Dad laughed, "You should see your face. Try it again, and keep a straight face. I'll give you half a crown if you can." I did it, and he was quite surprised about that. But it was easy because I couldn't taste it that time.

I felt a bit dizzy, but it was nice, but not when the Indians got trapped in the camp, and all the kids and mums were shot and trampled by horses. I cried then, and Dad gave me a hug and stroked my hair. The Indians that were left wrapped all the dead people in blankets and took them to the burial ground of their ancestors and made peace with the cowboys.

Dad said it would be best if I slept with him until I calmed down a bit. He didn't like to see me so sad. I wish I could go and be sad on my own. He stroked my face until I was asleep, but I woke up when Dad carried me to my room.

There are cobwebs in the back corner of my windowsill now. I can see the spider in the moonlight. It's a big fat spider. It looks nice now the stones are there. It makes a shadow on the opposite wall, but not so high. And it really does look like the moon. The spider is an alien that has survived from the ages. He is trying to catch some friends in his web.

Chapter 14

I was glad when Mum got back. She only lasted three days. Derek brought her back because Janice said she was better off at home. Her life was different to Janice's, that's what Uncle Derek said.

Mum asked me to help her make a nice dinner before Derek went home. Uncle Derek said I didn't look well. I didn't feel very well actually. I felt shaky and I had guts ache. Mum said I'd got the bug, and I could sit and read a book in her chair, while Dad and Derek had a chat. It's like the page of this book is angry, squeezing and punching the inky letters, so they are swelling up and getting fat, so I am just pretending that I am reading now.

Derek is on the edge of the settee. He is leaning forward with his elbows on his knees, and his hands are making a steeple at Dad. I wish it was the head of an Indian spear that would stab him. Dad is by the mantelpiece, watching Derek in the mirror. Derek said that Mum is at the end of her tether, and Dad had to seize the opportunity to make things all right. He was proud Dad had a job now, and he had all these lovely kids – he had to keep going and not mess things up or Mum would have a nervous breakdown if he doesn't share the load for a bit. She couldn't take much more.

Mum is crouching down by the cupboard, gulping a glass of sherry. I can see her under the other side of the table. She comes back up like a rusty old jack in a box and carries on cutting up the chips. I bet Dad saw her in the mirror. He said to Derek that he was doing all the hours that God sends, and he should try living with her. Derek said she was a good woman. If Aunty Janice and Dad died, I wish Derek would marry my mum.

We had to pull out the flaps of the table so we could all fit round. The boys were really good because Derek was there. Matthew told him the story of the game they were playing about the hunters that were trying to protect the bear that was getting attacked by lions because they had made friends with him. Matthew and Luke were the hunters, and Mark and John were the lion, because otherwise the twins forgot what they had to do, and just did Indian hollering and forgot their horses.

Derek was kind because he listened, even when all the boys were talking, and he talked like it was real, and the boys got excited, and they went out to play it again when they finished eating.

Derek said he had to be getting off soon because he was on the night shift at the factory this week, and he is the foreman, so he can't be late. Mum said I was being a bit quiet, and I had to stop playing on it and do the washing up. I was carrying everything over to the sink and organising it, and mum said I was being noisy, and she couldn't hear herself think. Derek said it was a nice dinner, Mum said she was glad, and it was encouraging to get compliments because she might as well make cow pats for all the thanks she got from us lot. Dad snapped at her and said that she did most of the time, so Mum turned on me. I didn't realise I was scratching my arms. "You picked up bloody fleas or something. Stop that! You'll start us all off!" I pretended I was looking out the window because I was crying. I couldn't help it.

"I don't feel well. I got a tummy ache."

And Dad jumped in, "See it's your bloody cooking."

Derek tried to calm things down and came over to me. "Alright Andy. Are you OK love? Here I'll do that anyway," and he took the cloth from me, "You go and sit down. Read your book or something. I bet those boys have given you the run-around these past few days." He put his hands on my shoulders, and I think it made Mum even more angry.

"She don't need no encouragement to read a book. She'd stay up half the night reading if you let her… that's the problem." I felt safe with Derek talking to mum, so I walked over and got on the settee out of the way. She let Derek carry on washing up, and Dad sat back with his arms folded, biting his lip and I could hear him tapping the table leg with his foot.

Derek just carried on talking, "Well there's nothing wrong with reading Hope. Wish we'd had more books when I was a kid. She might get somewhere."

"Not the stuff she reads. It's not like it's the bloody Bible or anything."

Derek laughed a bit, and then asked me, "What you reading now love?" I didn't want to say anything, but I tried to sound sensible.

"It's about these friends, one of them has a dog – and they solve mysteries and find out who the criminals are."

"See what I mean?" Mum said.

"What do you want to be when you grow up?" I wish he wouldn't keep trying to talk to me. Mum will think I was getting him to be on my side.

"A detective."

"You'd better watch it Andy, she'll bloody catch you out." I can feel Mum and Dad get angry, because it all goes quiet, and I can't hear Dad's foot tapping any more. I try to make it funny too.

"Yes, but on the moon." And it's good, because they all laugh at me, so I keep going, "But by the time I grow up there'll be lots of people living on the moon!"

"Mmm, well, you might be right there. I've heard that too." And he doesn't sound like he's making a joke of me at all, and I feel quite proud that I said it, but I keep quiet. Mum will think it's silly. She does.

"Oh don't bloody encourage her with these daft ideas. I want my kids living in the real world, where they can keep an eye on it. There's some right bastards out there," and she turns to Dad, "Don't sneer at me!"

"Oh shut up. Want her to turn out like you do you?"

"See Derek - I told you - this is it. That's the problem," and she walks over to the cupboard and gets out the sherry.

"That's the fucking problem! Look at the state of you." Mum holds up the whiskey bottle, and it's nearly empty. And I feel bad. Like I am a cheating liar, and Dad is going to tell her that I've been having some too.

"Like you ain't got a fucking problem."

"Oh come on, I barely touch it. You know it."

"I suppose it just evaporated. Or may you had some fucking slapper in."

"You want slapper - I'll slap you!" Dad throws his hand towards Mum, but Derek grabs it and holds it still in the air. Dad turns to look at Derek, and pull his hand back, but Derek keeps it still.

"Aye! Aye! Come on. Less of the talk. There are kids. April, love - go and see what the boys are up to," and I'm glad to go. As I get past it's like everything is still, like a photograph. Mum and Dad seem small, like kids, and they feel caught.

* * *

I'm sat on the wall by the gate reading my book, watching Matthew and Mark showing the twins how to do Indian whoops, so they can chase them in their cowboy hats. When Derek comes out of the house he jumps into the porch and makes monster sounds, they jump up and run whooping at him. Derek puts a hand to his mouth whoops too, whilst he slips his other hand in his pocket and jangles his change, and then shares it out. Matthew and Mark get all the silver.

He gives them a hug before they go in to show Mum and Dad, and tells them to behave, or the Boogey Man will get them. When he walks up the path, he talks to me different, like I'm a grown up, "You look rough. You go and get tucked in. They've calmed down - all kiss and make up - as usual. Always been the same them two."

He's never talked to me like that, and then he puts his hand on my shoulder, and I don't know what will happen next, so I stay still. "Look - your mum doesn't mean it. She's got a lot on that's all. Trying to keep this family out of trouble. She's proud of you. I would be if you were my kid. You take no notice - keep reading." And then he puts his other hand on my other shoulder, so I look at him, and he kisses me on the head. I show him my book.

"I'm a fast reader. I got given a whole box, and I read about a quarter already." He looks me right in the eye and puts his hand in his back pocket and gets his wallet. He opens it up and gives me a whole pound note.

"Here - you go and choose some for yourself and read them for me." And his eyes are sparkly, and then there is a tear, and he walks forward as he pats my back, and jumps into his car and drives off. I watch his green car drive over the crossroads, and along the road until it disappears as it slips off the hill.

Chapter 15

When I walk through the gate it's buzzing and peaceful, birds are flitting in the bushes, but the Toffee Man isn't there. There are lots of flowers that are going to seed, and they need deadheading. I am quite pleased because I am quite good at that. When I walk up the path there are lots of weeds growing up between the cracks and along the edges, but I can do that too. A week is a long time in nature. I try not to make a sound when I walk past the window to see the cuttings, so I can surprise him with all my work if he is having a snooze by the stove.

But he is sat at the table with his back to the window. I stand quiet by the edge.

He is looking at some photos spread out on the table in the sun rays. His hands are big and fumbly. He is looking at one of a little boy with a man and a lady in really old clothes from history, and her hair is in a bun – they look like royal family people in long coats and dresses. He looks at that one for a while. He is taking them from a box on a chair by his side, and making them into piles, along the table.

He looks at them and places them, one by one, stroking round the edges to take out the creases, even when there aren't any, because he wants to touch them. Like he is cutting them out and putting them in his mind.

He starts coughing, and takes his big hanky out, and he is gobbing up into it. It takes all his air from his body, and it hurts him. I can feel it. His back is jumping, and he is wheezing. He will get embarrassed if he sees me, so I crouch down by the window. He is coughing up so badly it sounds like guns, and dark thunder, and the birds fly up from the garden. I hear his chair whistle on the stone floor, and he walks to the sink and gets some water. He chokes it back, coughs a bit, and spits in the sink a few times.

The birds have come back.

I heard the chair scrape in. I crawled back to the path so that I could stand up and pretend I just got here. I get ready for him to see me, but when I look at the window, he is looking through the box again.

He pulls out a little square plate that was down the side. It says 'HAROLD' – and the letters are like little bushes with bluebells all around them, and red roses that go round the edges.

He is Harold. I know it. And he is the baby in the pictures with his Mum and Dad. And then he is getting pictures of men in the war – sat on jeeps and tanks, like in the films. Laughing and smiling, their arms across each other's shoulders. Then there is one of two ladies, and they are dressed up in bright clothes for a party. And they are with the soldiers by the tank. The next one is close up of one lady and she is blowing a kiss. She is wearing lots of make-up, like Gloria from the caravan site, but on her hands it looks like a man.

I think it is a man pretending to be a lady, like at Christmas plays. He holds the picture across to the light, and I can see he is crying. Very quietly.

I step back from the window and walk backwards down the path, until I get to the weeds, and I bend down and start pulling them up and putting them into a pile. I have done all the way up the path, just past the porch, when the door opens, and he comes out. He claps and smiles, and he looks really happy to see me. And I feel nice because we're both cheered up. "I got something to show you," he said.

I follow him as he walks over to the pots. I don't know what to look at because they haven't grown. I told him they look like they might be dead, but he says to me to look again, and I can see, I can see the shoots have got a tiny bit bigger, like sneaky green eyes. But, he said, the real magic is happening inside the earth, and the mystery of life is hidden.

Every one of them was still living, and I could take them home with me. He went to the shed and got an apple crate, and we lined up the pots inside, so I could carry them easily.

I had a good idea. With all the twigs that needed tidying we could make some little crosses to remind the people that bought them that will come alive again. That they were just in the tomb like Jesus. He agreed, that was a good idea, because it was a true idea. He liked that. The tomb of winter. When they came alive in the world again, they could be all over the village and be like a message.

The Toffee Man helped me make my idea, and he cut all the string for me, and he snapped all the twigs to the right length, because my small fingers were better to make the knots. We put one each in each pot. I got some dry leaves from the compost to put on the top after we watered them, to keep the water in, and it made them look pretty.

He said I could make a plan of what all the plants were on the tray, so that I could make labels for the stall when I got home. I really like making diagrams to explain what I mean, and he had some colours too, so I could make a coloured star to show people what colour the resurrection would be. And he said they could be called the unknown soldiers, to bring a message of sacrifice.

Before I left, I helped pick the dead heads. We shook some of the seeds on the bird table because he said the birds will pick them up and take the seeds all over the place, and he saved some for himself. I didn't say it, but I know they will eat them and carry them in their stomach until they shit from the sky. They don't even know about it, but they are making something good in the world.

He made a cup of tea, and we ate some toffee, and watched the birds flock around the seeds. We sat together, both thinking about things, and watched them fly out into the sky, over the valley. And I thought about all the happiness we had made, and I think he was too.

I couldn't take all the plants home. It's too complicated. Mum wouldn't even understand that they weren't dead. So, I took them straight to the Fisher's house.

Their house is a huge big house. It's like a palace. It's really posh big windows are all painted white, and the door, which has a big golden lionhead knocker. I bet God would prefer to live here, instead of the Chapel. But I liked the Tabernacle best, so God might like the Chapel. I expect he comes here to show Reverend Fisher how to do the talks for us.

Miss Fisher answered the door, and the green carpet went back everywhere in the house, like a field in heaven. She was a bit shocked to see me, and she didn't understand about the plants, she didn't want to. She doesn't like me. She called Reverend Fisher, and first he looked shocked too, but then he got pleased that I had brought them. He asked me about them.

I explained it was OK, and they were coming alive again like a resurrection. The Reverend said it was a beautiful idea. I showed him my diagram with the names of them, and I said I could copy it out if he liked. He said they had a special machine, and I could come to his study. He said to Miss Fisher that perhaps we could all have some tea and biscuits.

I never seen such a beautiful room for real, ever in my life. There was a wall of books, and a ladder to move along, which went right to the ceiling. Lots of the books were red and brown with shining gold letters. It all smelled so nice, like the church, but of nice cakes in the oven too, it made me want to cry.

Reverend Fisher took my notebook and put it on some glass and covered it with a lid and then he pressed a button. Wings of bright light burst out, moving along the edges of the lid, but it made a noise like a submarine. A piece of paper came out of the end and my diagram was in the middle, exactly the same, with my writing, like the page of a book. Reverend Fisher asked me if I wanted one too, and I said yes. I will keep it forever.

Mr. Fisher looked at it and said he could read it very well. He asked me about the 'Unknown Soldier', and why did I call it that? I said Uncle Derek called it that because I didn't know what to say. He said he was a thoughtful man. And then it was spoiled when I had my tea and biscuits, because I had to make the lie even more. I said that Uncle Derek brought the plants back, but Mum said we could use them for the fete because our garden wasn't ready yet. I felt really bad because Miss Fisher was watching me carefully, and she knew it wasn't right, and so did God.

Chapter 16

We are fighting the flames of fire from the sky. Clapping, and shouting the sound of the canon, boom! The sheets are hanging down from the beams, and the windows are open. The sheets blow up like balloons over our heads, and we are sailing across the land in our beds. We fly up, out of the forest to get away from the pirates. They tried to steal the catalogues so they could spend all their treasure on new furniture for their old ship, but we set light to it, and sank it in the piss bucket. And we have won.

Mark is sat on the windowsill, crashing his cars into biscuits, and crumbling them like rain out the window. The sun is making his shadow and the bars of the window across the floor and up on the bed, so he is on the twins. They have gone to sleep, and it is like he is pouring dreams in their heads.

Me and Matthew are making a list of numbers for the things we want to buy on the order form at the back. It won't be until we get older, but it won't be long. We are doing it properly from the catalogue, so you have a list of the numbers, and what it is, and how many you need. We are putting five sheep skins so we can all have one each, just the same, by our bed. Mark is testing me for the numbers, so I know them off by heart because I am the oldest, and in case I lose my book. "We need some shelves," I said, "Then we can put everything in the right place, and it won't get broken."

"No! No! No!" said Matthew, "Shelves are boring. It takes too long to save."

"I'll get them with the babysitting money from Mum when Dad's away and she is at the club."

"I'm not a baby," and then Mark said he wasn't either. I don't want to spoil everything now. The sun is like fire. We are all golden in the light.

"Mum said we'll all get some pocket money anyway. I will get the shelves." I tickled Matthew and pulled him over to the window.

"Isn't it brilliant," and I don't know who said that, because we agreed in the quiet as we stood still. And then I felt Luke's hand pulling on my dress.

"Can I see?" I picked him up, and Matthew went to get John. We sat them on the windowsill with Mark, and I felt like we were the Royal Family, as I waved goodbye to the sun like The Queen.

We have been there a long time in the quiet, in the warm air, and in the magic gold of the sun. And I think I know what Reverend Fisher means about when Jesus gets a home in your heart and makes you have a joy unknown. I can see him all around us. And I feel like he is worshipping us, and in this minute of the world we are the most important people he has made.

The valley looks like a great big bonfire, and big golden ribbons fall from the sky across the trees and fields, and the shadows of the clouds slide across. We have never seen something so beautiful in front of our eyes. If I could use all the wishes I would ever get in my life I would wish Dad would go away and never come back.

When I creep quietly down the stairs and open the door on the landing I can hear Mum singing with the church on the radio. I walk carefully down on the last bit, on the smallest part of the stairs where it doesn't creak, and I watch her through the edges of the door. She is wearing her Church dress, with the collar and big green flowers, and even her shiny black shoes with fat white buttons on the front, but her lipstick has gone on her face a bit at the bottom, like a blood drip from her mouth. Like she is a woman that swallowed a woman that is trying to get out. She doesn't look fierce though. She is drunk and crying. She is holding her hymn book tightly which was a present from her mum and dad in the long ago past. It has a message in joined up handwriting on the front that I saw one day, but I couldn't read it. They might have asked someone to do it, because there aren't any kisses, or with love from, because I could read that.

I can't see her feet, but she grows from the shadows, and her singing is too greedy for the songs, and she is choking. I want to sing with her and make different words and make her laugh. I don't know all these words, but my lips pretend they do, 'And did those feet in ancient times'.

A giant snake is curled around her ankles and I push my face closer to the crack in the door and his head moves up to stare at me with his big white eyes and the silence that is inside me like a bubble grows big and big and pops, and I am covered in its shiny white spit, and the tongue of the snake slips through the crack, while his eyes make me still as a mouse. I can't move forward, so I creep quiet as a flower back up the stairs to my room.

I can hear Mum singing downstairs while I am on my bed watching the birds lining up on the wires like they are waiting for choir practice.

Chapter 17

I've been thinking if I should let The Toffee Man borrow my book 'You will go to the Moon' or not. Some people wrote it even before I was born, when they were still trying to explain the plan. I don't think The Toffee Man read it though. I read it quick again to remember, and I put it in the shopping bag in case I get a chance to see if he wants it.

I can see his feet, under the table up the path by the porch. I open the gate as slowly as I can, and it doesn't make any noise at all. I think he oiled it. The hinges are shiny black, and the rust is gone.

The Toffee Man is sat in a chair at a small table. He's got all his tools set out on his cloth. He turns to nod at me, but he's concentrating. I stand in silence and watch. Inside a clock is full of wheels spinning like a bike race, I say. When he finishes, he sets the time and puts his ear to it, and he says yes, but they all depend on each other, and they all win. If even the smallest wheel goes wrong the clock won't work. And I put my ear to it too, and we listen together, and it is the truth.

"How do you know what time it is?"

"Ha! Well, it don't matter much. Got it working," and he moves the duster gently over the curve of the wooden case, "It's a good one this."

"But what about when they come to get it? It won't be much good for them if it's the wrong time."

"They can sort that out for themselves. People have their own ways."

"But what if they haven't got a TV or radio, like you haven't?" I start deadheading the flowers like he showed me, and pulling the weeds he said that take over the edge of the path and in between the stones.

"I suppose that they could go up to the phone box and ring the government, they've got a big clock that tells exact right time. They put it on the telly every night at ten o'clock."

"You should be in bed asleep by then – should think I am myself. I've always found plants pretty reliable." And he tells me about the different weeks of different flowers growing, and when they open and close in the day. They all have their times, and you get to know. He said I could learn for myself by drawing a flower clock when I notice.

He takes the clock back into the kitchen. I have to speak more loudly now. I'm not a kid. "I have to baby-sit at night now. That's why. My mum's got a job in Gloucester, and it's a long way, so sometimes my dad has to drive her there, and they can't come back till morning … so I have to watch telly in case the boys wake up. It's good there's news and films and programmes about people's lives everywhere."

He comes out with a different clock. A prettier one. An oval face, like a lady with curly hair. "If people minded their own business and got on with their own lives, they'd be a lot better for it. You'd think people would have enough to do without gawping at someone else's business that they don't even know."

"Well, it's not just about people – about how mountains are made... wild animals... insects that might get to be big enough to eat everyone if the people don't do what they're told."

He looks from fixing the clock and swats a fly. "Shouldn't think it'll come to that!"

"Well, it's alright if they do – because by the time I grow up, it will be normal to go and live on the moon – that's why we have to learn how to understand aliens, in case they're not very friendly, so we can explain about how we don't want to hurt them… but we have to find out about their language first," and I try to think about words from space because it probably won't be the same, "knicky, knacky, noo - gura boo – doiyoing -"

The Toffee Man laughs, "Oh, I'll be dead by then. And glad of it by the sounds."

"Well, the… you might be on the moon already… or in space with the angels… I could come and see you in my spaceship."

"And where you gonna get one of them?"

"Oh, when it's normal, you'll be able to choose what kind you like from the catalogue. I'll probably get my own record player to put in it as well."

"I expect them angels will be moving on then."

I pretend I am the Angels putting their hands on their hips and complaining "God, this is such a racket!" I burst out laughing, and for a minute I think he is going to be cross, and he starts laughing too. It is a nice feeling. We're friends who laugh. Like me and Eli. I don't know what happens because suddenly I want to cry, so I get the trowel and it scrapes as I push it along the cracks. I am strong. I can feel him watching me. My heart is fast. I made too much attention.

"It won't be that noisy when you get to the moon, because you can't open your windows and you have to put your garden and your spaceship into a bubble, which is tied to a rock, or something stuck right in the moon, because otherwise, everything floats out into space and they'll get lost… if they're not a proper ghost."

"Ah well, no peace for the wicked, eh?"

He goes into the house and comes out to hand me a small parcel in paper. I know it's toffees. "Not much left now," he says. "But the next crops are doing well. Those apples and beets are ripening up." I open it to break a bit off. His toffees taste of the best things of the earth. I close my eyes and suck and chew.

"I suppose with all these foreign languages you haven't got no time to learn some manners. Close your mouth when you're eating – keep them flies out. Like my old mum said: you eat with your mouth open, and you eat with the devil!" I close my mouth tight and open my eyes wide. He shakes his head, but he is smiling, "Where is your mum?"

"She's gone to the moon."

"Has she now. And you'd better run along or that's where your mum'll think you are. I don't want no trouble!"

I pick up the shopping bag and I pull out, "You will go to the Moon," and I put it on his chair, "It's for you. So you know about it."

"Well … thank you. My eyes aren't so good now – but maybe you could read it to me. Maybe your mum would like that too?" No, she wouldn't. She wants me back home because she's going out.

"She said she don't care about the bloody moon, but I'm going. I'm going to be a detective there." I want to give him a hug, like friends in films, but we shake hands. And his hands feel full of clever and wise. "See you."

He's coughing when I'm out the gate, hacking like sudden branches ripped from the trees in the wind that nearly hit the van, and mum said it would be the death of us. They weren't though. It goes quiet. I stand outside the gate a minute, until I hear the scrape of his chair and the tap of his tools on a clock. And then across the green I hear the engine. I look up. It's Dad. He's in his truck, and he is looking at me for a second, grins, and drives past. He's going to tell Mum, I know it. If I get back before he does, Mum will go out before he gets there.

When I get to the crossroads, he's parked up like he couldn't wait, not even put it in the pub car park. Mum is waiting at the door and starts shouting at me straightaway, "Where the bloody hell have you been? I was meant to get the last bus to meet Mary in town! He's only just got back. I told you. You were meant to be five minutes. You've been nearly an hour. You know I can't leave the boys." He hasn't said about it. Mum would have said by now. Then Dad walks back in from the bathroom. He doesn't look at me. He goes to his chair and open the newspaper, so he is hidden. But I see his fingers pricking up.

"I've been reading."

"Reading what? Where?" and I remember I haven't got a book and my heart gets fast, but Mum keeps going. "Well, why didn't you come home and read? You're bloody mad you are! What are people supposed to think. Sitting in the village reading like a homeless tramp. Showing off more like. If I find out that you've been at that bloody old bloke's place again, I'll knock your bleedin' head off. You'll understand one day. They'll take you away if you go down there!" I don't know what to say because he's kind about people. And he even told me to behave as well. Mum glares at me, and I duck my head for a slap, but it doesn't come. She stares until she's pink in the face, then turns to Dad. He's not saying anything. "Bloody do something Andy. Will you tell her for Christ's sake. I'm at my wits end!"

He stays behind his paper, "Nothing to do with me. She's your kid."

"That's right. Start that again – not going to be allowed to forget that mistake am I?"

"Like I said, it's your kid. Bloody women, always trouble!"

"Well, she don't get it from me! Just like…"

"Who? Don't bloody go on she's here now, isn't she? Why don't you take some of your pills, you know they make you feel better. You can get the next bus."

"The only way I'll feel better is when I take the bloody lot," and she storms up the stairs.

"Make us all feel bloody better," Dad mutters to himself. I'm standing behind the sofa waiting. It's like Dad to say something, even to me, now Mum is out the way. But he doesn't. I don't move. I better wait for Mum to come back. And maybe he's saving it.

Mum comes back downstairs, picks up her coat. She comes right up to me, "Well, don't just stand there you dozy cow. Put that shopping away … and since he's here, you can get upstairs to bed. Bloody hour to do a bit of shopping." This time she catches me out. I get swiped round the head, and I trip to the side, over the shopping bag. "You clumsy idiot. I'm warning you. If you've been up to anything, I'll hear about it." And she walks out and slams the door. It's dead quiet, and I can hear the boys playing round the back.

Dad folds the paper into his lap and watches as I put things away. When I've finished, I stop before I go upstairs to my room, so he can say it if he wants. He still doesn't.

I lie on the bed looking up out the window. I'm trying to think what I can do. Mum is getting worse nowadays. I wish we were back in the caravan.

I hear him coming up the stairs. I turn and face the wall to pretend I'm asleep. In case he comes in. And he does. He walks right over like he knows I'm awake and sits on the side of the bed. "What were you doing then? I saw you."

"Just talking and stuff."

"Come on, I wasn't born yesterday. Old men don't just have little girls around their house by themselves to 'just talk and stuff'!"

"I was digging."

"Digging? And what was he doing?"

"Nothing … just talking." He puts his hand on my leg, rubbing it.

"I don't want to do nothing; I don't like it … I don't want to do it no more."

"Is it because you're doing it with him? You like doing it with him don't you?"

"He don't do nothing like that!"

"Well, that's not what your mum reckons. He does it with all the little girls, and boys - even did it with his own mum! That's what killed her… because she was too old!"

And I know that it's not true. Why can't he see that, "He didn't, he looked after his mum. He liked her all the time and nobody else goes there, except for people with broken clocks. He's my friend!"

I'm crying now. And he's saying, there there, and he's rubbing my leg higher, and with his other hand he pulls my hand to his lap. I try pulling it back, and I'm crying even more. "I want mum."

"Well, she's out... And probably just as well, because if she knew what I knew, she'd probably be very upset. You heard what she said."

"Why? He's only talking to me…"

"Well, he can explain that to her." And I know Mum would make him do it. And I imagine myself reading him 'You will go to the Moon' loud in my mind so I stop crying.

"Don't tell her." I whisper. My teeth have gone numb, feel soft and rubbery. My eyes and ears are slipping round my face. All the sounds and shapes spin, spin in and out. I hear his voice.

"Well, how about being my friend then? And, if you don't tell her, I won't tell her. Fair's fair. Agreed?" He wants me to say yes. "My baby," and he strokes my face.

"She's not seen you. What the eyes don't see the heart don't grieve for. The sooner you learn that."

"Yes." He stands up.

"You'd better get undressed for bed." His voice is gone now. I hear the buckle of his belt fall on the lino. And when I look up from the bed, I see the clouds. I am the ship comes sailing by, sailing by. And it stops for the lady with a tray of biscuits, like a giant pile of biscuits, so many they fall off into the water, and she shouts watch out. And they're all crumbs now, falling from the sky onto my head, and I try and catch them all in my mouth, keep everything tidy, put them in to my mouth, too many toomany tomommany whaoh whaoh – I'm choking but there is no sound. No sound. I can't hear. No sound. Vroosh. River rushes through my ears, screeching round the corner.

Dad stands at the door now. Matthew is calling for me from the bottom of the stairs. Dad opens the door, "Can we go to the park with April?"

"No."

"Why?"

"She's been sent to bed by Mum. She's been naughty. Do you want to play soldiers?"

"Yes! Yes!" and he runs down to the others, "Dad's gonna play soldiers," and they all rush outside.

Dear God, Miss Fisher says the parables will always help you when you are in trouble. But I don't know which one. I lied to mum. You know it. I think she knows it. That's why she is angry with me. But The Toffee Man isn't bad. I don't know why people say it.

It's daytime but there is a whole cloud moon in the sky, like a ghost – and it stays still as the other clouds pass by, watching me – and it looks like a mirror of the earth with shadows of seas and land, and I am there, too tiny to see – just like for me in there. Maybe when some more men go to the moon, they will get a telescope and they will see me, and they will see about the truth in the world. About Dad. Maybe they will tell Eli. And he will come and tell Mum. Or God, could you tell her.

I fold the letter so its long and think and poke it into the hole in the plaster behind the box. I hear it skitter down the wall. Only God can get it now.

Chapter 18

Abracadabra! Mum is walking to the pub with me. She said to Dad that I couldn't walk on my own – it was too late. Fucking hell! I'm not really swearing. Not saying it out – just in my mind. I can't help it. Fucking hell! It keeps shouting in my head, going on over and over. I'm not saying it! I'm not being too excited, or she'll change her mind. Dad is watching me. I pretend I'm concentrating on reading, but I'm remembering catalogue numbers for when I have to get things to take to the moon.

Fucking hell. I just want to talk to Mum. About anything… I have to be calm. Not a mad bint. If mum reckons that I want to talk to her she gets fed up about it. I've noticed it. But if I wait and see what happens, she laughs, sometimes, and then you can talk about all sorts.

Sometimes, when she is playing her records, she likes it when we make up new words together – and sometimes she sings swear words out loud, and so do I, and she doesn't mind. She laughs. We get so crackers. Other times, she doesn't laugh much, and you can feel that she is busy inside her mind.

It's kind of because of Dad she's coming with me. He said I had to go and get fags and lemonade from the shop. But, Mum said it's too late and only the pubs are open, "She's only fuckin' ten!" That's just what she said.

So he says, "Well, she can go to the fucking Offy at the fucking pub then."

And she says, "It's too fucking dark to go on her fucking own. Anyway they won't serve her."

I say it quick. "If mum comes with me, I'll carry all the stuff."

And she says, "OK! OK!" Then she sings, "A–a –a-a –pril, come-she-will," and I feel nice, because I am April.

He says, "Taken your fucking pills have you! Fucking pair of mad slappers!" He's screwing his finger against his head and sticks his stupid fat tongue out.

I say, "Fucking tough shit dad!" In my mind.

Mum is putting on her blue raincoat and white shiny stilettos. She backcombs her hair a bit and puts on her shiny pink lipstick. She sits in her chair with a compact mirror and she really concentrates. I sit on the arm of the chair and watch. She is rolling her lips inwards and outwards and blows a kiss to me. She smiles at me… well, she is smiling her lipstick in the mirror, at my reflection.

She sits still for a minute when she's finished. Just looking in her compact. Not smiling or looking at anyone. It's like she's forgotten everything. She is far away. But I can see her. She is really pretty. Like a Queen.

She looks like a lady off the telly who is in films, apart from her pointy tooth at the side when she smiles. It is yellow and black stripe like a bee. She doesn't like smiling very much. She looks like a Hollywood woman when she does, but then she puts the back of her hand by her mouth and taps her teeth with her wedding ring and she does a crazy stare. She said it's a bad habit, but it helps. People get scared and leave you alone if they think you're crazy.

I think Mum gets embarrassed. She could be in films if she went to the Dentist to fix it. She's gets big soft brown curls like a doll when she does her rollers. One day when I get a job I want to save up and send her for a perm because she said she could do with one. A perm means permanent, which means for all time, I asked my teacher. So it's worth it. Dad said she looks like a fucking slapper when she doesn't do her rollers. I might write to the television place and tell them about my mum when she's been to the Dentist. That will shock Dad.

Tonight, Mum is laughing. She is laughing, then she stops; then she laughs again – and I don't know what started it. I think she might be on the booze. She likes having booze before she works at the club. My dad gives her lift. Most of the time he stays until Mum has finished her work, but sometimes he comes home and goes to pick her up in the morning. After. When it's a long night.

I don't care if he does. So what? I can watch TV until the end of it. I like watching some of the things about the moon and the stars. If it works out, when I am grown up, there will be cars that can travel to the pub quicker than me just saying it. 'Let's go to the pub'. There I am! Already there!

At least Mum is happy and laughing, and almost as soon as we are out of the door she grabs my hand. My guts are churning up; I need to hold her hand. It's like I am on the flipping moon or something.

But Mum makes me feel like she is trying to hurt me sometimes. "Pick your bloody feet up and stop dreaming!" she laughs. And she sneaks a look at me. I walk straight and fast as I can, but she squeezes my hand really tight and twisty. It really hurts.

"Owaa!"

"Sissy. It's just playing!" I make my hand forget.

It's nice and warm. Mum says it's an Indian summer, and it won't last for long. Everything is dying and there are clouds coming. We close the gate and walk on the soft grass bank, to the crossroads. Mum says it's like we live on a hot cross bun.

Outside it's sparkly in the dark. You can see the stars as they fall down from the sky, into the fields on the other side of the valley. You can see the lights from the houses and lampposts, and the car headlights make fast, flicking shadows as they drive along the valley roads. And, because of the moon you can see the river and the shapes at the end of the land. Actually, I can see the really big cloud coming. Mum was right! She let's go of my hand and she is racing over the crossroads. Her metal on her spiky heels scratch and scrag the road, and I watch the sparks flying from behind, into the invisible. "Abracadabra!"

"Get a move on, slow coach!" she shouts. There're nine streetlamps down the road before the pub. I just counted. They zigzag down the road, like monster teeth. I ask mum if she gets scared on her own, because I do. What crisp flavours have they got? Can I choose? Can we get red pop? Can we make a cake – I mean on another day? I wanted to tell you. I wanted to tell you… I don't like staying with Dad. He says I ha-"

"Will you shut the fuck up? When did he ever say anything good about anybody? Don't be so bloody soft." She stops under a light. She gets her fags and matches out of her pocket. She's trying to strike a light, but the box is squashed and it won't go. She's pissed off with it.

"But, he wants … he puts …," it bursts like a star in her hands, and her arm rises like a wing, and she breaths deep and quick, and puffs out smoke rings. Like windows into – BANG!

She slaps my ear hard. It hurts. I can't think. I stand there. "Fuckin' 'ell, now look what you made me do! Oh darlin' don't cry, I didn't mean to. I just thought we'd have a nice walk out the house. Just me and you… Why do you have to go and spoil everything? Huh! Huh! Huh!" She is shouting. It's really loud. Mrs Pearce looks out her window like we are on telly, watching from far away and then the curtain jerks closed.

Mum tries to grab my hand, but I turn away, "Sorry mum. Sorry." I want to show her good things I can do. Make her proud. Make her laugh. I do a cartwheel. And then I just keep going. I'm the best. She's clapping! She's got her fag in her mouth, and clapping. "Nice one – that's my girl!" I do another one – and another – and – I'm feeling a bit sick, and the zigzag lights and stars are spinning a bit, but it's alright, I can skip backwards. "Look! Look at me mum. I can run backwards." She's laughing again now. I'm running, using her eyes as my mark, a balance trick we learned in PE. She follows me, smiling and clapping, with her fag bouncing in her mouth, until it drops onto the road. She bends down to pick it up.

BANG! BANG!

I can't find the ground; I put out my hand out, but my arm buckles and I am skidding and crashing.

BANG! BANG!

My body is jumping like the ground is pushing me off; every time I open my eyes the sky is sick into my brain. "April. April … you all right." I can feel her giant hand turning my head. I can hear a fast river in my head. Angry fishes swim in me.

"April! April! Get up now! You're scaring me". I open my eyes. Mum is crouching beside me on the road. I can see her knickers. She quickly takes a last drag of her fag, throws it to the ground. She stamps it under her foot.

"April! C'mon, get up! Let's go and get a drink, you'll feel better." I sit up, but when I try to push up with my hand it really hurts. I stare at it; the skin is curled and bleeding, broken with dirt and grit. Mum pulls me up by the back of my jumper and starts brushing me down hard.

"Where's your other shoe?" says Mum. My red jellybean sandals with silver buckles. My best thing in the world. I look round. We are by the top of Church Lane that goes down into pitch blackness. The streetlamp shines down and her eyes are black shadows. I feel my fingers through the soft grass, 'Mum, I can't find it! Help me.' The grass is dry and scratches my sore, and I try not to cry, but tears come out my nose.

"Oh for God's sake April! We can't go along the fucking pub without your shoe … and with all that bloody snivelling. STOP IT! Or I'll give you something to cry about! If you didn't spend all your time trying to show off, this wouldn't have happened. Find your fucking shoe, before I get back – they don't grow on trees!" I duck to avoid another swipe. Mum turns towards the pub, and I watch as she walks away, sparks fly behind her like dragon spit, until she turns the corner.

I can hear her shout, "Find it! I'm sick of it."

I want to find my shoes. I'm sick of it too. I can't see it under the light. There are bushes round the lamppost and in front of the wall. I pull the branches back, and then thump. It's my shoe. Like God is helping me. And he is saying Mum got it wrong. I sit on the verge to put it on.

My hand is stiff with hurt. I am crying again. This time I can't stop. I don't want to stop. I don't have to if I don't want to. I crawl behind the bush into the porch. I sit at the top of Church Lane, hiding, and I cry until I don't care, even when it starts to thunder. I'm glad I'm scared. I shout back, 'CP87214 DX89465 FD52431. It's the catalogue numbers of furniture for when I go to the moon: and I made a spell, and I shouted the co-ordinates of the Kant craters, so they know where to go. And it's a secret.

It's raining. It's raining harder. I stand up and push the branches to get out, and walk down the lane. Into the darkness. I shout all the numbers and I am not scared. I hold out my hands, turn my face up and feel the water splashing on my eyes and chin, and rushing over my face, cleaning my blood and snot, and I rub my face with my hands and push my palms into my hand while I suck out the last bits of grit

For a while, I just stand there with my eyes closed and the rain is drumming on me, sending me a secret message. I feel what it might be like if I could grow roots and never have to leave here. I could be part of the arch that walks everyone through to the church on Sundays when they are doing their best. I could sprinkle the sun blades on their hair and shoulders.

"April! April! Where the fuck are you now?" I can hear my mum's voice, slow and angry. More booze. I open my eyes and I can see my mum and a shadow of a man at the top of the lane. They're both swaying about. They look stupid. "APRIL! April! C'mon darling. I've got some crisps for you." I keep quiet.

They're laughing. The man says, "C'mon love, give us a feel. She's not here. Gone home when it started to rain."

"Fuck off, I'm a married woman – and so are you! Married!" They start laughing. I need to go or Mum will get mad with me. The man's voice sounds mean.

"C'mon – give us a feel, you dirty bitch. I bet you ain't got any knickers on – 'ave ya." She has. I see his hand go up my mum's dress and then they fall onto grass with him wriggling on top.

"Get off me, you dirty bastard! You fuckin' messed up me work clothes now." Mum is grabbing his legs, but she is too drunk "Gotcha!" I can hear Mum's shouting. It's raining harder and harder. Everything is a messy blur, and I'm running now.

BANG! BANG!

I kick him. I kick him. He tries to grab me. I pull his arm. I stamp on his guts.

BANG! – BANG! BANG!

He's laughing at me, and he's dribbling, "You little bastard. I'll 'ave you an all." I kick him in the eye. Kick him in the mouth. Pull his hair. Pull his ears and lips. "You shit head fucking bastard! You fucking – fucking – dirty bastard. I fucking hate you! I wish they would put you in the prison forever." I laugh. I can hear my mum screaming the words. No. No. It's not Mum. It's me.

I kick him until my feet are sore in my wet, red sandals.
BANG! BANG!

"STOP IT! April! Enough! What the fuck? He's pissed. Just an asshole! THAT'S IT!"

The rain has stopped. It's quiet. He stares up at me. I spit on him. My mum sorts her coat. Pulls down her dress. "I'll get you back for this Hope, and that little bastard kid of yours." I spit on him again.

"Oh yeah!" Mum laughed as she picks up the bag with the crisps and the lemonade. She looks at me like I'm a stranger, "They only had white," she says, "You'll have to make do."

Mum grabs my hand and drags me off. The water in the drains sounds loud. The world is upside down on the wet road. And I look. No sparks in the rain. We walk back in silence. Mum holds my hand tightly, and it hurts. I'm glad.

"What the fuck happened to you two?" said Dad.

"We got caught in the storm. Summer is well and truly over," Mum says. "I'd better go and get changed. We'll be late." Dad knows she's pissed. She gives him a kiss on the way to the stairs.

He gives me a wink, "I'll see you later." Dad goes out to the car.

I am sitting in mum's chair when she comes down. It's all right. I can. When she goes out to work. She sits on the arm and rubs my grazed hand between hers. It hurts. I don't care anymore. "If your dad asks you about tonight, you say nothing right! Right!"

"OK!"

"Well, you know what he's like … just, some things are best left unsaid! Now behave yourself. See you tomorrow!" The car doors slam, and it revs as it pulls from the gully.

I can hear thumping floors. It's the boys. I'm going out the back to have a bath before Dad gets back.

I like the sound of the bath running in the quiet of night-time. I sit on the toilet and watch and wait for it to fill. I've put lots of fairy liquid in. I watch the mountains of bubbles grow, and keep swishing them to the other end, until the whole bath looks like a snowy mountain land where Polar bears live. When I get in my head pokes out – it's like I am the Queen of the Snow. I blow through the land and make commands with my arms for a road for my carriage.

When I get out, I pull the plug and dry myself. The bath is still full of bubbles. I carry them out and stack them on the table in the kitchen. I make it look like a statue of my Mum's head. I am trying, but it doesn't look like her really. I blow a big hole right through the middle and blow her face away. I can see the mirror on the other side with my face doing it. It's good. I look crazy like Mum. I just keep blowing bigger and faster breaths until all the bubbles are gone, except a few lumps that stick to the chairs and what's landed on the floor. I can hear the quiet ripping sound as they disappear. I won't get told off. There's no proof anymore.

I jump up on the sofa and watch myself jump and dance in the mirror, dancing and smiling with my hair swinging. I know that I'm never going to tell Mum. Like Dad said, "What the eyes don't see the heart don't grieve for."

Abracadabra.

Chapter 19

You just must think of something good when you feel sad. You start at the top of the lane, and you jump from shadow to shadow, like this, except when the gap is too big, and then you must stand in the light and count to ten, do three turns and clap hands, like this. The long straight path is the King, no, the Queen into the Kingdom, and you must perform tasks to be allowed to pass through her grassy cloak along her brown dress, but you must step on her big stone buttons. If you step on more than one little button at a time you must do a star jump and then sit on your heels, balancing, without putting your hands against anything. If you can count to ten, no, six, and hold it, she might let you find some treasure for your pocket - and you are blessed and live to tell the tale. She might let you find a golden leaf, feather, or an insect, or something, but if she sees you're cheating then you would just get covered in slugs and dog poo, a sting from a bee or a nettle. And be asleep for a hundred years. And those are the rules.

I want to make a better game.

The grey stone wall outside Clara's is covered with dabs of yellow and white lichens, and moss grows in the shadowy between the stones, with little golden whiskers poking at the light. I press my arms and face against it, and I warm in the sun. And I'm thinking the wall is like the village of the Queen. When I press my ear against the gate, I can't hear anything except the wind, rushing around like the whispers and songs of dreams in the world. I put the latch up quietly to open it a bit and push my head through the gap. Sometimes you just want to cry because you are happy at the thing you see, because it just explodes into your guts. More beautiful than any of the catalogue pictures, or the shop windows in town, or than even my teacher can say. I can't see Clara. And it's OK to just look for someone if you're just helping them.

Quietly, quietly, I try to push the gate back into the wall without scraping. I walk around the edge of the long grass. Slowly, through the long grass and flowers, around the van. She's been painting the outside, and it's green, with white doors, and some red round the windows. It fits in. The trees at the bottom are full of shining red and golden apples, and there are wigwam canes of tomatoes and beans, surrounded by little feathery forests of green. Over the bumps and hollows in between the beds, the grass is making lots of different greens. Then I see, in between the trees and the canes, a blue dress is flapping up with the wind. Clara is asleep on the big pile of grass. When I get close I can see her face is happy and smooth like a big pearl button, and her headscarf has slipped a bit. Her white hair is blowing like smoke from her face, and she looks like she's looking what to do next, holding a rake by her side, with her other arm reaching out. I go and get some grass cutting to put under her head.

There's a bang and I jump; it's just the caravan door swinging in the wind. She must have left it open and fallen asleep. I stay still for a minute, listening to the sounds, watching, waiting for her eyes to open. She doesn't wake up, even when I stroked her eyebrows, like I've seen on telly. I put my finger under her nose, and I can feel air going in and out. I don't think she's dead. She's probably just tired from raking this field. People get old and tired and die like Granddad did. I wonder why God made it like that. It would stop the people who didn't die getting sad if he made it stop. And if he made it so they didn't get things wrong with them, we won't need the hospital.

If God is so great, he could have made it so we could just go to the moon when we wanted anyway. And in space. I can imagine it. Maybe that's what God wants us to do. If we imagine things and then we want to do it with our bodies, our mind makes us try hard. Sometimes we can imagine about what someone else would like and we can make it for them. Because we are making the effort to make it for them, they know that we think about what they imagine, and we like them a lot. Like when I make the beds for the boys. It's not like going to the moon or travelling in space, but it makes it nice so they can save time and imagine other things just for themselves. I don't think anyone does things for Clara. I could do something in her van. Then it will be a surprise when she goes in, and she will think that she was in God's mind.

I thought if she woke up while I was going up the steps she might think I was stealing something. They're steep, so she has a blue rope to hold onto and pull yourself up them. I did take my shoes off because the green paint is worn away in the middle, and the steps are smooth. I put the door on the hook so it didn't bang anymore.

It's not like in The Caravan Family. The bed is made with a big black crochet cover like a web, and some brown blankets folded and stuffed in the corner. In each corner, it's got a dark wood post going up to the ceiling, and it's carved with animals and flowers. It's got her name on it on the headboard, carved out in curly joined up writing. There's a mirror on the chest of drawers at the side, and underneath a big oil lamp, is a silver hairbrush and a wooden box, painted with pictures of women with baskets on their heads, and men with carts of hay and dogs watching. At the other end is the wood burner, with some big pots and a kettle hanging down of the hooks. In the middle, there is a little table and two small armchairs, one of them full of newspapers with a big gold magnifying glass on top, and knitted squares pinned together, waiting to be stitched onto the blanket on the table. On the wooden floor balls of wool are being unravelled from jumpers.

She's got oil lamps. I opened the curtains, and sat in the chair, so I could see what to do. Everything is tidy, but it's dusty and dark, and I could change that. The bed posts are dark, and all the little carvings are nice. I bet she doesn't even see them. I leaned over the table to look out of the window, and she is still asleep on the grass. If I am quick I could make it light. I have imagined it; imagined her smiling when she sees. I saw the tins of paint under the caravan. If I use the yellow and white, I can make it like the lichens on the wall outside, so she can see it all the time.

When I got the paint, I took my dress off and put it by my shoes outside so that I don't get paint on them, and I got a sack to put on the bed when I do the posts, so I don't get paint on the crochet. It's really fiddly to paint all the carved bits, so I'm just doing the side facing into the room. She'll be sleeping inside the bed anyway, so she won't mind if she can't see it as much.

I have painted the wall around the stove, and it already looks better. I am glad I took my dress off because I already splashed paint on my chest, so I painted triangles and straps so it's like a bra.

When you paint things white it makes you see how dirty the old white is, so I finished the wall all along the back. There's a lot of paint, and before I know it, I've done two walls. I tried to clean the drips on the floor, but it was spreading, so I made that like daisies in the clouds. I can't stop. I just want it to be perfect. She will know I perfectly love her, and God is loving her from me.

My hand is thinking with the paintbrush, and I can make an answer, and I feel like am speaking with God. And he wants me to speak, and every time I stop, he says no, don't stop. Don't stop. And above the clouds there is a kingdom of white halls, and every one of them is a Kingdom of Ends. And every person has their own special hall, and in the middle is a table with steps up to their book. And it is full of all their favourite things, pictures and words, and all the people and things they think about. And I am in my place, and it is so big I can't see the walls of it. Just white and white, and I am spinning and I can't see any directions. I can feel my book in my hands. I open it up to see what is inside, but it's all blank. It's my notebook, and everything is rubbed out, blurred and smudged, and I paint it 'til it's clean and gone.

When you stand in the door of the caravan you are high up so you can see into the attic windows and the roofs of everywhere. I am in a big and beautiful pea green boat, and they are all around in the sea, like islands, rising from the sea after a storm - when the ship is wrecked.

I look back in the caravan. The wall where the paint was running out looks like clouds with the sun coming through, and I made it like the feathers of birds were falling from them, so she can imagine herself flying from the sky, even higher above the world, swooping down to pick people up with giant talons and put them in the right place. I think she will like it.

I walked around the field and got all the petals from the flowers that were dying, and different kinds of leaves, and scattered them in a circle round her head so that she could see them when she wakes up. She has a path of leaves from her feet, right to the caravan steps to make her curious, until she sees her surprise.

I pulled my dress and socks back on, and the scrape of the gate feels like trouble as I close it. I put all the brushes and tins back, and it's all tidy. She'll see the paint is like nature.

Chapter 20

Fred was pushing up the knot of his tie when there was a knock at the door. He only had fifteen minutes of his lunch break left, and he still needed to get to the toilet. They could come back. Information was clearly set out and framed on the door.

The tie was taking some careful adjustment. He couldn't fasten the top button; the starched collar chafed now. He used his fingers to prise it from the fleshy tenderness around his neck and released it to a more comfortable resting place, which was proving difficult to find. He usually went straight to the bathroom after meals, but his mother held him in earshot with her (often repeated) story of how his dad had rounded up stray sheep on his bicycle.

He'd agreed with his mother initially that a bit of weight gain and a carefully shaved beard to 'link up those sideburns' would add some gravitas and increase his prospects. He needed to do his father's legacy proud. Decades of rationing and the long bicycle beat, circling and threading the hills and valleys were what had finally seen him off. That, and the disappointment of seeing his son wasting a hard-earned education, and increasing demands for financial support. His mother was determined that she should reclaim him from the ashes of a 'fashionable' city lifestyle, which he had probably enjoyed too much, and to his detriment. As much as he resented her, he grudgingly agreed.

The knock came again, more urgently this time. "Is that someone at the door Frederick?" she lowered her voice, "Leave it for now. You've still got quarter of an hour. Come and finish your pie, and let your food go down. They'll use the telephone if it's urgent."

"I've had most of it. It'll keep." He headed for the station room toilet. His mother used the upstairs bathroom. It was at the end of the counter, through the storage area, and round the corner through a thick wood panelled door. It had once been a holding cell. It had become his sanctuary and gave him the privacy he needed at this point in the day; his vomitorium, as he and his old friends had called the destination.

This time the bell rang out. He stopped for a second and turned back. He had to answer.

When he opened the door he saw Miss Carter, scuttling back down the path, almost at the gate, "Can I help you, Miss Carter?" She immediately turned and made her way back, with the determined look of someone who was heading into a storm of perpetual crisis. He remembered the first year of school, sitting among the others with folded arms, all wide eyed and fixed on that face, fearful of what they couldn't yet see.

"Oh, Sergeant Pilcrow. Thank goodness. It's Clara. I've called an ambulance. She's not well. I don't know what's happened - but I know she was up to no good, running around covered in paint, naked as a savage."

"Clara?"

"Oh no Sergeant Pilcrow. That Smart girl. I saw her. I was thinning the hedges. They get a bit unruly at the end of my garden. I saw her, through the branches, rushing around and then getting dressed and leaving. I thought it through; I could see no purpose to her behaviour, and I could see no Clara. I did not want to be so rude as to call through the thicket and so I decided to call in. I found her laid out, unconscious, in the middle of that - field, surrounded by dead flowers." Frederick had to agree this didn't sound good.

They hurried down the lane, and Frederick noted the open ambulance doors backed up to the other end of the lane. They turned in at the gate, and Frederick looked across where Miss Gomer was emerging from the caravan with Clara's bag. Clara herself was being secured onto a stretcher by two attendant volunteers. Clara's accent was thicker than ever as she instructed Miss Gomer, but she was smiling, and Miss Gomer seemed to understand well enough.

Miss Carter walked slowly but purposefully ahead of him, and he gazed about the scene. The smell of fresh paint hit him in heavy drifts through in the air and became stronger as he came to the foot of the caravan steps. He was curious to see inside. He was surprised at the level of detail that April had gone too. Clearly a purposeful attempt at something.

Miss Carter took it upon herself to repeat the details of what she'd seen to both Clara and Miss Gomer through the open doors at the back of the ambulance, as the medical aids tried to keep a straight face. Clara, for the most part, was also a little amused but for the clearing of the paint on the old wood, but Miss Gomer assured her it could be removed with a bit of elbow grease and sandpaper, and she would speak to Reverend Fisher about gathering a few helpers. Miss Carter became quite irate, insisting that punishment was the only way in which people learned. Clara, was though, quite adamant that she wanted only a warning for such a young child. She didn't want her getting into any serious trouble. She asked that Frederick would do what was appropriate, as his father had done with children before. And this time, he thought, it may be necessary to speak with April's mother, or father. A thought he did not relish. Both could be quite volatile.

Frederick had always found Clara friendly enough when they met in the village lanes, but had not had cause to step beyond her gate before, not since he'd been a young boy anyway. He remembered they had entered as a dare one winters night when it was still dark before time. Even then the glow of the lamps from the tiny windows seemed like eyes that glared above the jaws of the craggy foundations, the half-built walls and doors that had frozen and began their decay the day her husband died. His father had thought them decent people, and was among those to help move their caravan into the heart of the empty space that Clara's husband had made to be their home. He imagined her with her husband, on starry nights, sharing their dreams of what it would be. The blackened crumbling stubs and crevices now housing poles and tools, back then when they were children, through the post war years, other worldly, a land of monsters and Gods. Now, finding the world as he did, it was beautiful and simple.

After the ambulance had departed, and Miss Gomer and Miss Carter parted ways, Fred walked back up the lane to secure the caravan and the field. It occurred to him that he might find somewhere he could get rid of his dinner here, before it was too late. However, he found that the sanitation was quite rudimentary – and although he felt sure he could regurgitate his food within a few seconds of keeping his head over the hole in the ground, that he couldn't flush it away didn't feel appropriate. And he felt the same about the compost heap. He could not see that the worms would survive his bile. He slipped the Q-tip back into the little packet in his breast pocket. He had to accept it wasn't always possible to purge himself. On this occasion, he needed to pop round to the Smarts and deliver a little warning.

When he arrived, he saw April at the bottom of the garden. He wondered whether it might be possible to call her over or walk down and have a few words with her alone. From what he understood from Eunice at the chapel meetings, April was prone to a little trouble, but she had always seemed to be a very responsible child to him. Probably more responsible than many her age, and certainly more pressure to be so. Her mother's medication, coupled with her drinking, didn't bring out the best in her. It didn't bring out the best in anyone. He'd learnt that the hard way, but he'd been able to get protection from the worst of himself. He'd come home to his mother. He didn't have a large family. He'd been able to start again. The last thing a young girl with her background needed was a record.

"Can I help you?" Hope appeared at in the porch, before he had even turned to the door.

"Ah Mrs. Smart. Yes. I just came to see April. I just need to have a quick chat, ask a couple of questions."

"Can't you speak to me first? Do you want a cup of tea?"

"Well, that would be lovely." She turned to fill the kettle, and he saw his opportunity. "Perhaps I could just borrow your bathroom?"

Chapter 21

When I get back, I slip down into the garden. I'm just thinking into the sky in the grass down the bottom of our garden when I hear Mum calling me. I jump up and I realise as soon as I look over that I'm in trouble. The policeman is there, and Mum is shouting at me, "Don't deny it." I don't know what I've done, but it must be bad, Mum is going bonkers. She's shouting that I'm bloody stupid, even in front of the policeman. He is trying to look kind at me. Why does Mum always think I've done something bad?

I know I have to go. Anyway, it can't be worse. I'll just wait and see what they say. I walk over and avoid mum's glare, and as I look down, I see there's white paint all over my arms and legs. I stop in front of them. I don't know what to say. Mum pushes my shoulder. Here we go. "Don't bloody deny it. Look at you." She jabs into my clothes across my chest, down to my stomach. "Are you fucking deaf or stupid? Say something!"

She tries not to slap me because he's standing there, but she can't help herself and grabs both shoulders and starts shaking me. Dad, and Mum, always says the policemen are horrible, but they're afraid of them. Mum is fuming. She's shaking me so hard her voice is wobbling, but he steps in, "Alright. Mrs Smart." And he moves himself between us, and he stoops to look in my face so he can be serious, but calm, "OK April - now this could be very serious: trespassing; theft; vandalism. Luckily for you the lady doesn't want to press charges - she's selling up, but WE have to take your behaviour seriously." He looks more closely at the paint on my arms that goes under my dress. "What on earth did you think you were doing?" Not cross, but gentle.

I just stand in silence. It's hard not to cry when someone is nice to you. Suddenly I don't understand what I was doing myself. I look at him right in the eyes, and I want to tell him everything, and my head is shaking, like no, no, no, but I'm looking for an answer. He keeps looking at me, like the question is still there for me to answer if I want. "We'll be keeping an eye on you, young lady. I'm sure your mother doesn't need this kind of behaviour. It's a worry for her too, isn't that right?" and he turns to her. "I'll leave you to have a chat with her Mrs. Smart."
"Oh I've got plenty to say to her. Thanks."

We both watch as he leaves and turns the side of the house up to the gate. Mum grabs me and drags me into the house.

She pushes me into a chair at the table. She is ranting, more and more angry and I feel scared now because it's like she could do anything. More than before. She slaps the table, and then me. It's like the furniture is just for practice. I know whatever I say it will just make her madder, so I don't. I'm still trying to think about it. And it's like her and Dad make me feel bad, but mum makes me feel even more scared, but I know she's not well. God, you need to tell her.

"What the fuck do you think you were doing? Do you want to destroy everything I've done? You're fucking mental! What's the matter with you? It's not me who needs fucking tablets... You've been slowly destroying my fucking life since you were born... and you try and pretend... You're a fucking curse."

And my mind is doing flips. Sounds rush through like trains out of a tunnel. And it's like everything that ever happened is happening right now. I'm drowning. I can't even speak if I want to. Mum just grabs my face and pulls it to her. She stares right through, like I was an open gate, and she shouts into a field where she thinks I'm hiding, "Stay out of my fucking sight. You little bastard." Then it is silence.

I get up and turn to the stairs - and I want to say sorry, but Mum shoves her hand into my back and I'm falling forward to the stairs. I don't breathe all the way up the stairs in case she hears me. I close the door and even when I sit on the bed, I try to keep it quiet.

I hear Dad come in and Mum is shouting straightaway. I can't hear the words. It's like when my head is in the bathwater. I know what she's saying though. Their voices make me want to hold my breath forever, like if I could stop the world like a photo. But I can't.

Dad opens my bedroom door and Mum shouts up the stairs. "I wish you'd knock some fucking sense into her. I'm going to get some fags, and I'm taking the boys with me."

The front door slams, and Mum calls for the boys, "Kids! Coming to the shop with me?" and I hear them run round to follow her up the path and being excited, and Mum is telling them to throw their sticks down before they get onto the road.

"Hey. So, what's going on? What was that all about?" and Dad sits close and puts his arm around my shoulder and rubs my arm. The warm of it makes me cry a bit, even though it hurts a bit because my shoulder hurts. He pulls me into his chest and I just cry so loud. I'm making up with breathing now and I'm crying my guts out. And he strokes my hair until I quiet down.

"Come on. Nothing's that bad for long. Nothing stays the same forever."

"Mum just hates me now. She said I destroy everything in her life … I was just making it nice for Clara."

"Hey, come on. You've got me … I'm here, aren't I? Aren't I? I don't hate you. You trust me, don't you?"

I nod. He wipes my cheeks with his fingers. I feel cold and still and stare up through the window at the clouds. And Dad says, "I know what will make you feel better." And he walks off to their room and comes back with his whiskey. He unscrews the top and takes a swig. He hands it to me, and I take it with both hands. "Have a few swigs of that. It'll calm you down and cheer you up." And we sit on the bed, laughing about Mum, and drinking whiskey, until he says he better put it away and get downstairs before she gets back. He brings me a glass of orange squash in case Mum smells it, because it has to be our secret.

And when he's gone I feel happy. He didn't do anything except try and make me feel better. Maybe we really are going to be friends now. And I feel fuzzy and warm, and I get on a cloud and fly over the hills and along the valley to the Tabernacle. And I run in, but it's not big anymore. It's a long alley with a glass roof. I keep running, and it gets smaller and smaller until I slip down onto my back, and it's a glass tube and I keep racing through until my feet hit the end. Outside, the stinging nettles and the grass are all around, and I can only see tiny bits of sky. The glass is tight and smooth on my arms and my eyes can't close. Insects crawl over the lid, over my face, and some are giant, like there are telescope lenses by my eyes. But now there are hundreds of them, so heavy, and I am sinking into the mud. Into the dark.

I wake up and I can hear Dad and the boys outside my bedroom door on the landing. The door opens, "I need to talk her round. She's taking a few days in her room."

He pops his head round, "Sorry love… leave it with me." He winks at me. Matthew starts chanting from the stairs, "You been naughty. We got sweeties." I don't care, but I don't say it. I just sing it in my head.

The door closes. I get my notebook and I write a note to God. Maybe it is working a bit, and I just need to let him know that I mean it.

I'm trying to finish reading my book before it gets dark. I hear Mum come upstairs and I keep reading, but listen to see if she will come in. She does. I see a plate with sandwiches first. "They're Jam," she says as she comes in. She smiles briefly as she comes over to put them on the drawers. I can smell she has had a sherry. She's more kind now. I put my book up on the side.

"I'm sorry Mum," but she's not looking at me, she's looking at my book.

"You're not sorry. You just don't bloody care do you. It's no punishment … probably happy … I'll wipe that bloody smile off your face!"

She pulls my book box off the drawers, picks up all the other books and she crams them into the box with all the others, and drags them out of the room. I hear her drag the box down, bumping down the stairs. The Jam sandwiches are flattened on the floor. But I'm starving, and I peel them up and eat them anyway. They're not really dirty. I get out my notebook.

I keep writing until I can't see. I hear the church bells, cars, the tv and the boys go up to bed. No one comes in again. Like I've been forgotten. And I wish I was really forgotten, and I could just go to America and get a job in space.

As I fall asleep, I imagine the end of the Famous Five book when they all have a campfire, wondering what their next adventure will be. And I have been listening behind the tree, and then I come out and I'm introducing myself, and explaining that I am a detective from the moon. And they all shout hurray, and share their ginger beer with me, and I drink and drink it, because I am so thirsty.

Chapter 22

This, he thought, might be the happiest he'd felt in a long time, striding back across the freshly cut summer grass, as it shimmered in early morning dew. This vast stretch of green behind the Rectory was rarely used, or seen, by parishioners, and one of the few places that he had privacy. He felt a sense of magnanimity, that he had gifted and so carefully prepared it for the annual church fete today. It had grown long and unruly. He'd initially cut it with a scythe, quickly teasing out the cuttings with the rake, before completing his work with the mower and the heavy roller. His arms had ached so much this past week that he'd had to hide his struggle to reach and realign the hassocks after services. But now, they shivered with pleasure as he leaned into the cool brick wall, his head bowed as he looked out over his glasses.

He watched the birds swooping and hopping across the striped lawn, so evenly aligned that they ran before him to a perfectly realized vanishing point. A blackbird crossed the lines searching for worms, finally upturned and pulled a snail from its shell, its cruel but frail claws glistening in the dew. And up above, the sky was peppered with swallows preparing for their long journey home in the coming weeks. The grey surly skies with their foreboding red streaks illuminated the first blushes of red and yellow in the leaves, and the filigree of their veins seemed to throb with the force of life. Ah! How could one doubt the presence and movement in and of God in all things?

As he turned back to the house the first rays of golden light broke and threw a shadow of the house to the side, and the conservatory became a temple, reflecting the magnificence of all that surrounded it, reassembling into a glory of broken colour and meditations, coming to know themselves anew.

He stopped just inside the door. The conservatory was full of boxes piled high on every surface, waiting to be unpacked for this afternoon's fete. He could already hear Eunice in the kitchen preparing for her final bake before she would call him to help with the buttering of bread. Bread that she had baked yesterday afternoon, and he had blessed before supper, before they had shared their Agape feast, with Liz, Jasper and Fred from the Chapel.

Of course, the Agape was an opportunity to share not only food, but to explore the thoughts that constituted their religious experience, and the doubts and barriers they came across that challenged them on the long road to Christ. This year had been particularly troubling with the arrival of the Smart family. On the surface, the problems had been practical and basic; the more disturbing problem was Mrs. Smart's mental health, and her drinking habit. They'd all agreed that Mr. Smart had proved to be more able than his prison record suggested, but Eunice said she herself had found the children particularly testing in Bible class, and mainly April, who seemed to lack any proper humility or instinctive obedience. She seemed entirely set on destroying any chances the family had. It was true, they had all agreed, this last act of vandalism on poor Clara's van seemed to place her in possession of the devil himself, that having found Clara asleep in the garden, or, as later discovered, collapsed from a stroke, April had surrounded her with dead flowers, removed her own clothes and painted the caravan and everything in it completely white, including herself. Despite Fred's reservations, it did indeed suggest some devilishly inspired state.

Ezekiel had spoken to the child himself and had not been able to draw anything more from her but tears. As he passed through the conservatory, he firmed the loose soil around a few bases of the twine crosses that April had brought to them a few weeks earlier; the twine crosses that were to provide the stakes for the dormant life beneath the soil.

Secretly, he felt the light of the Holy Spirit was in her, and he considered how he might encourage others, and April herself, to see that light burn more brightly.

And, of course, he reflected, this year had brought Eunice to confront her own secrets. Secrets she had not brought into the light of Agape meetings, or even with him, but secrets that remained shrouded in the dark murmurs of furtive prayer that he would fall asleep to, as her conversations with the Almighty, shuddered along the silent corridors, and through the walls to his room at all times of the night.

Not that Ezekiel felt he could speak to her about such things, but he did understand this to be a difficult time for a woman, particularly one who had not married; but they had never been apart, except for the short time during the war when she had been called upon for nursing, and he had never known her to indicate any sense of lack or loss without marital union. Indeed, she had been devoted to their work together, to his calling. A destiny they had always sensed and yearned for, as one. That they had been called to earth the very same day. She embodied the echoes of his father's widowed prayers. And perhaps, he considered, as he shuffled his feet on the mat, that this was why she was so exasperated with that young girl's behaviour.

He checked her progress through the window, before disturbing her. Food preparations had always been an outlet for reflections from which Eunice did not like to be distracted. Her brown eyes attended only the task in hand, like the thick dark grips that held her greying hair in place, but there was always a grace and softness in her attentions. As she slid the tins into the oven, he could see the bread had already been sliced and placed to one side of the table; the assembly line for the sandwiches was in place. He reached for a butter knife. She looked up and clapped; a punctuation that signified completion that he was always glad of, but the clap was not so bright, and lacked its usual rhythm. He put the butter knife to one side and stepped forward with a gleeful rub of his hands, "It's a magnificent sunrise. I've cleared a little space that we can take some tea before we begin."

Eunice stepped back to the cooker, "And eggs too? I think that's quite sensible," she said. "I don't think there'll be much opportunity later. Sally and Jasper are coming with the team to help set things up at ten. And, I imagine, any cakes and sandwiches that are not bought will find themselves a home," and he raised a brow and smiled to let her know he knew which home she was referring to, despite, or perhaps because of, her cheerful bustle. She tore off a small piece of crust and buttered it to taste, approving her work.

The sky was magnificent. Eunice placed the breakfast tray on the low table at the window. She placed the teapot on the mat, and the coddled eggs and buttered bread onto plates, and they sat back in the wash of colours, cups and saucers in hand, and admired it. He turned to reassure her, but saw that her eyes were glazed with tears, searching for some fixed point above the horizon that could not be easily identified. He turned back, searching for that same distant point, but before either of them could find it, she spoke, "No, Ezekiel. No more. I have been too long in the shadow of your righteousness." He wasn't sure if he'd heard her correctly, but in any case, he felt compelled to lighten the tone. But she held his gaze and he felt forbidden.

We could despair Eunice wanted to say. How many cycles of seasons and religious observations since their world began. And the thought of any sudden separations rendered her mind barren. Her tongue fumbled with a small seed set behind her teeth, she worried it with her tongue until it was freed, and she swallowed it. She had taken the time to slow her heart and distil the heat of her breath to something that came more readily, more coherently - something more purified than the jagged heat of guilt, and jealousy.

That Ezekiel was not her real brother, and her guilt as a foundling had long been discussed with both Ezekiel and their father; and that they understood her to be a gift from God himself when Ezekiel's mother had died at his birth. They had vowed that they must always minister to the truth. She had not.

"Ezekiel. I have kept secrets from you, from so long ago I had forgotten they existed," Ezekiel raised his hand as if to reassure, "No. Ezekiel, now is the time… There is… You must have… I have felt the heat of God's test, scorched and searing to the depths of me. No. I mean it sounds like I think it was God himself – or worse, the fault of another, but it was a pain of my own making. I thought it was for the best, at the time, I see now…"

He was watching her, with such carefulness now, such patience. He took another sip of his tea, "Eunice, you don't have to -"

"Days I, we, have lost…"

"If this is the Smart's, April, then we can -"

"Oh Ezekiel! It is not the Smart's – and if April has played on my mind, it is that I am jealous."

"Jealous? Of April?" He stood up and walked to the door, as if the answer might be found on the threshold. He turned to confirm it was not there. Eunice, having composed herself with the turmoil of her first revelation could not stop.

"That my son had given her a gift I had refused."

"Your son?"

"That they had such a friendship. That he had such a friendship with the Smarts."

"Your son?"

"How do I tell you? Elijah. American. He came to the chapel last year, but I kept him from you as best I could." He'd taken a seat again. As he sat back, she saw that he looked at everything as though it were unrecognisable to him. "He came to find me. His father died recently. He never married."

"When you were nursing? It was then?" she could see that Ezekiel was assembling any information that he could retrieve, to understand how he did not know, to understand how he did not know Eunice. "How – why did you leave your child? Was he a good man? Tell me?"

"He was a good man. He loved me, Ezekiel. I loved him."

"So why return to the Chapel. Why turn your back on your child? On love? We serve God in honouring our responsibilities, Eunice. You did not need to make such sacrifices. I would have -"

"I didn't sacrifice anything Ezekiel. I loved you more. I love you."

"Yoo Hoo!" It was Liz, and Jasper with arms full of Tupperware, appearing from the side gate, walking towards the conservatory. "We thought you might be here."

Chapter 23

The afternoon sunshine was alive with the sound of children and laughing and shouting, or jeers and groans of disappointment: the buzz of the bell, from those failing to hold the ring from the wire; the thud of wooden balls that missed their mark at the coconut shy, and the crisp knock, and whoops when they toppled their target. Pennies rolled, numbers were called, card tricks baffled, and children scored goals in jam jars with tennis balls. The jam jars had quickly proved popular, not least because Mrs Peters, in a bid to take less space, had failed to consider the need for a space between the open-mouthed jars on their sides, so that prizes were not inevitable. Initially, she had been as excited as the families had formed a queue but began signalling Ezekiel for help in her coy manner, as she was quickly running out of prizes, brushing aside Mr Peter's who was encouraging parents of reluctant children to move to his 'roll a penny' stall, although less so as Mrs Peters turned every other jar end up. Ezekiel continued to intently organise the books alphabetically, which required focussed inspection. Occasionally he felt he was being watched from the cake stall, but whenever he looked over Eunice was chatting to customers as she bagged up cakes and counted out change.

Hope Smart's arrival caused only one or two turned heads and signals, but it disproportionately increased the self-conscious performance she gave; the children grimaced as she polished their teeth with a handkerchief and licked her hand to smooth their hair. Ezekiel hoped she would interpret the limited attention as acceptance, but he doubted this was her way. For him, although he had yet to grasp the full details, if he had not embraced them into the fold fully already, he now felt tied to Hope's brood by strings of more personal nature, especially April. Unsuccessfully, he politely tried to bring the small transaction he was engaged in on the bookstall to a close, so that he might hurry over and make them welcome.

He looked again over to the cake-stall where Eunice and Liz were now busy replenishing and rearranging half empty plates of frosted fairy cakes. He had failed to catch Eunice's attention since this morning's revelations, and it was Liz who caught his discreet signals, and rushed over to Hope with friendly enthusiasm.

Eunice frowned as she watched Liz walk Hope over to the Bingo tables with the twins, and they sat together, making easy conversation, whilst April seemed to calculate a moment to slip away and dawdled towards the cake stall. After a brief smile of recognition, she inspected every cake with an awestruck intensity that Eunice found disarming, finally choosing two particularly large cupcakes. Eunice visibly faltered when April presented her with a ten-shilling note but gathered herself to accept the tender April and give change with grace. Nonetheless, he felt an anxiety about Eunice's declared 'jealousy', and it did cross his mind that April was subject to some complications from a vexed world. He tried to clear his mind as she turned toward the bookstall whilst glancing round to check on her mother who was enjoying the admiration for the twins, and Matthew and Mark now proving rather skilful with the Jam Jars.

He watches her, as she catches sight of her cuttings on the plant stall, where the two Miss Fanshaw's have removed their gloves to touch the delicate twine crosses and admire the tiny green shoots that will ascend. They announce they're thrilled and decide to buy six of the pots. April's face lights up, and her step lightens.

She notices, and comments on, the alphabetical order, and she carefully returns each book to its rightful place. She looks up, "Reverend Fisher, which books do you think I should read now. I've nearly finished all the books from Sally. My teacher says I should get some classics. Which ones are classic?" He assumes that the teacher is talking about Dickens and the Bronte's and picks them out. But she has spotted The Secret Garden, Little Women, Tom Sawyer, Tom's Midnight Garden, and she built a sizeable pile, and she knows she can't carry them all, so she says she'll read Dickens and the Bronte's another time. Of course, he says, he understands – and he tucks them into a box under the table and marks it with a cross and asks for a shilling.

"Your cuttings have been popular, haven't they? You've done well. Your family have been generous with their time." He sees her cheeks have flushed, "I hope you enjoy your new books." She's quiet now, awkward, and embarrassed. She searches out her mother again, who is walking across to the Punch and Judy show with the twins, along with most of the people that are there. It's about to start. "Thank you, Reverend Fisher. I'm going to ask Mum if I can go home and read them." And she darts off to her mother, and after a quick exchange circles the outskirts of the garden to the drive, and leaves.

He sees that Eunice is alone clearing away the stall. He's hesitant to walk over to her, to speak. He looks for more of the classics that April's teacher may have had in mind. There is no one else there as a diversion, should it go wrong. He's frightened of what there is to be added. He's had to work hard against some force since their talk this morning, since Liz and Jasper arrived and suddenly everything had to be as it had been yesterday evening. He wished it was. But there was something else. He was afraid to touch her now, a hand of reassurance, even to her shoulder. Throughout the day, boundaries had been dissolving, crumbling. He feels warmth, like the sun has shone deep into his bones. Yesterday is a lifetime away. Another life. He orders the books alphabetically, in their genres.

Punch and Judy finishes. The announcement is made for the raffle, the sweets in the jar, and the thanks. As people flood back through the stalls, they generously rush to buy the remains of the perishables; garden produce; cakes and ice creams, and those that aren't taken are put into a box which Eunice takes to the gate, where Ezekiel is waiting as he personally thanks everyone for coming.

It takes Hope some time to gather her boys, and she is among the last to leave; she tucks in their shirts and pats and smooths their hair. And perhaps a little too enthusiastically he clasps her hand, "Mrs. Smart. I'm so glad you came. The children have been a joy. Wonderful to see them enjoying themselves. And you too."

And Eunice stepped forward, "I see the cakes went down well, and I wondered if you'd do us the favour of taking these away for them. I don't know if you could take the vegetables too?"

"It's been a lovely day." She takes the box and puts it on the tray under the pushchair. "You're always very kind Reverend, you, and Miss Fisher. You must both come round and let me make you a cup of tea."

"I shall be sure to try in the coming weeks - see how April's getting on with those books. She is such an imaginative child."

"It's not always easy with her - she's got her head in the clouds. You know."

"Well, I'd love to see how the garden is coming along, she's certainly got an interest in that too." Hope looks quizzically in the first instance, like she thinks he's making a joke, "Well, we'll get it clear for her to get stuck in one day."

"She's getting well prepared. Now that's what I wanted to say: thank you so much for sending us the cuttings."

Eunice seems to sense some well earned praise will help too, "April did a wonderful job with the crosses - and even a little plan with all the names. They sold very well - a wonderful contribution on the part of your family." All they get from Hope is a frown.

"This is news to me? I better get this lot home and find out."

"Perhaps I've spoilt a surprise she was planning. I think she said her uncle had helped her."

"Not any uncles that I know about … but I intend to find out?" Hope walks off, calling the boys to follow.

"Oh Dear." He found himself saying softly. And he felt a hand on his shoulder.

Chapter 24

I see him through the window, his hands leaning into his table, with his head drooping and tired. It looks like he's in misery. But he's coughing up into his hanky. I never seen him get in a misery – he just misses people.

I put the bag down and walk away from the window into the garden, so he can see me when he's ready. I imagine I'm a princess, and all the people of the palace have left me in peace. Silent shadows of bushes guard across the paths that wind through the red, orange and yellow of the flowers, and the trees and hedges are starting to go yellow and red too. And when I stand still with a breeze in my face I can hear the sounds of people still at the fete. And I feel happy that Mum is there, and the boys. We are becoming part of the village now, and people are friends with us.

And I feel sad to the tips of my fingers when I hear him coming down the hall and his breathing crackles like the radio trying to find the words out in the airwaves. When I hear the lock go, I swivel round and down to take a cake out of the bag, and up 'Ta Da! His eyes are bright, even squinted through his wrinkles, and his face is white and shiny with sweat through the folds of his skin. He dabs it with his hanky.

"Look at you. All dressed up." He smiles and stoops to take the cake, but it makes him cough again and he has to cover his mouth. I wait until he's quiet. I think he's embarrassed. I get out my books so we can think about something else.

"I just went to the fete. I've got some books like they got in the library van now, and they're all mine to keep."

"So what you got there then?" And he's still got his hanky in his hand and pulls out his chair from the side of the porch and sits down. So I put them in his lap as I get them out. And it feels even more interesting to see them with him.

"Look, Little Women, Tom's Midnight Garden, The Secret Garden, Treasure Island, Reverend Fisher helped me. Him and my teacher said that he thinks I should read the best classics books now. I looked for a book about how plants can make you better, to get some recipes - I need to know it anyway, for on the moon." He makes a little laugh at me, and starts coughing really bad, and I wish I had a special recipe right now. He's bending over as he stands, and I know it's painful. It's like a big tree being sawed. "I'm going to look for the things we should grow to make you better," and he has to spit in the flower bed and keep coughing it up. And he's never done that before. "You've got to stay warm. I could make you some tea and you could eat some of your cake."

"I'll save that until later. That'll be a treat." He goes into the house, and I see him through the window breaking some toffee off the tray with his little hammer. He puts a piece in his mouth, and he stands there sucking it a bit. He breaks of some other pieces, and I know he's going to bring them out for me. But I don't want to go. Not yet. He stops to look at his photo with his friend from the army days. He curls his fingers on the frame and strokes his thumb over them.

When he comes out, he's cheered up, "This is the best recipe I know, but you are right - you could look up some tea that we can grow. That would be nice to have, some toffee with a cup of tea."

He hands the toffees to me, and I know that I'm supposed to say goodbye, it's like a signal - but this time, as he hands it to me, with the other hand - he ruffles my hair, I can feel his warm fingers through my hair. And I get frozen in my guts. And I feel sick. He never touched my head before, or any of me. And I'm thinking a hundred things in a second. I don't want another boyfriend. Maybe Dad was right. And I want to give him his toffee back. Just in case he wants a favour. I hold out the toffee, "I think you should keep this. You're running out and you need it for your cough. Mum gets the shop ones." And he takes it and stands back to look at me, "But I'll see if I can find a medicine plant to make tea."

"You know. You're a good girl. A fine soldier. Not many of you about. Your parents must be so proud of you. Now off you go and read those books - I'm looking forward to hearing about them."

His hand has slid to my shoulder, and I know it's a different feeling. Not like Dad at all. He really is proud of me. And I feel embarrassed about myself, and I don't know why. Except, how could I ever think he would want anything for a toffee. Toffees mean love to him. And that's why he remembers his friend when he has a toffee, the recipe from his mum. And I think of him sat in fields in France in the sunshine and getting a parcel from his mum and sharing out the toffee with the army. And for a minute I can see he was a man like Eli, just clever and kind as can be. Just fixing clocks so people can keep their memories of their family. I just say it, "You're the cleverest and kindest person I ever known … and you are my friend … and I want you to get better because you got to keep being my friend." And I'm glad I said it, because the clouds moved out the way of the sun, and the world was all bright, and it made him do the biggest smile ever, and he showed all his long, big black and yellow teeth and his sore red throat from coughing, and his sparkly eyes with his big white eyebrows. He's so beautiful and I'm so happy he's my friend, and he likes me. I think mum would like him so much if she would just talk with him. And my mum has got a black and yellow tooth. But only one is. Maybe she could come and have a cup of tea. Then she'll see. And I want to give him a hug, but he's too tall and I can't explain to him that he needs to stoop, so I take his hand. And I kiss it like he is the king in his kingdom with his treasures.' He laughs again, and I think he is shy now, and me.

"Well - you best be off - us friends have got business to attend to!"

"Yep!" I pick up my bag of books, and he has already walked into the house. I peak through the kitchen window, so I can wave like normal. He's gone back to his picture to look at his friend and him together. And I wish I'd knew him too. Next time, I'll ask Toffee Man about what the world was like when they were friends.

When I get home, I tidy up and make everything nice. I clean the table, and make the draining board, the sink and the taps all shiny. I put the cake on a plate and divide it up to eight and put the knife to the side. I put little plates to the side. Put the tea pot ready and fill the kettle up, ready to put it on when Mum gets in with the boys. I tuck the chairs under the table and put a cup and saucer with a shiny spoon on the side, by the tea pot. When it's all as ready as can be I go up to my room to sort out my books.

Miss Gomer gave me lots of different size wooden crates from the fruit. She said they are sturdy and it would be a shame to waste them. She thought that I would be the best person to think of things to do with them. Well it was easy – I put two long ones into a square one and made a shelf to go on top of the other shelf. I coloured in all the edges in black so now it's like a stain glass window, but instead of saints and their friends it's books in the window. Where there was enough space to draw on the corners, I drew suns with clock hands. The books smelled nice as I flickered through the pages, before I put them in their place.

I found a place to put my diary safe now. It's on a long piece of string tied around a baton of wood in the hole in the wall. You have to have kids' fingers, but Matthew or Mark would never think of it, and you reach your fingers to the baton and pull the string towards you, and up. The book comes up and I can take it out and sit on my bed next to the draw and write in it. Today I write about visiting The Toffee Man, and how kind he is. And I write that I am going to read all the books and tell him what they are, one every week. It's important to write it down. Writing it is like a promise. And I write that I am going to tell Mum as soon as she is in a good mood with me that she should give The Toffee Man a chance and come and have a cup of tea with him.

Chapter 25

I hear the door go, and the boys run in, and Mum is unloading the pushchair, getting Matthew to help. I'll wait until she notices the table all set, and the cake, and her teacup and go down, take her shoes and sit down for tea. "April," she's in the house now, "April!" and she's come to the stairs. She hasn't seen it yet. I run down, smiling – and she is looking at me strange. I can't tell.

"The Reverend thanked me for our contribution of the plants? Where were they from?"

"I made them… for the sale."

"You made them? How? You lied. He told me what you said. Did you steal them from that old woman's place?"

"No. I … made them. I… I'm trying to work out the right thing to say, I don't want to lie."

"What do you mean? You made them! Do you think I'm fucking stupid? You don't make plants. You grow them - it takes time. Someone's time. You know fuck all about plants, and it's not been happening in our garden." And I slip past while she goes to look out the window, just to check.

I know as soon as I say it, I'll be in trouble, but I can't think of anything else, "Mum, I got things ready for tea." And she turns to look, and she's mad because I went past her without her saying.

"Stop sneaking around. You're just determined to fuck this family up, aren't you?" and she slaps me right round the face. I don't move this time.

"We'll take some cake outside Mum," says Matthew and gives them all a piece and they head out into the garden. She just ignores them.

"Where did they come from?"

"I didn't do anything wrong. The Toffee Man growed them and showed me how to make cuttings. He's nice mum. He's my friend."

"I've told you! How many times?" She grabs my shoulders now and is shaking me hard, "What did he want? What did he fucking want?"

"I don't know Mum. Nothing. Nothing. He just talked to me that's all. He helped me make them for the stalls because he had too many… he just showed me -"

"When? I told you to stay away months ago."

"I just went a little while. When I went to the shops and stuff. He's not well … Mum he's really kind. Can't you just talk to him. Please. Please. Please?"

"He won't be very well at all by the time I've finished with him. I'm getting the bloody Police on him! You can go to your room and stay there until he comes."

I'm glad when I can be in my room, on my own, but I can't stop crying and crying. I nearly can't breathe. I close my eyes I'm running and running – and I don't know what I'm scared of, but I don't know what I'm not scared of. My shoulders hurt from Mum, but then I remember The Toffee Man's warm hand on me, and they feel better. And I just imagine I am in the garden with him, and his friend comes in the gate and I tell them both about the Famous Five adventures whilst we have a cup of tea and some toffee.

I am just dreaming when I hear Dad come in. I can hear Mum start on at him as soon as he's in the door. He says she always does that. I can tell she's had a few drinks. She's got loud with him. Dad tells her to keep her voice down, the boys are watching television and they don't need to hear all this.

"Right. Well I'm going to get the police round here. God knows what's going on. What he's getting up to - but I'm putting a stop to that dirty bastard. He's been getting her round his house on the quiet."

"Who? What are you talking about now?"

"Do you ever listen to me? That Bloody weird bloke in the village – she'd been round there making stuff for the fete. She told the Reverend it was Derek. Why would she lie? Something's going on! Since you don't do anything, I'm getting the police."

I hear her heels screech away up the path. Dad runs straight up the stairs to my room He closes the door and comes straight over to sit on the bed. I'm still crying, and he strokes my arm. It makes me feel sick and I push his hand away, "Get off me. Mum's getting the police, and I'm going to tell them the truth about everything. Even you." He starts laughing at me.

"Hey - come on - don't be stupid. Deny everything until proved guilty. Why would anyone believe you? All the lies you've been telling. Your mum told me. Lied to the Reverend she said." And he's just saying it all likes it's a joke.

"I didn't drop the weird sod in it. I didn't break our deal. Don't blame me. It was you from the sounds of it."

"Mum will believe me." I look him straight in the eye. He stops smiling and he takes both my hands and holds them down in my lap, and it doesn't hurt, but I can't move them.

He's serious now, "Are you sure? Even if she does, she isn't going to be very happy if I go away again. How do you think she'd cope?" He let's go of my hands, and strokes my face, and pinches my nose, "Look. I'm your friend. Let me tell you - we don't get many in this world. You don't want to make it worse for yourself. Or your Mum. Am I right?"

And then he's quiet. Mum has got back, and she's got Sergeant Pilcrow with her. She tells the boys to go and play in their room, and they make a huge noise as run up to the attic. "April. Down here now young lady. Andy!" She's putting on a voice for the police.

"You better go. Remember. You got to think these things through. Don't make things worse for everyone. That's growing up for you."

I get up to go, and I feel my stomach jumping and my ears got a rush in them. Most of all, I'm scared of growing up.

When I walk into the living room I want to run, but my heart is beating too fast, and I would trip over. Sergeant Pilcrow asks if he can use the bathroom, and whilst he's gone, I wait for Mum to speak, but she has her arms folded, like something bad is going to happen. Dad just goes and sits in his armchair and picks up the paper on the Pools page and starts checking numbers.

When he gets back Sergeant Pilcrow asks me to come and sit at the kitchen table with him and pulls out a chair for mum too. We are all sat there. Silent. He finally speaks, "So… what's been going on April? Your mum's very concerned … about it. I mean, I want you to explain it to us… so we can sort this out. Your mum's here. There's nothing to worry about. Tell us about Harold. What's he been up to." It's funny hearing The Toffee Man's name, said by a policeman.

"Nothing. He hasn't done anything. He's been nice to me. He's helped me - that's all."

Mum butts in, "So why all the lies? He put you up to it - didn't he?"

But the policeman turns and asks me, "April?"

"I only said about the plants to the Reverend because everyone thinks he's bad. He's not. He didn't do anything. He doesn't want any trouble. He just wants to be left alone." He smiles at me, and looks across at Mum, and she nods her head towards me, and he turns back to me.

"I'm sure he does, but your mum's making some serious allegations April, and it will make things much easier if you tell us a bit more. Are you afraid of him? Has he threatened you?" And it's not that he's being mean, but I just don't know what to say anymore, and my throat is a big lump and I start to cry again.

"Perhaps you'll feel more able to talk about this tomorrow."

Mum slaps the table, and even the Policeman sits back in his seat, "If you're not going to talk, then we'll have to sort it out. Unless you can call in Sergeant Pilcrow?" And it sounds like Mum is threatening him.

"Don't worry, I'll call in this afternoon." And I look round at everyone. I don't want to grow up. It's just like they said in Famous Five, grown-ups are mean and stupid. "April. I'm going to have to go and pay a visit to him. In the meantime, you must do as your mother says and stay away from there." He gets up from the table and puts his hat back on. "Mrs Smart I'll call in now. I think it's best if you keep her in the house for the time being." He looks at me again, and I feel like he wishes it was different, and he believes me. Mum walks him up the path a bit, and I can't hear what they are saying, but when she comes back she is being a bit nicer.

"Right. He's going to let us know tomorrow. Go to your room. I'll come up and see you later."

"Please mum, he didn't do anything wrong." I can't help it, I look over at Dad, and I want to shout it. Mum doesn't understand. She comes over and pulls my head to her shoulder.

"I'm going to get to the bottom of this. You're scared to speak. Twisting your mind. It's not your fault. Now go and get some sleep. I called in and cancelled my shift at the bar tonight. I'll put the boys to bed." They're both watching me now.

In my room it's not very light anymore. I get my notebook back out of the hole and write how sorry I am to The Toffee Man. How I wish I said that I'd been stealing the plants from someone. That I'd stolen them from him. Perhaps God is punishing me for not respecting my parents. But that wouldn't be fair, because really he is punishing The Toffee Man.

When I come down the stairs in the morning, Mum is talking to Sergeant Pilcrow at the front door. They can't see me if I stand still. Stay here.

"Well he seemed pretty upset by the whole thing, but he would be. He certainly doesn't seem well."

"And did you get anything out of him. Why all the secrecy?"

"He didn't know it was a secret. He just said she was interested in helping with the garden and called in to see him sometimes. She was good company. Mrs Smart, he has agreed not to see April again - and he understands that there will be 'problems' if he does. I'm afraid that beyond that, there's not much I can do."

"I think most of the village would challenge that."

"Well, they might. Look. I took the liberty of calling in to see the Reverend. He said he will call in after lunchtime for a talk with April." I see her hand come round to the latch and start fiddling with it. Mum does that when she's changing her mind, fiddles with things out of sight.

"Sorry if I've overreacted. It hasn't been easy … and with April, it just seems ... It's not like her … all this."

"Mrs. Smart. It's understandable. She's growing up! You're taking a normal interest in your daughter. That's nothing to apologise for." Mum goes quiet, and her fists are clenched, as she stares at him.

"Thank you." It comes out all strangled. I think she's going to cry.

"Oh, and he said he should return this book that she'd lent him." He hands her 'You Will Go To The Moon', "He said to let her know he liked it very much."

And when he says goodbye, I watch her push the door closed and lean back against it. I step back into the stairs. She looks around the room, but she doesn't see me on the steps. She walks over and checks herself in the mirror. Pats her face and pushes her hair into place. She picks up a Secret Seven book that I accidentally left on the side and looks at it, and she reads the back. I think she is going to throw it away, but she holds it to herself with 'You Will Go To The Moon.'

"Normal interest. Normal…" She says it like it's the happiest word. She puts down the books and walks over to the dresser and gets out her sherry bottle. She takes out the cork, and walks over to the sink, and pours it down the plughole. "About bloody time!"

177

"Mum," I say. And I'm scared because it's like I might break the spell. She comes rushing over and just pulls my whole body into hers. I feel like I am a baby. This time when I cry it's different. And when Mum moves me back to see my face. I can see she's got tears too.

"It's alright. It's been sorted."

'What's going to happen to him Mum?'

"It's all fine. He said he doesn't want to see you again, and so long as he sticks to it - nothing. That's all I want love, is for us to be safe."

And she pulls me in again, and I feel like I might be a bit crazy. Is this what growing up is like?

Chapter 26

Ezekiel was struggling to maintain a sense of calm after the weekend, and so it had seemed incredulous when Frederick had called in to tell him of developments in the Smart household. He knew of Harold of course. He was a coarser thread in the fabric of village gossip.

When he and Eunice had first arrived in the village, he had heard first-hand the ungodly cries from his house, as he had passed by in the early hours, after delivery of the death rites for Col. Fanshaw, who had confessed to the substance of his own dark nights since the war, from his ancestral bed, much to both his daughters' consternation. So, it was with a heavy heart he heard Harold Gardner's' cries for the Nesbit boy, for whom his mother had installed a bench of contemplation on the village green opposite the cottage.

He had approached Harold on several occasions, and done his best to engage him, rehabilitate him to the community. Harold was always polite, but Ezekiel found him difficult in respect of his faith. When he, the new Reverend, had commended his service to God through his care of the garden, he'd stated he was in service to nothing but nature itself. What can a man mean when he says he is in service to nature. It could lead to such unnatural acts as Hope was accusing him of. What is nature if not God's design?

It was an awkward silence, and once Hope had handed him a mug of tea, she stood at the end of the table between them. He looked across at the raw red rimmed eyes of April as she poked a pencil into the crevices of the table. He had to begin somewhere.

He looked up at Hope, "Perhaps I should have a little chat with April on her own." She looked uncertain, but nods her head in agreement and walks over to join the boys who he felt were enjoying the game of snakes and ladders they were playing enough to keep his talk with April private enough, but not too oppressive. "Your Mum tells me that it was Harold that helped you with the plants."

She looks up, "You mean The Toffee Man! That's what I call him," and adds a little more softly, "I'm sorry I told a lie. I just thought it was a little lie."

"Even small lies grow April. We all have to learn this as we grow." And he found himself grimacing as he recalled Eunice, and forced himself to a smile, "So April … Is there anything else you'd like to tell me?"

"No. It's like I said. He just talked to me - and showed me how to do the plants and things. He let me use all the spare ones he usually puts on the wall the fete." And Ezekiel did indeed recall the careful prepared seedlings that were placed outside Harold's house year on year. He'd taken a few himself. He saw Hope glance across. He needed to be more direct.

"Did he give you any special presents? Or ask you to do little tasks for him?"

"Just the cuttings … and some toffees that he made. He got me to help with the cuttings, so I learned to do it. He's not…" and April looks at him, and she wants to say – something - he knows she does, but her open mouth is silent.

"Things are not always as they seem April. But God, he can see everything. He knows the truth." April looks across at her mum and her brothers, and turns back, and tearful.

"I think he's like Jesus. You know, in the church – the window with the children in his garden… and they were happy. I am happy in his garden."

"Did he say that April? Jesus is different. Jesus was the son of God."

"Yes - but yes but the people in the bible days didn't know that – because they killed him." Ezekiel is a little taken back.

"That was part of God's plan April. What do you know about this man? What else did he talk to you about?"

"We just talked about the garden and the moon and stuff. He doesn't like people talking about other people. He just wanted to be private. I got a stomach-ache - can I go to the toilet now?"

He tries not to show his frustration, as she leaves the table. That's the trouble with children with these troubled families thinks Ezekiel, they look for and find inappropriate friendships. He wonders about Elijah. Of course, it's a different situation, but Eunice herself spoke of the feelings he had expressed for this child. What would be the basis for that? Whilst one could sympathise with hardship, one could not embrace the evident moral failure. Elijah will have inherited some of Eunice's fine qualities, but she played no part in his guidance through life. But that she was drawn into a moral failure of her own in the face of an agent of temptation, and that this boy was a product of that – acquiescence made his uncertainty boundless. But that she delivered that child to an unknown future… but that she loved him. And this father of his, what had he felt for her, and now this son, what did he want from her, what was his hope? All this, and she loved him, and the burden was too great, too pressing. He was untethered.

It was Hope that brought him back to the table, to the problem in hand, "Can I make you another cup of tea? She'll be back in a minute. She'd spend half her life in the bathroom that girl." It occurs to him then, as he looks up.

"Look Mrs. Smart. I know things have been taken care of, but I feel that something is still amiss with April. Something she's not saying. I think it would be a good idea to take her to the Doctor." She takes a seat. He is relieved to have found a solution that she can act upon. He holds back a sigh as he looks to give her a beatific smile of reassurance.

But Hope was impervious, "Take her to the Doctor? What for?" He looked now to his own clasped hands.

This is exactly what he needed his sis – Eunice – for. "For an examination. There are … how can I put this? Ways of telling if … If you see what I mean." And he wasn't sure what he meant. He knew there were ways. Eunice had intimated at other points in their ministry. These things were complex. The health authorities often picked up on complications.

"Ways of tel…? Oh! Erm… Yes, I do. Is that necessary? I mean … I think April would have said if … I would know … I mean we had a good chat this morning and if -" and it was necessary to assert himself now, if there was progress to the relevant authority to be made.

"April has said a few things that sound - almost defiant - as if someone of more mature years had been encouraging thoughts."

"She's always been the little grown up round here. But if you think it would sort things out once and for all. it can't do any harm. if there is anything to worry about, that old gi - man - should be behind bars." He wasn't able to engage in any further discussion on the matter and tried to draw a conclusion to the meeting.

"Good. I shall alert him to the importance - and delicacy - of the situation." As he rose from the table and put his coat on April came back into the room. She looked as comforted as he felt at his imminent departure.

It was not with joy that he left the house, but he did feel a certain lightness. When he got to the gate he stopped and let out a long-awaited sigh. He put out his hand and steadied himself on the square gatepost which gave him some much-needed sense of stability. Some sense of form that he did not need to create for himself. It also gave him pause and impetus to push himself to turn and take a route the opposite direction he'd come from. He could not go home, just yet. He would call in and speak with Dr Wright first.

He was wearing his summer coat, and the cold buffeting wind made him stop to button himself up to his collar and pull his gloves from his pockets. Discovering they did not match, but were right and left, he put them on and put his hands back into his pockets. He felt insufficient as he walked to the top of the hill and across the park.

In the play area a blue scarf twisted and streamed from the handrail, tied, and forgotten, like the wings of the bluebird forever flying over the White cliffs of Dover, between the known and the unknown. And in the wind he heard the swell of the voices outside Buckingham Palace that day. The joy, the hope. He'd always had such a clear sense through his calling, his march forward through the parishes he'd served. He and Eunice had what he had understood to be a holy alliance, with a purity of intent that he had never had cause to doubt. He felt now as if an abyss had opened before him and swept all memories to the base of it, as detritus.

And he thought of Eunice's return. It was her face among the station throng that he found, no other. He saw that face alight with love at the sight of him, and an embrace that held his very soul to up to God in a note of silence. And he had felt like the luckiest man. Did he know of her feelings then? Had he understood his own. But it was hard to comprehend, this resentment she harboured for April, a child; one whose only crime had been to unknowingly befriend her son.

In the far corner of the park, the Ravens laughed unkindly as they gathered in the fiery autumnal trees sharing tales of the day. He thought of the ancient myths, and the Ravens as the appointed of Odin, reporting sight of new wisdoms, and treachery, from across the world. How he wished for such insights now. He, who just less than a week ago was so sure of all he knew, now felt the pure fool, as Parsifal.

He saw the front door open as he walked up the steps. And there she was again, clear amongst the throng of his thoughts. Of course, there were never any bluebirds over those cliffs, but those in his heart. He had to fall and begin again before God. He knew. He had always known. But love was a difficult business. And he had seen his father struggle with the loss of love. He had deceived himself, and Eunice, believing he could protect them both from that. What a child he was. And look at her. Always willing to live in the full glare of that loss, until she could no longer endure the pain.

She held out her hand, and as he stumbled through the porch he fell before her and began to cry, and she stooped to stroke his hair, "Let's go inside, and talk."

Chapter 27

We had to wait until it stopped raining to go to the Doctor's house, but when we got to the door my sandals were still got wet on the bottom and I made footprints when I walked in. Mum wiggled her feet on the mat in the porch, but I didn't realise until we got in, and when I looked back some wet leaves have come off me. The next-door neighbour of The Toffee Man was there, and she frowned at me and tapped her friend's arm to look at me too and talk about manners.

Mum said hello to them, and they said hello because they had to come past to get magazines off the table and take back to their seats. They pretended to read them while they did sneaky looks at us. A Doctor's waiting place is worse than the prison visitors room when you wait to go in. People don't know who you are coming to see, and they don't stay so quiet. Nobody, not even the police guards care if you do forget to wipe your feet or if you look sad. I'm just not smiling because I don't know if it's going to be good or not. I'm thinking about it.

Mum said the doctor has to check me because I'm going to be grown up soon. He's going to check that everything is in order. I don't know what order is the right one or the wrong one. She said she doesn't know, but doctors can tell from looking at you if you're not, but he might need to ask me some questions. I don't want to answer more questions. It's hard thinking about what to say to stop things going bad. So much things are going bad.

I keep thinking of The Toffee Man coughing and trying to do his garden tidy, and I write into my notebook about going to help him when I am dreaming. He is alone in his kingdom now, and he thinks I've said bad things about him, and he said he doesn't want to see me. He is still my friend, like Eli is my friend even when he is so far away. Except, it is worse because he is not far and now, I won't even be able to go to the bench on the green, because it will be bad if he sees me from the windows, or I see him. Mum's right, I just make trouble.

There're two doors that have labels that say Private on them, and one that says Dr Wright, and that is the one that opens, and the old lady from the top of the caravan lady's lane comes out. She catches one sight of me, stares like she's seen a devil and then rushes off. Then a man pokes his head out, "April Smart!", he says my name like we're late and disappears, leaving the door open.

We go in, and there's only one chair for the people, so I wait until mum closes the door and wait for her to sit down and stand next to her. He looks across, and mum is about to speak, but he looks over his glasses and stops her. "Now, no need to speak. Reverend Fisher explained the situation. April. I want you to take your pants off and pop up onto the couch there." I turn to look at it, and it's really high. It's like he hears me think, "Use that step at the side if you can't manage." Mum doesn't say anything, but just keeps looking across the desk, even when he gets up and gets a packet that's got gloves in it and puts them on. He comes and stands beside me, and the gloves smell of gone off milk, like someone makes a hole in the top of the tin with the tin opener and puts it on the shelf and because they can't see the top, they forget it's open and leave it there, and it starts to stink. And he's really tall and thin, and my head is by his waist, and he looks down at me and says, "Come along now," and he breathes his words down at me, and his spit falls on my face. I imagine I'm drinking a secret whiskey to burn away the bad, and I take my shoes off, then my pants and I climb up the little steps and sit on the side of the bed. He looks at me in silence for a moment. And then he talks to me like I am a stupid baby. "Now lie down on the bed. Raise your knees, put your feet together, and let your knees fall apart." And I hear footsteps through the ceiling above, and it's like everyone is gathering to see, and I look through the next one and the next one, through the roof, and way, way up through the clouds and into space, and I say in the beginning was the word, right through, until the end when I hear him say, "OK. Now if you could pop your pants back on and sit on the couch while I speak to your mother," and he walks over to his desk and starts to write notes. I don't know why he says to sit here because I can hear everything they say.

"Now. Mrs Smart. It is my opinion that April has had full intercourse… there is an infection … so I'm giving you this prescription. I will make out my report for the Police. Obviously, this is a serious matter for them, so I suggest that you keep April in the house for the time being."

Mum is still looking at him, but she is still. He hands over the paper he made for me. "Do you want me to make another prescription for you whilst you're here. These pills seem to have been quite effective for you - keeping you on track - so I think we'll keep you on them for now." He has written her paper anyway, which he gives to Mum.

She sounds like a Dalek, "Thank you. Thank you, Doctor." Mum looks across to me, we're going. She holds my hand tight as we walk through the waiting room, and outside into the park. She lets me go when she stops at the phone box and makes me sit at the end of the wall. I hear her shouting. I don't know all the words, but I have to take tablets. She grabs my hand when she comes out and squeezes and pulls as hard as she can. She lets go as soon as we're in the door. She kicks off her shoes and takes off her coat as she watches Dad reading the paper, but he doesn't even look up, even though he knows she's there because the boys are playing on the carpet in front of him and Matthew asked mum if they can have biscuits. She tells them in a minute, but she can't say anything whilst they are there. Dad knows it. I look at everyone just all frozen. I don't care anymore.

"Mum. What's going to happen mum?" She doesn't look at me.

"I want you to go upstairs and read a book. I'll call you when I need you." So now she wants me to read. She never wants to know anything I think about anything, and usually she doesn't even want me to read. I've never seen her like this though. I might as well make the most of it. I'm only a few steps up when she tells the boys to go upstairs and play too. She tells Matthew she needs to talk to Dad, and he's in charge. Matthew doesn't need mum to tell him he's in charge more than once. I hear Dad folding his paper and putting it to the side with a little laugh, "What's up love? No prescription?" Before she gets the chance to answer there's a knock at the door. Mum answers, and straightaway I can hear the policeman. Dad would usually say something else by now, but he's quiet. And for the first time, I wonder if Mum has guessed about me and Dad.

"What's up?" I hear Dad say, like he wonders too.

"I'll tell you in a minute." I hear her clear, she said into the house, then she's talking into the porch again. The boys are all in the attic now, and I go to the landing window and open it a tiny bit so I can hear.

"I want you to arrest that old fucking bastard now. If I have to go down there myself, I'll kill him."

"We can't just arrest people on accusations Mrs. Smart - we need evidence."

"Wait till you get the Doctors report - there's evidence. She has to take medication. I want that pervert locked up."

"I understand how you feel. But there's little to go on ... even April won't confirm it."

"Well the Doctor has. Or is there someone else in this village you want to charge? I want you to let him know I am taking him to court for rape - and corruption of my daughter."

"I can go and let him know of the developments - and I'll take a statement. We can go from there. I'll let you know." I watch him walk away and pull the window to and lock it again. I lie on the landing floor with my head as close to the top of the downstairs door as I can." Mum flops into her chair.

"So what's April said? What's this about the Doctor's report?"

"Nothing. She won't say anything. But the Doctor reckons she's definitely … had it - she's got an infection for Christ's sake. She's fucking ten! The dirty bastard wants stringing up." Mum starts to cry, and I hear Dad move over to her.

"We won't let him get away with it. We'll sort it out." I get up as quietly as I can, then pretend I've opened and closed my bedroom door and go downstairs. I watch Dad cuddling mum, and then he sees me, and gets to stand behind mum, "Your mum's upset - we'll have a chat in a minute."

Mum turns to me, "Why? Why are you covering up for that bastard? There's … evidence now. I know the truth April." And it makes me cry because she doesn't. She doesn't know it. Even when I do it's a waste of time. Mum holds her hand out to me, "Come here," and mum takes my hands, and soft now, like the Toffee Man did.

"He's just trying to make you as bad as he is. He's going to go to prison for this April." And I'm crying from my guts again. Mum pulls me to her lap, and she's hugging me. "Why didn't you tell me darling?" I feel Dad's hand stroking my hair, and I move it away to bury it into Mum.

"I'm sorry I made so much trouble."

"I don't know what's going to happen. We're trying to make a go of everything. It's not just for us - it's for you too - all of you. Make it easier for us. I need you to tell me." I curl up and I want to disappear back into Mum and get born again. Mum pulls me up to face her. "Tell me!" and I look from her to Dad, to her.

"Just go to your room until it gets sorted out." And I get up and go upstairs, and I can feel them both staring into my back. I am nothing now.

Chapter 28

It's like the worst thing has to happen before things change. Sometimes that is because they think that a person not being in the world is a good thing, even if they are wrong. Or maybe it can be because they think a person not being in the world is the worst thing, like me, but they change because everyone starts getting better.

Mum is being much nicer now. It's like she is on the telly now, and she looks straight at me when she does a nice thing, with a big smile showing her teeth, and doesn't try to hide the bee one. And it's like things are not real, because Dad is kind of copying her. Like he is being a dad on the telly. Like when we came in from school today and all the tea was on the table on plates, and all the knives and forks were by the side ready for us. Dad was doing his Littlewoods pools and she told him to come and sit at the end of the table and have his tea with us, and he did. He didn't moan or say anything about it. He just came and sat down and asked us what we been up to at school. And when we all finished, Mum said we could all go and do something while she tidied up before she got the bus to work.

I came up to read Little Women, and I'm writing a note about it to the Toffee Man, and Eli. Jo has a friend, Laurie, who are not called their real name. It's got lots of difficult decisions, and people make up and say sorry if they do silly things. Like Eli said friends have an enti… integra … entangle - ment. Like they are together when they think about it. I think if I put them in the wall then they might get tangled up with other places that have people you love in them, and I think that means even if you are in heaven, or far away. It's the same thing. You can still speak to them through your mind.

Mum calls me downstairs to say goodbye before she goes to the bus, and Dad has already got the boys in their pyjama bottoms. She gives us all a big hug, and even kisses Dad on his face. He takes the boys up to bed. They do everything for him much easier than me and Mum. I go and have a quick look in the cupboard where they keep the booze. There's no bottles at all. No Sherry. No Whiskey. The meter has run out on the telly, but I stay downstairs and keep reading.

When Dad comes down, he's got his whiskey. He goes and pours some for him in a glass, but he doesn't ask me if I want some. He bends over the telly and puts two-bob in the meter and turns it on. He doesn't say anything much, just pretends he's watching, even when I go back upstairs. I want to watch it because it's about two detectives, and they are friends, and Hopkirk is gone to heaven because he got deceased by a car, but he comes back to help Randall solve the murders.

When I go back down to the toilet Dad's head has fallen on his chest and he's snoring a bit, so I watch the end of the detective show before I go back up to bed. Maybe even if you don't get to be something before you die you can get trained if there are dead detectives in heaven, or you could just come and practice by yourself. Now Hopkirk can't get in his grave for a hundred years because he didn't get in before the sun came up, so he's going to solve lots of problems. It's easy for him, because only Randall can see him and he can get through walls and one place to another in a blink, but he's tangled to his friend now.

When we got up this morning, Mum was already up and had a pile of toast on the table and was watching another lot under the grill. She asked me if I wanted to help her make some flapjacks. Miss Fisher had given her a recipe so we could all have a treat. So that's what we are doing now. Dad is playfighting with Matthew and Mark, while Luke and John are tickling them. It's nice because they are all laughing, and it makes me and mum laugh too when we're just pouring the butter and syrup over the trays. It smells a bit like when The Toffee Man makes toffee, but his has got flower medicine too.

There's a knock at the door and Mum hands me her jug and wipes her hands. It's policeman Fred. Mum goes into the porch and pulls the door to, but there's still a crack for sound to get in.

"Mrs Smart - I have some news for you. Mr Harold Gardner has passed away at his home and -" and I pour the golden sauce on the oats really carefully, making sure some goes into every crack. I look to see what Mum is going to say.

"Who?"

"Mr. Ha - The Toffee Man as April..." He catches my eye through the crack in the door, and I look down quick, "Reverend Fisher has just contacted me and ask that I come here - "

"Bloody guilty conscience that's what did it." She's trying to keep her voice low. "So that's it now, is it?"

"Do you want me to come in and explain to April?" And I wish he wouldn't. They're going to start talking about it all again. I don't know what to say. The smell of the flapjack is sickly now. But it's too late, they've both stepped in and he's holding his hat like a doll. Mum is standing against the closed door.

"Of course, Mrs Smart, April, this impacts on the … situation. We'll continue to keep a close eye on you April, but -" and I didn't even know they were watching me. Just in case I went to see him. And I wish I had. I don't care. He thought I was a busybody and told lies.

"No bloody justice is there? What about us? What about April?"

"It's difficult … the Reverend felt that any 'spiritual' confusion could be repaired through attendance of church."

"Right." And I can see mum itching to shout, but she doesn't. She looks at him, and steps over to open the door, "Well at least it's over. Thank you for calling in." And he nods at us both. When I look over Dad and the boys are still playing. I know Dad heard it all. I saw him keeping a sneaky eye on us talking.

Mum closes the front door and Dad glances up at the policeman walking past the window and keeps pretending. Mum starts washing the jugs out. My hands and my face have gone all tingly and I sneak upstairs. All inside my body feels like it is gone now, and I've just got bones left. I think carefully about how to move. I am tangled up. The next thing I am sat on my bed, but I can't feel my breath even though I can see my chest moving in and out quick. My lips are curling back tight on my teeth. I get my notebook to write him a letter. I'm sorry. Sorry. Sorry. Sorry I wasn't there. I draw a flower clock. The flowers for each month of the year, and the hours of the day they opened and closed. Like he told me. I can't write words. I can't think of them.

I hear Mum coming up the stairs, so I push my book and pencil back down the hole in the wall. I push back my bookshelf so it covers it, and it looks like I'm just looking for a book. "I looked in the bathroom for you," she says, and is looking at me suspicious. For a clue about something. Detectives have to learn to hide things too. She comes and sits on the bed, but she looks away from me now. "God knows what he put into your head, but it's over now." She's looking at me now. Don't touch me Mum. Don't touch me. "April … you're not … bad … I know that. It's all for the best." But she does. She puts her hand on my shoulder. All my guts come back at once. All my breaths come rushing out. I'm shaking a bit. I'm crying. "Stop it! No – you go on. Let it out. It must be a relief after everything… It's enough to make you bloody drink all this."

I turn to hold her hand to me, "No Mum, don't."

"Oh - I won't. Don't worry. I'm going to trust the pills to sort me out." She holds my face in her hand. She's trying to be nice. I know that. "You're not a kid any more are you? You need to toughen up. We need to toughen up." I look at her. She wants it to be good. I reach up and put my hand on her hair. My mum. She is beautiful. My mum. I hear someone creeping up the stairs. They've stopped by the door. I know it's Dad. "There's shits like that everywhere darlin' - preying on the -"

Dad comes in pretending like he's just come up normal. "Ooh look. Nice to see a little love in." It's like he's a bit nervous. But he's being jokey, "Are you going to get them things in the oven, or what? The boys are asking."

"Huh? God – yes!" and she just gets up and rushes down.

Dad smacks her bum on the way, and she laughs.

I thought he was going to come over to me, but he doesn't. He shoves his hands in his pockets and licks his bottom lip. "I'm sorry … about your mate. Not nice. I don't know what went on, but it's not my fault … and uh … we'll leave things for a bit."

I just don't want him to know anything about what I think, "Well, he was old anyway."

And I kind of feel strong when he raises his eyebrows and shrugs, and I go back to my books. I hear the door scuff closed, and his footsteps down the stairs.

I lie back on the bed. And I remember him, and I imagine if he has got young again like Reverend Fisher said we do when we go to heaven, and all the people who loved us are waiting, and his friend will be there, and his mum and dad. And all the birds and nature will be there and flowers and clocks. And then I am laughing and crying and dreaming… two birds are flying across the sky and then towards the window. It's so fast I think they might crash, but they sit on the windowsill, looking in at me. And then one of them puts its wing through the glass, like a magic trick, and opens the latch from the inside. They walk through onto the big sill inside. They walk from side to side, as they do, they are becoming little people – and it's the Toffee Man and his friend, like they were in the photo. And they finish getting ready for the show and sit on the ledge – and they sing a song about flying to the moon, like the man on the telly.

Chapter 29

Mum is playing her records downstairs. Sometimes she puts the same one on and leaves it to play over and over, and it's annoying. But I like this one, it's just 'paint it black'. I want to do that. I wish they would play music like this on the radio for music and movement at school. I just finished reading Little Women, and I want to be like Jo and get a school, and then you can teach what you like, and I would have music and movement things much better than we do. It was like a hundred years ago, and I bet Jo would do that if she was starting a school now. People just know what they know about their time.

The Toffee Man died six weeks ago now, but I promised him I would read the books and tell him about them, I've been doing that nearly every day. I tell him what they were doing and the new things I am learning – and lots of words too, so I can explain it to him better. I think now he's in heaven he will just see everything anyway, but it makes me think about things better when I talk to him. So it's like he's still teaching me about things.

It's dark at nights now, so Mum doesn't take any notice if I go up to my room when the boys go to bed. Matthew and Mark stay up with her sometimes now. And they stay up with me when she gives us money for the tv meter when she has to go to work. When Dad's not away driving jobs and he's at home he doesn't speak to me much. When he is away though I drink a bit of his whiskey sometimes and it makes me have nice dreams when I'm reading. And I stick my map from Eli over the bookcase and imagine the moon places, and I just got a book about space and the stars from the jumble sale now, so I make sure I know as much as I can about where things are in space. And I talk to the Toffee Man about that too.

Mum asked me to go to the shop for some tinned milk. She hasn't asked me to go for ages. She's worried about the rumours. So we only really go out to school, and to church. I don't mind anyway. I want to go. Now I've got all the Bazooka comics I have to send them to America. So I think that I could send them to Eli, but I don't know how to do it. I'll ask Miss Gomer if she wouldn't mind. I don't think she will because she won't want them to go to waste. I worked out that I've got enough to get the important things, and my ring for Miss Gomer, because I promised her. I packed them up into the right number of comics and labels for the A & K rings, a telescope, a zapper and magic strings. 'Dear Bazooka, I have sent you these so that I can have the things I want for my job in space for the future. Thank you for doing it, April Smart'. As well, I'm going to ask her to check I got everything right. I made a card for Eli too, to explain it, and so that he knows that we got a house and I'm doing all my learning for the future, like he said.

It's cold and windy on the road, so I'm glad when I walk into the shelter of the lane. When I walk past the Caravan Lady's place, the gate is blown wide open. The van has been moved to the bottom of the field, and builders are making the walls that got started high, up into a house. There's the spaces of the doors and windows now.

When I get to the shop, everything is just the same. It's neat and shiny – and warm, and Miss Gomer says my name like I am important, "April! I haven't seen you for a while. How are you?" and she come from behind the counter to shake my hand.

"I'm fine. I've been learning. Miss Gomer - I've come to ask you a favour. Could you post my letter to America? My Bazooka Joes. I don't know if I need special stamps. I got it ready. Can you check it?" And she takes the envelope from me and empties it onto the counter." She reads the labels, and my letter.

"You've done a good job April. Of course, I'll post it. I think we can get the address from the one of the wrappers."

"Can you send it to my friend Eli. He lives in America, and then he can send it to me."

"You have a friend in America?" And then I have to tell her the story of Eli when we lived in the valley, and he lived in the vestry when he came to find his mum. And now his work address is the NASA space rocket station of Florida, America, which I got from the telly. "Oh, my goodness. You are certainly a girl full of surprises." I give her a two-bob bit for the stamps.

"Thanks Miss Gomer. Can you ask him to send them to you? Just … so it's a surprise when I show Mum."

The builders have got a trolley of sacks up the lane, so I can't go up. I didn't want to walk past The Toffee Man's house, not yet. But when I think about it, I have to face that too.

I keep my eyes closed as I go round the corner, and then I stand still and open them. I was expecting it to look empty and quiet, and I could see what's left in the garden, but there's a van parked outside, the back doors are open, and it's stacked up with his clocks. Two men come out pushing the grandfather clock wrapped in a sheet on a trolley, with the face poking out the top. It's like a Royal coffin. As they tie it to the inside of the van, I see the picture of The Toffee Man and his friend with other pictures leaning against the wall by the gate. I walk up the side and crouch down. It is him. In his eyes it is him. He is happy. His friend's hand is over his shoulder with his hand hanging down onto The Toffee Man's chest, and hand is reaching over his heart, and the tips of their fingers are just touching. It like something that happened in the picture stopped, quietly waiting for heaven, like when it says 'to be continued' on telly, when it ends at a good bit, and gets saved to next time.

"You want to buy something?" I jump up. It's one of the men from the van.

"No."

"What you after then? Piss off." I look over into the garden. They've emptied the shed and most of the pots are broken, and the earth and seedlings are fallen out.

"I'm just looking. He was my friend." And I point to the picture, so they can see. So they know it's a person that lived here.'

"They look right queer to me. Here look at them Dave." And he's laughing. Dave gets out the back of the van and looks." He winks at me.

"Leave off Jack. Let her have it. You're right, no one will want that."

"Don't be soft. That frame will fetch a few bob." Dave takes the picture from the frame and looks at it and carefully rolls it up and ties it with some string. He gives it to me. And then I see my book on a rubbish pile, 'You will go to the Moon', and I go over to pick it up, "Can I have this too? It's mine. I just lent it to him."

Jack is still being mean, "There! Take it. Now piss off. If I see you grabbing anything else - you'll get a clip round the ear."

I run up the road with my book, and the picture, in my hand. When I get to the top of the green, I turn and shout, "Oi! Jack! Fuck off you ugly pig face." And Jack starts to chase me, but he's too slow.

I'm a bit out of breath when I get to the park. I sit on the swings and untie the picture. It's funny how people get old. It's hard to think about them being young. But it's hard to think of being old too. And what we will look like. I can see it's him, but like his nose was bigger, and his skin was coming unstuck. I think that maybe he played here when he was a kid too. So I tuck the bottom of the book and the picture into my belt so it's across my chest and swing high, so it's like they are with me. And I take them on the slide, and on the roundabout.

There is roar in the sky, and it's a hot air balloon, and I lie down on the grass and make a star shape. People are waving from the basket, and we are waving back. And then the Girls Brigade band practice come marching down the road. We go and sit on the wall. The people in the houses by the park come and watch too, and they are clapping. And we are clapping and cheering too. And then I hear the church bells. It's four o clock. I kiss them goodbye and put them inside my book and under my cardigan with my arms folded.

When I get home there's smoke blowing up to the gate and all over the place. Mum's chopping all the dead grass with a hand sickle. Matthew and Mark are picking it up and throwing it onto the fire she made. Mum says just go and get any rubbish to keep it going.

"There you are. Where's the milk?"

"Oh no. Sorry Mum. I watched the Girls Brigade march. Can I join next year? Can you ask Reverend Fisher. You get badges! Make -"

"We'll see. Miss Fisher says it would do you good to do more practical things. Depends what times?"

I don't want to join, but it made her forget about the milk. She always wants Miss Fisher to be pleased with us. Miss Fisher is more interested in my ideas after the plants got money for the church fete.

When I get in the kitchen, I take out the picture on the table and look at them. It's the first time The Toffee Man has been in my house. "Who are they then. New friends?" I nearly jump out of my skin. I didn't even notice him. "Dad!" I can tell him now. He won't say. "It's the Toffee Man with his friend when he was young. They were chucking it out."

"They do look pretty friendly don't they." He pats me on the head. "I've been missing my little friend. A little drink later … when she's gone."

"C'mon cheer up. Your mum's happy… Thought that's what you wanted." He turns to look through the kitchen window, and watches mum.

"I'll tell."

He picks up my photo, "Tell her about this too? She'll burn that right away." I snatch it back and run upstairs. I roll it up and put rubber bands round the middle and both ends, and tie in a piece of string before I pull back the shelves and lower it down into the hole. I put the book on the side so he might think the picture is still in there if he comes.

My heart is going really fast, and I sit on the side of the bed. I can't think. What if he just tells her anyway. I think he likes it that Mum's just gets mad at me. I can't say anything. She won't listen. When I put my hands to my ears it's really noisy in my head. My blood is running fast from the thumping giant feet stomping through the land of me, running through a swarm of bees, flocks of squawking birds, a cloud of angry butterflies. It's like I've made another funeral for him. Buried him. I punch my bookshelf box. It tips over and falls off the drawers and crashes to the floor. They all get mixed up, the Secret Sevens, The Famous Fives, Toyland and the Caravan stories. I get my moon map from Eli and stick it up over the hole before anyone comes up. I stand still. But it's dead quiet downstairs. I then I hear them in the back garden through the window. Dad's telling the boys to put some old boxes of newspapers from the shed on the fire. They're excited they'll get a bigger fire, and Mum says it will help burn the grass. It sounds like fun. Everyone's happy.

I have to empty the rest of the books out of the shelf so I can put it back up and tidy them. I put the box back up, and I look at the mess. Some of the pages got bent too. I get an idea. And I put the box on the floor again, and I just cram all the books in, any old how, and I drag it across the floor, and bump it down the stairs, out to the garden. They are still round the back. I drag the box to the fire. It's just smoking now. I rip some pages from Mr Meddle and hold it to the red ashes while I blow until they catch alight. One by one I open the books and hold them over the flames until they catch alight and add them to the fire. They are blazing now, and each one I add I remember the story, or the people and say goodbye, and thank you to The Naughtiest Girl. It's okay, because we are tangled now. I am concentrating hard, so I don't notice when Mum and Dad and the boys have come to the fire and are watching too. "What's got into you?" says Mum. "I never thought I'd see the day when you were burning them books." I look up, and Dad has got his arm round Mum's shoulder. He shrugs.

"They're not kids for long. She's growing up." He looks a bit sad.

I turn back to the fire and carry on. Matthew starts putting the grass on. It gets smoky again.

Chapter 30

We are stirring the ashes with sticks, and Matthew is too. Sometimes there is a whisp of smoke, or we find a glow of red at the bottom from where Matthew had put some dead branches when Mum made the fire yesterday. It catches the bits of paper that didn't burn, and we watch the tiny flames lick around like snakes. When the ashes are cooled down, I'm going to spread them on the garden. The Toffee Man said that ashes make good food for plants when the rain comes and washes them into the ground. And I think about all the words in the books and if they will go into the ground, and if they will be like seeds and grow into the trees – and it will be like a garden full of Faraway Trees that take you to different lands from the books when you climb to the top. Or like Jack and the Beanstalk, and we all get rich. Mum is watching us from the porch. It's nice, because she is smiling and she has a tea towel in her hand, "Come on you lot. Tea's on the table," and the boys run after Matthew and throw their sticks into the grass, like he did. Mum made a Shepherd's Pie and it's their favourite now. I'm just turning to go into the house and a big hand of wind scoops up the ashes and blows the curls and whisps that make ghosts of us the day we came here. I look at me so small, pulling the book out of my jumper bag, and Mum, unlocking the door. All the ashes fall to the ground again, and I go in for Shepherd's Pie.

Mum said we can get good lamb mince now that she is working, and she has made a friend of the butcher and as well, he cuts more of the fat off now she goes with Sally's mum. She goes to have coffee with her sometimes when we are at school, and they talk about cooking and house stuff. Mum said Liz is more of a laugh than she thought she was, and she's not stuck up. Sally won't come to play with me here anymore though. She plays with Susan now, and Susan said she doesn't want her too, because her Mum said I get up to no good. And Sally said that she heard her Mum and Dad talking and they said I caused problems. Sally said not to ask her again. I just said okay. I didn't cry in front of her.

All the Shepherd's Pie got finished. Mark scraped all the edges of the pie dish with a spoon. Matthew kept taking some of mine when Mum wasn't looking. But I didn't mind. I get full up quick now. Mum is trying hard to make nice things for us and have dinner with us before she goes to work. I keep saying to myself that it is making her happy. That is the best thing for us all. It makes a difference. I feel happy and sad at the same time. There are more clouds now, and I'm finding more people, even Sally was in the clouds, and I make a play of us being secret friends in the mountains.

The twins are in bed, and Dad, Matthew and Mark are watching a film about horses. I stack the plates on the draining board. I look out and there are no clouds. It's getting dark early now. I can see my reflection in the window. I pretend like I'm watching myself. I speak without making a noise, like on telly with the sound turned down. I'm like Jo in Little Women, but I'm acting like she is living in my world.

Mum is finishing her make up, getting ready for work. She puts her make-up and compact in her bag. She dabs her perfume on her neck and wrists whiles she talks to Dad, "Get there for 1 o'clock before we close for the party mind, so we can get a decent table near the boss … staff do is the only time you get near him. He's looking for a bar manager now Penny's up the duff."

"I told you. I'll be there. If you don't get a move on, you'll miss the last bus."

"And you two – bed by 8!" And she turns to me, "Make sure you get to bed at a decent time too. I need you to sort the boys out in the morning. No reading all night … well, I don't suppose you got anything left to read. I don't know what got into you."

"They were just for kids," I say. I see her watching me in the window, but I pretend I don't notice.

"Walk to the bus with me?"

"Okay."

Dad calls over, "Make sure you come straight back. It's dark. I can't come looking for you," and he turns to mum, "I don't want her out there on her own … you know, with everything that's happened."

It was freezing when we left so I put my anorak on. Even though the zip is broken so I have to hold it closed I like it better than my coat. It reminds me of the caravans. I can't take Mum's hand when she holds it out. She's a bit ahead of me, so she doesn't notice. We walk all the way to the bus stop in silence. Her high heels don't scratch and scrape the road to make sparks anymore. She's stabbing the road like the drum in a song. I thought she might be a bit upset with me.

It's really windy. When we get to the bus stop, we sit on the stone bench in the bus shelter. It's set back in the wall with a roof on, so I didn't have to hold my coat together so tight. I leant on the side wall. Mum sat down and got her bus fare ready. "Come and sit with me," and when I did, she put her arm around me and had a big sigh. "You know what? Next pay packet I'm putting a little aside and we're going to go and get you a brand-new dress. Like that? Seen something you fancy?"

"I like the trousers - from the catalogue."

"Not from the catalogue! And not trousers. We'll go to town find something nice, together. Something a bit more grown up. Make a day of it."

"Really. Just us?" I hug Mum so tightly she laughs. She strokes my hair from my face.

"You know darlin' – I'm not always …. I'm trying. You know that - don't you? And your Dad, he's been worried about you."

"I know Mum." And then she squeezes me, and we're holding each other tight as the wind sings like a hundred years of church choir practice and I wish me and mum could go back to a hundred years ago before Dad was born, and we could be old and dead by his turn.

"Now that nasty … business … is finished … I'm taking my pills properly … I'm happy -" and then she lets go to stick her hand out to the road. She's seen the bus. She kisses me on the head and walks away as it stops and the doors flip open, "We'll get that dress next week. And a coat too if I get that promotion. Now, go straight home."

"I love you Mum." It felt urgent to say it, but I think she thought I was too loud. She smiled and turned away.

"I know darlin'. Now go home."

I watch mum find a seat and we wave at each other. I watch as the bus moves off full of bright windows that light up and disappears down the hill.

I sit back down in the bus shelter.

Soon as I got in Dad asked me if I wanted a drink. I think I'm like Mum a bit. I do like a drink, but not much. It never tastes that nice, but you get used to it and it makes things soft and blurry, like a nice dream. And it's easier to pretend you are somewhere else. He said we need protection now, after all that fuss. So, I didn't have to worry. I wouldn't get any problems. He is the problem. He's getting ready to go. He said he's got to get more dressed up than usual because he has to help Mum get a better job. He could be around more often then, spend more time with us kids.

He takes the last gulp of his whiskey and says I probably shouldn't have any more. Make sure I take Mum's negligee off and get myself to bed. They'd be back before we were up, but I'd need to help out when the boys got up. I'd be in charge. I just lie on the bed whilst he buzzes around. He said he can't give me a cuddle before he leaves because he's got his aftershave on now. He winks at me when he leaves. I hate him even more when he does that.

When I hear the door shut, I get my pencil and paper out of my trouser pockets and write about Mum and me going shopping one day. Why does she think that Dad cares about me or even her. I write down the rude things he says about everyone, and what he said to me. He doesn't care what happens to any people so long as they do what he wants. He says that everyone does what they want in the end, it's just that a lot of people aren't true about their feelings. They don't believe in much. The Toffee Man was a thousand times better than that. He believed in things, but he said it mattered what other people believed in too.

I go to my room pull up my picture of the Toffee Man. I feel so angry at Dad. I decide I'm going to have some more of his whiskey anyway.

I don't take too much. I sit in the window seat, and I put the picture at the other end so it's like we are having a conversation. When I drink it on my own I can pull the faces it makes me feel, and I have to pant to cool my mouth down. It's nicer drinking on my own. It's so hot it makes me laugh, and it looks like their smiling faces are laughing with me. The light of the moon is shining on them. I turn off the light. Their faces are more real. It's like we are having a party by the light of the moon. I don't want it to stop now, so I pick up my clothes and take them to my room, and post my notes down the hole, and I go back.

I am acting that we are having a conversation about the books, and I am telling them about all my favourite stories, and the secret seven, and how they solved all the mysteries and found out all the bad people. In the end the Toffee Man said that nobody is all bad. Even when they were fighting the war, everybody had a reason. You must learn to be happy with your lot and do what you think is right. His friend agreed with him. I told them that is what I think Mum is trying to do, and now I'm growing up that I want to try and do that too. I want to be the best girl she could have, because I am the only girl she's got. I love her, even though she is angry with me a lot. I made a mess of things. She just wants me to be good. To be happy.

I look across the bed and it's all messed up. By the side the glasses are there, and the whiskey bottle is in the cupboard underneath. I pour a little bit in. I put the cap back on and put it carefully back in the same place. And I see two little brown bottles at the back; 'Mrs H. Smart'.

In my hand they are shiny and beautiful. I can see why mum always looks at them with a happy face before she swallows them. Like a bowl of diamonds shining in the moon. Hidden treasure in your belly. She won't miss just a few, and I could see if they make me happy so I can be like Mum. Maybe the doctor will give me some if they make me feel better. And I don't know if I should steal some or not. But I don't think Mum would mind if they made me less trouble. I am growing up, and it is hard.

They don't taste of anything anyway. I've had four – five now. I'm not taking them all at once. Mum doesn't take many, but that's like when you have seconds at lunchtime. You just have a little bit after you got used to it. The boys always get seconds at school. The dinner lady says it's because the girls will get too lazy and then they can't get married. I feel lazy. And I can't even get up to put the bottle back in the cupboard or put mum's nightie away. And I just seen I dropped my knickers on the floor by the door. I can do it in a minute. And then I see that The Toffee Man, and his friend, have been watching me the whole time. But he's still smiling at me.

"You won't tell will you? You're with your best friend now, and your Mum. I wish my mum could know how nice you are. But I can't change it now. Mum couldn't be alright on her own. I will be the best girl she could have. And wear a dress …"

I start to cry. I don't want to cry. I want to be happy. When will they start working. I just need to stay still, and soon they will work. Be patient, like my teacher said.

I Will look after Mum - and be her friend. And she will help me practice to be happy. We don't need Dad!

I feel so lazy that I take the last two pills. Like the Lord's supper. I make my promises to God. I'll get better - just like mum. Honour thy mother - be happy for her - make the garden nice for her- be good in my schoolwork - be happy - be happy - be grown up - be happy - happy – happy…

I can't move any more. I'm still away though. I practice whistling. And I can. I do it. I sound like a bird. A real bird. Big. Like an angel bird.

Over our garden and next doors, the light comes on. The lady who lives there is in the kitchen with her baby. She gives it a bottle and walks around patting it's back until it is still. The lights go off.

Chapter 31

It's been a fucking all night victory march Hope thinks, as the key crunches into the lock. The hard rhythm of her heels pounding down the path had her reliving a memory of youth. She turned to the Grenadine sunrise, fanning her fingers in a vain attempt to stir the colours between them, until the door gave way behind her, and she staggered to the back of the sofa, suppressing a giggle.

You and your husband are so deliciously modern, he'd said. And you. You know what people want. You are exactly what we need.

She'd been uncomfortable as his hand landed on her knees, slipping down and up between her thighs as Andy watched and winked, before distracting him with another cocktail. Andy had left it off with the boss right away and played his card well. She'd enjoyed the attention it drew to her whenever she joined their conversation. As he'd promised them all, the blue pills they had just made her want to dance, to talk, remember the best of herself.

"I think we'll do alright there," Andy said as they drove back. And for the first time in a long time, she looked across and believed him, yes, they would.

Suddenly Andy was in the doorway laughing, "Fucking Hell, what a night!" and swung it shut.

"Sshh! I don't want them getting up yet," Andy leaned into her, bearing her down into the sofa, as he pulled at her dress. "Stop that – what if -"

"Just you wait until we get upstairs. You try keeping quiet then!" This time she looks him in the eyes.

"I'll be ready for you, big boy!"

"Oh. You better be." He puts his hand on her knee, and slides up between her thighs, "I saw you. You liked it didn't you." He watched as he pushes up her dress, "Hm! Just going for a piss."

Shoes in hand, Hope creeps up the stairs. April's bedroom door is open and as she reaches in to quietly close it she sees her bed is empty. She's in the attic with the boys. There's no sound from up there. Still fast asleep. She can see it now. She smiles. April will have been reading with them until heaven knows what time and fallen asleep with the boys.

It's a long time since Hope has seen the dawn. It's usually still dark when she gets back from work, and she sleeps with the twins if she needs to catch up in the day. The magnolia walls are glowing pink and gold now, and she resolves to race for every sunrise.

As she walks into the bedroom, she sees April, right before her. Curled awkwardly on the window seat. "April, what are you doing?" but, she is asleep. The little madame, she's wearing her nightclothes, dressing up. Being mummy. And that's nice. She thinks of their chat, at the bus stop. The dress. She can't wait. She'll wake her up. Get her to her bed before Andy comes up. She walks over to shake her.

Something is wrong. She knows that straight away. She shakes her shoulder. Her arm flops to the floor and her knuckles hit loud against bare floorboards, but she doesn't stir. Doesn't move. Hope starts to panic. She's breathing for two now. "April? April? APRIL!"

She kneels by her side. Feeling her head, grasping her for signs of life. There are none. "Andy! Andeeeee…"

As she calls out, she searches, things out of place lurch into view – a picture of two men leant at her feet, the unmade bed, empty glasses – two, her knickers... Scenes flash through her mind – senses arranging, rearranging, accepting, rejecting -

Andy strides along the corridor, hushed and hissing, "Hey. Don't wake the kids you said!" For a moment he stalls, scans the scene. Their eyes meet and she recognises a glimpse of her darkest fear. In silence it scuttles to the back of her mind. It is gone. Andy crouches at her side and holds Hope's face to his, but she twists and rises.

"She's dead. She's fucking dead." She walks to the bedside table, glancing at the empty glasses from above. Her eyes rest on her bottle of pills. She picks it up, and shakes it, before unscrewing the cap, and empties the few remaining into her hand. She holds the bottle out to Andy, bewildered.

"Why? Why? I thought … it was better. She's wearing my nightdress Andy. Why would she do that – and this?" She throws the pills to the bed.

She stares at Andy. He shakes his head, looking to the floor for time.

"Darlin'. I should have told you - on the way home. I wanted to wait until you'd got some kip. I'd told her that we'd all have a chat about it today. When we got up."

"What? What did she tell you?"

"Well - she - she broke down in tears last night - when she got back. She was ready to tell you what had been happening - with that Toffee Man bloke. The bastard. You were right you see - That old git had been interfering with her - She was frightened to say anything … He'd told her that everyone would blame her.

We had a long chat - I thought I'd said the right things … she was OK. I said we'd talk today. I told her you wouldn't be angry - nobody would - you'd be glad she told the truth - but she thought she would upset you. I really thought she was OK. I didn't think she had anything … like this on her mind. I feel so…"

Hope knows. She knows how he feels. She can see it all now. She was right. But not with April. She feels the weight of it, and crumples. Andy is there to catch her, holding her up. "It's my fault. It's my fault."

"Come on Darling - you can't blame yourself. See - you were right all the time. It was him. Now look what he's done." Hope looks over his shoulder at April. Her nightdress. The picture at her feet.

"Who are they?"

"Who?"

"In that picture?"

"'What picture?" He turns to look. "I don't know. Probably from one of those books of hers." But he keeps looking.

"Look - you need to go and call an ambulance - I don't want to leave you on your own here. We need to sort it out straight away."

"Yes. Yes. I know." She begins to cry again.

"C'mon. We need to do this. It'll begin to look suspicious. You know what they're like."

"OK. Give me a drink." He picks up a glass and pours her a drink, and hands it to her. She gulps it back. She slips her shoes back on.

"Now off you go. Don't forget - tell them about your pills. We can tell them the rest when they get here, and there's the two of us. Go quietly. Don't wake the kids."

He looks at her face. He wants to slap it. Why? What was the fucking point in this? Just when everything was finally going their way. He can't stop and think about all that now. He needs to check the room. They'll be here soon. Even Hope had a moment there. He didn't want anyone catching them out.

He picks up the knickers. He wipes the outside of the glass at the back of the cabinet. His glass. He straightens out the bed. He turns to April. It has to be done. He lifts up the nightie and parts her legs to give her a wipe. They'll be concentrating on the pills though. He's going to have to stir up Hope's anger about that old bloke when they're here – be smart thought. He will. He needs to get rid of these. He doesn't want to – but just get them out the way for now. Time is short.

And he realises this is goodbye. This is it. And it hurts. It does. This isn't what he wanted. She chose this. Stupid cow. Stupid little cow. It's probably for the best though. And he can't stop himself. He walks over and kneels at her head. Strokes her face. An angel. An alabaster angel. With his finger, he follows the ridge of her brow, over her cheek and round her jaw. He brushes his thumb across her lips, and back again. Is he imagining it. The tip of his thumb feels warmth, like a light kiss. He places a finger under her nose. He did imagine it. Then. No. Again. He feels the gentlest warmth from her nose. No. No. Fucking no. He can see now. For the first time. It hits him. What it means. And it's instinct. He closes his thumb and forefinger. Scissors. Cut out the evidence. Fucking cut it off. The breath will speak. Don't bruise her. Gently now. Just hold it as you will. There's no resistance.

'Andy! Andy! They'll be here any minute. What the fuck are you doing?'

From the first call of his name, he twists himself to hold her nose and ducks down to resuscitate. He just keeps going long enough. She's still breathing.

'I just thought I'd give it a go. It's working. I need to keep going until they get here.' And he continues.

And Hope sits on the bed gathering the counterpane into her clenched fists, laughing or crying. He can't work it out. He needs to think.

Chapter 32

It's blackest night, but I can hear my mum's voice. She is shouting, but I can't understand what she wants. It's like she is in the radio when it gets interfered. I think I might be in trouble because I fell asleep in her room. I can't see her. I'm trying to call to her, but she can't hear me. I can feel the warm of her hand around mine. A slap on the face, soft, but my head falls. I can't make me work. I hear her crying. Why can't she see me? I try to concentrate. I can't do any of the things I need to do so she can hear me. And then dad starts talking. He's saying she is right about The Toffee Man. That I told him that. I didn't want to upset her, he says. The red and green of my fists and my feet hurt. I want to tell her she isn't right, she wasn't right … and the voices fade, and the air peels off in slices, falling across the blackness, past the earth into the distance, all stirred and muddled, like the voices of walkers in the woods.

It's dark again. All for one and that is all. And I am lost forever. I reach into the black and I can feel a flat dusty ledge, it must be the windowsill. Mum, I'm coming. Can you see? I sit up but it's too big. My legs dangle like ropes. I hear a voice. Not a broken radio. Here. With me. 'Jump in April. Don't go thinking too much.' It's my friend.

A star explodes, and a rainbow of threads and strings fill my dark and start plaiting and weaving, and I can see my mum's face again, and tears, and tears, and it makes her so sad to love me, and I don't want her to be the sad. And then I can hear Dad's voice again, and the strings knit up his hands, taking her face and turning it to his and he is telling her, we just got to stick together, and I know she will never believe in me, and she finds her sad in me. And I hear her walk from me and the sound of steps get so small.

Beep. Beep. They are gone.

I slide down fast into the slope of a giant bowl then I'm scooped up and up. The first surprise is how high, and how slowly I fly; like a swan with my big heavy wings, so bigger than me, are like a slow rush beating of a heart in my ears - woowaah woowaah woowaah. I'm not afraid. I am dead.

Beep beep!

For a while, I circle and criss-cross the crater, swooping and gliding through the dark, and it comes, light, as I spin and dip my feathers and fingers into the well of inky blue. And as I race up and I feel that if I fly up and up higher, I could reach the tips of my wings into Mum's sky, and I could write my words into the light.

Beep. Beep

The second surprise. It was The Toffee Man waiting for me when I came back down to rest. I was trying to think about if I was dead like him. Or maybe we don't die, we just come to space, or wherever we like, and he has been here all the time.

Beep. Beep.

I was just standing on the wall of the crater. He was reaching his hand across to me from standing in the air, above the bowl of black, and I couldn't see the bottom. It felt more frightening to fly out alone to someone's hand.

Beep. Beep.

So I laid down on the side of the lake to think of getting brave, quiet and still, and as I was looking out, chandeliers of stars began to appear, and then I saw one big star, and I thought it was the moon.

Beep. Beep.

And then I remembered it was the Earth, because it was in the book about space that Eli gave me, and like they said on the telly, and like the song on the radio. It was blue and blue and blue… And then I knew I was on the moon. That's when the first star exploded, and all the whispering strings came past.

Beep. Beep.

And now I know, I'm very far away from home. Home is a shining ball of blue in the blackness. You can't see people from here, but the sun catches the tips of the highest hills and tallest trees that poke into the dark, and sometimes I can see the flicker of a bird that flies too high, and dips, or a cat or a monkey that got chased to the top of the trees.

Beep. Beep.

They miaowl and chatter and screech, but quickly disappear when they see the emptiness of space. They don't give themselves time to get used to it.

In between and far away there are glittering stars. Far away they hang in clusters, like the chandeliers in the hall at my old school, huddled above and below, all around.

Beep. Beep.

Sometimes they grow brighter and spin, folding in and out like a kaleidoscope, and sometimes when that happens, one of the stars will explode into a hundred thousand strings of light; they breathe and whisper and sing as they scribble and lace themselves into words and stories in the dark.

Beep. Beep.

When they get close it feels like the sounds are in your body. If you catch one and close your eyes it can take you to all the places in the back of your mind, all that you can remember or imagined. You can travel anywhere through the dark in no time at all. It is always now.

Beep. Beep.

When I can't understand the words, I reach out and catch one, it whips round my hand like a lightening flash and thrums, connecting me, and wrapping itself around the sound until I can see the shape and colour, and I can see what was invisible, even with my eyes closed.

Beep. Beep.

Sometimes it's just an ear with hair tucked behind, moving round to an eye and the bridge to a nose, or a finger smoothing the creases of a dress or collar; fraying threads and hairs all get tangled up, and they might turn out to be my mum, Hope, or my brothers, Matthew, Mark, Luke or

John, or even Katy Gomer with a bagful of Bazooka Joe comics.

Beep. Beep.

Or it might be a place from somewhere I used to know … another time… not now. Sometimes I can bring things back here with me, through my mind; there's a whoosh, and here they are on the moon when I open my eyes. And I can order things from the catalogue, I say the numbers, and they are there when I open my eyes.

Beep. Beep.

It's only me that can do it, because I was the last to get here. I got all the things from the removal truck that they were taking after the Toffee Man died. And he was so happy. His cough has gone, and his friend from the photos was already here when he came.

Not people. The strings will bring them if they sound. But things, that other people won't miss - like the tall trees that were sucking up the epidemic, up through trunks and branches, and along the canal in the valley meadow, where our caravan used to be. Their leaves are bright yellow as they disappear, and nobody can see them in our place on the moon.

Beep. Beep.

Our crater is just over the horizon, but we made steps so we could get up and peek over the edge to look at the earth world when we want to.

Beep Beep - Beep Beep - Beep Beep.

And I can feel Dad's hand pretending love on my face, sliding across my lips, across my cheek to cover my nose. This time I fall into the darkness, but as my eyes get used to it, it's not dark at all; I'm a bubble, rolling and falling then rising from the wispy tangled mist, and I make my dead arm tingles fly.

Beep… Beep…

There he is. I can see him waiting to catch me, so small, like the tiny farmer in the play set, among a patchwork of colours; big fat fuzzy felt pieces finding the right place on the ground, I'm flying to the big yellow sun, but then as he catches my hand everything becomes clear and sharp. It's his garden. Only it's bigger. It's like I am looking at everything through a magnifying glass, like at school, only it's not just one thing, like a fly or a flower, but everywhere, everything, looks like you're close to it, all at once, no matter how far away it is. It's like everything is already in your eye.

Beep…

And it makes me dizzy. And I thought my heart was going to be crushed at the end; rushing like a train, screeching to stop at the black; pictures, feelings and strings of light tumbled and cut through my mind, like if you opened the great big doors of a giant's cupboard, and everything fell out, all the memories of a thousand days; of blackboards and books, of fields and forests, of Sunday school and sermons. And all the strings came rushing from the black and wrapped themselves around me.

Beeeeeeeeeeee…

Then I felt the rumble of The Toffee Man's voice until it exploded in my heart, 'April. We see you. Stay with them April. STAY WITH THEM.'

Chapter 33

Hope was seething. It wasn't her daughter's bloody funeral, but it might as well have been, and hers too. She could see it in their stony smiles. They'd made up their minds. And what could she say. She had too. There was no getting away from it. If it hadn't been for Andy, it bloody would have been. She saw he liked that story of him got around – 'the kiss of life'. But it was of her own making, and how she had explained it when she'd tried to make sense of events with Liz.

That first week, when Reverend Ezekiel had insisted that they both attend the church for prayers and support, Andy had squeezed her hand in excitement when he'd seen the nods of respect. It wasn't the affection she hoped for, or for April. He hadn't visited the hospital with her. The distance between them was more visible now, but she felt strangely relieved. She'd let the club know she couldn't work now, and lost the promotion, so she couldn't begrudge him being crowned the hero of the hour. The reluctant hero. He'd sealed that status as he took every long-haul job and bit of overtime available. They'd had to minimise his absence that night. He'd just popped out to pick her up. They were doing their best to pay their way; make a fresh start. Again. This time though, he really was different. Not one complaint that she wasn't working.

Her nails dug into her fists in her pockets as she nodded to the congregation outside as they left the chapel. Eunice and Ezekiel spoke for her if anybody enquired about April. Whilst it was important to not to hide your face, they said, one should show humility. Every week prayers were said for April, for the family. She felt crushed by the weight of their pity as they passed. The boys, standing still as a row of fence posts, with straight backs and upturned faces, basking in the attention of this cold winter sun. Following their dad's example.

The school had taken the twins into nursery class a few terms early, in the light of events, and for the first time since April was born, Hope had time. Now Andy was barely there, she had time to herself. And she realised this was something she'd never had. She'd been chivvied along by the demands of others her whole life. For the first time to find rhythms in her day, sitting in the park, sitting in the woods. Time to think. She'd lagged behind the days for so long, and now she walked quickly, weaving through roads, fields, visiting the many churches and walking in the graveyards, reading the headstones, the families, the children – and lost words rushed up from the very ground and found their place in her thoughts again - sweeping back and forth like a pendulum over and over and over that morning. That initial stab of terror when she had returned from the phone box and stood in the door to see Andy's hand over April's face, his head bent towards her. As she had cried out, the image had shattered – had rearranged itself in a flash. And since then she had woken to it, frantically reaching to hold it still, but it crumbled and fell away too soon.

That first week at the park a man had sat down beside her on the wall as she watched the empty swings gently twisting in the wind. He was nice enough. He introduced himself immediately as a reporter from the local town. He wanted her story. The story of a watchful mother rising from adversity, and heroic father. She had steeled herself. And she began. She hadn't been proud to sit there and say she had been at work. She did it. Strangely, once she started, she couldn't stop, even when he seemed to reconsider when she talked about giving up the booze. She told him about that picture in her mind, when she had first walked into the room. And he asked for some detail. Well, the image of two empty glasses. And when she returned, there was only one. Of course, she was imagining the second glass, as Eunice, the Reverend's sister, had said when she told her, that second glass represented the guilt that April, her child, was learning from her. When he had finished his questions, the reporter stood up and shook her hand. He said he would be talking to a few other people in the village. He asked how he might contact her again if he needed to.

The following day, Jasper came to visit in his capacity as the family lawyer and told her he'd spoken to the reporter and made it clear that now that April was expected to survive, he felt the story was of limited public interest. Jasper advised that things had become too complex for simple minded newspaper stories, eager to invite speculation. He was anxious that Andy's probation was not affected. He asked when she expected Andy to return. He needed a final signature regarding April's inheritance as sole benefactor of Harold Gardner's estate. She looked shocked. It had been an unusual turn of events, he said, but not to worry. Andy had taken care of things. He'd wanted to protect Hope from, in the light of events, from what was, at the least, a distressing questionable generosity. Hope had sensed Jasper's impatience with any questions she had. These are things she needed to discuss with her husband he said firmly. He had found Andy exemplary, with her support of course, as to how a family could turn its life around with support from the community: and she couldn't deny that it gave her a sense of pride to hear Jasper, of all people, say this.

When Andy returned, he had no time for her questions either. It was though, he added, the least that they should expect, for all the bloody suffering that old bloke had caused this family. Of course, he'd been surprised. He'd needed to take advice from Jasper about the legal aspects of this legacy. It seemed it wasn't insubstantial. He'd also been worried for Hope. She'd needed a chance to sort out her mind with so much going on. Jasper was right. At some points it was hard to believe he was the same man. And, she agreed, it made sense that if April did recover properly, they shouldn't speak about what had happened, or the inheritance with her, not straight away. Jasper would see what could be done. For everyone's sake, leave the past where it belonged.

But the past has a way of returning, and not always for the bad. One cold December morning when she's just got back from taking the twins to nursery, Hope answered a knock on the door. Her heart had momentarily sunk when she caught sight of a man in a smart blue suit and short hair. It took a moment, but, as he stood there smiling in his suit and wire rimmed glasses, she saw it was Eli, with a Christmas Tree leaning against the wall of the porch. "It's good to see you Hope."

"Bloody Hell - Eli. What are you doing here?" It was good to see him too.

She had thought of him when she watched some bit of news or interview about the moon, something of dark and empty spaces. The bloody unthinkable distance spoken about by news reporters between the earth and the moon. It had all seemed unreal back then, those astronauts in such emptiness. And that one, the one that had stayed in the rocket, unreachable on the far side of the moon. She had found herself caught up in that, fearful of his disappearance, not returning. Lost to the world. Untethered. But where? When they had regained radio contact with him, she found herself crying. Now she understood.

And she remembered Eli telling of the journey across the Atlantic through the moonlight and sunrise and how he 'saw the magic of England loom into view like an emerald in the crown of a diamond encrusted ocean'. April had been open mouthed in wonder. Hope had laughed at the time. The sea holds the memories of all that ever was, he'd said. It returns to the sky, and it always finds its way back to the beginning. Idiot. Yet, now here he was.

"You've come back to see your Mum then?" She reddened, wondering what he knew. How far had it spread, with recognisable names and details that could bring him to her door, certain enough to bring a Christmas tree. But she couldn't deny the warmth she felt inside to see a friend. "How did you know where to find us?"

"Well - yes, her too. But, finding you was down to April, Bazooka Joe, and the persistent Miss Gomer, who tracked me down at work asking for a favour from my friend, April, and for me to arrange a special delivery to her shop. The number for the shop was on her letterhead, and so I called her. She told me about April was very unwell. In the circumstances, this was a delivery I wanted to make myself. Oh, and Santa asked if I might drop these by," and he handed her the bag of presents, "For the kids. And you're right, I had some unfinished business. How are you? Are you going to invite me in?"

"Of course," and as he stepped into the room, she felt lost again - they struggled to locate each other in this unknown world, until she remembered the Christmas tree and they brought it in. Layer by layer the branches sprung open as she cut the strings. They quickly reached a pause where she could no longer talk without addressing the 'developments' as he had referred to it, and 'was her husband still away?' And before she knew it tears rolled down her cheeks, and he reached across the table and held her hand.

"What did she say? About April."

"To ask you. But I got some details from my… where I'm staying in the village. I understood it was a close call for April. Lucky he was there."

Of course. His mother lived somewhere hereabouts, a Godfearing woman, much like her own. Then she felt her words falling forward. Her words, sensing a soft landing, sensing a hearing. Words that she had been forming, defending through the weeks.

"He's not the hero I dreamed of, but look, he's a good man for all that. He saved her Eli. Saved me. He may not be her father, but he gave life to her when she needed it. I have his boys. They look up to him. Boys need a father they look up to. She will too."

"Hope – it's alright, he's doing a good job by all accounts. And so are you."

"So why did she do it Eli? There's been some – bad business. But we'd got through that." He squeezed her hand.

"You don't have to say anything Hope. I know. I can't imagine…"

"It's okay Eli. I mean, I don't want to talk about … that… but since that night, something feels different. I don't bloody understand it myself Eli, but he feels … dead to me. In that very moment I saw when he had found her breath and kept it going. Brought back her life… I saw other things too. When I walk, I lose myself a bit you know, like after a few drinks, and imagine something more like … he's not saving her at all. You know, the opposite. How ungrateful is that. I need to be thankful. Thankful is a feeling on that I can build on. I am building on." She got up and went to put the kettle on. A habit she'd trained herself into instead of going for the sherry every time she felt in need of a drink.

"You've been through a lot. You're probably just feeling misplaced guilt."

"Funny, Eunice said something like that. The local Reverend's sister."

"She did?"

"Probably right, I've got a lot to feel guilty about. You know I watch her face now she sleeps. And for the first time… Now the cares of the world have fallen from her face. I think it's probably the first time I can see she's just a kid. I don't think I've let myself see the kid in her. I just saw punishment for my sins. Good for the likes of you that indulged her. I'm thankful for that."

"You weren't as bad as you think. She adores you."

"Sorry, but thanks. I feel alright to say it with you. A cup of tea?"

"That would be great. I'm beginning to like tea – a lot." He laughed. "My English roots are taking hold."

"Oh yes! So, where are you staying? I presume it's not with your mother."

He paused for a moment, "At the Rectory actually, with the Fishers. They've put me up – it was through the church."

"They've got the room. That's a lovely place. He's alright. She can be a bit uptight, but she's not like that when you get to know her. She's been a rock."

"That so good to hear. I've found that too."

Chapter 34

When he'd received the letter, Eli had laughed at April's ingenuity. Letters addressed to NASA arrived from children, and even adults, all over the world. Usually, they were addressed to Neil Armstrong or Buzz Aldrin, so when he was called to the post room to verify receipt of a small package from the England he was met with a few raised eyebrows and a fair amount of ribbing. Although he'd thought of his mother every day since his return, he'd tried to accept that although as she said, she was happy to have met him, he understood that his contact was a difficulty in her life. He froze when he recognised the sender's address immediately as in his mother's village. When he cautiously opened it to find bundles of Bazooka comics and a note from April all that he held inside tuned into laughter. A note on headed paper from the shopkeeper clarified that Hope and her family lived in the village.

When he went to send for the prizes, the address for exchange of the comics was actually in the UK. He'd called the shop and spoke to a Miss Gomer to explain. It wasn't the best line, and she was so measured and calm in her manner that it was hard for him to believe that she was saying that since April was in hospital in a coma. The cause wasn't clear. He'd had to ask her to repeat it several times. She'd advised that he send them back to the shop at this time, as her parents were in great distress. April's future was uncertain. She didn't feel at liberty to give out the family address. She'd suggested he might call the Rectory and Reverend Fisher, or his sister Eunice, who were working closely with the family, and she gave him their number.

He'd practiced an English accent in case the Reverend answered the phone. When he got through and the Reverend answered, Eli had redialled so many times to a busy line, he forgot himself and asked for Eunice in his own voice. 'Is that Elijah?' came the reply. Friendly and warm enough. He could only say yes. And so, she had told her family. He had been acknowledged. And before he could think or could say anything his mother was on the line, and when she confirmed with details of April. He asked her what he could do. Come home she said, come home. And he could hear from the break in her voice through the static on the line, that she'd found a way out.

It had taken a few days after he'd arrived before he felt he could go and visit Hope. Eunice and Ezekiel, as they asked to be called, were with him almost every minute of the day. They had talked a lot, around things, and he sensed there was more to come, but he was keen to talk about April, how was she? That was for Hope to say they'd said. But what surprised him most was Eunice's confession of her jealousy of April. She told him of April's presentation of the map. How she spoke of such pride of Eli's work. His friendship. How she had perceived April as taunting and testing her. How she had come to realise her selfishness, her pride in not taking the opportunity that he, Elijah, had offered for reconciliation. She must pray for courage to explain herself further, but for now, he should know that she was thankful that April, through God's will, had brought him back to her. A second chance. She requested one thing. That he should not share that she was his mother outside the family. Not yet. And one other thing. She was a foundling. Left outside the church the day of Ezekiel's birth, and his mother's death, his father had raised her as his own. It was complicated.

Eli was still working through what might constitute complications in his mother's life when he found himself face to face with Hope. He had always thought of the Smarts as he had found them, set against the elements, as he had been. In that small magical box, which folded into and out of itself to what was needed, and she the bird that sprung up and made the music. In the cocoon of that valley which he had dreamt of so often since he'd left. What had been so at odds with his world had rooted itself deeply into the crevices of his reasoning, drawing from hidden streams as its softness crept towards the light. If he had found himself trying to navigate undercurrents with Eunice and Eli, with Hope he sensed riptides along the line of their conversation, and suddenly found himself pulled far out at sea. But she was also in need of some help decorating April's room, preparing for her return, and he was happy to clamber aboard a task.

For all his thoughts this past year, he was not prepared for the feeling when he pushed back the door. He put down the pail of soapy water and the handle fell to the rim with a chime. The map he had given her was hooked by a wire coat hanger to the sill of a high window. Above it, a pathway wound its way to the window through a landscape of stones, twigs bound with coloured wools into bundles or structures to the clouds drifting through the cold blue sky.

Below, near the foot of the bed on a set of drawers a partitioned vegetable crate served as a bookcase. He lifted the crate to the windowsill so they could begin to move the furniture out and make space to work. The crate caught the hanger which fell from the ledge, but the hook of the hanger had caught in a hole in the plaster. As he went to put it back, he saw there was a string, which he pulled – and up came a small notebook. He'd recognise that writing anywhere. He put his fingers into the gap as far as they would go, behind the strips of wooden lath it was crammed with papers. He heard Hope on the stairs. As he pulled out those he could reach, he opened them up to the lunar seas and craters mapped to the village. Hope was behind him now, "What's that? Can I see?" He handed her the notebook as he continued to reach for the papers. "Just pull the plaster off," as she sat on the bed, "probably one of her science projects. She'd been keeping that stuff out the way since Eunice told her it was ungodly."

"I know, she told me about that."

"Eunice told you?" Hope looked up. Eli stopped, and shrugged, "I guess she was just trying to figure out answers," and he took out a penknife to score the plaster so he could pull it away as neatly as possible. Hope had begun to read.

When he pulled away the plaster, he'd had to carefully cut the rotting wooden lath strips to get at what was boxed in against the stones: among the feathers, pencils, marbles, eggshells, dried flowers and leaves, plaited wool bracelets, pebbles with pencilled numbers which he recognised as map co-ordinates, were notes and newspaper cuttings of the moon landing, and predictions and speculations for the future. He began to dust them off and sort them into neat piles, "She'll want these. Have you got something to store these things in?" He turned to Hope. She was still reading. She was pale and focussed. But an inner turmoil broke out through the surface through her fingers, flicking pages back and forth. "Are you OK?" she didn't reply. "Hey – I didn't think. This is hard right now." And he sat beside her. She continued, and he waited, until they heard someone open the front door, now making their way upstairs.

"Andy!" she said sharply, in a way that seemed to invoke a defensive curiosity in him, and he glared at Eli.

"What's going on here?" it was said to be a friendly comment, Eli could sense that, but it was also intended to be unsettling.

"This is Eli. He's staying with the Fishers. He's come to help. We'll go down for a chat." She took the notebook with her, and ushered Andy downstairs, who turned and gave Eli a strangely conspiratorial look, "Thanks mate."

The chat was very brief, given that she said he'd been away for a few weeks this time, but he figured they were familiar with time apart. Ezekiel had said Andy wasn't workshy, and supported his family the best way he could. All the same, although he couldn't hear most of what was said, the tone was furious and terse between them. It was silent for a moment. Then Andy came upstairs, along the corridor – and went back down again after five minutes dragging what he presumed was a suitcase. There were a few more exchanges, until he heard Hope say with a performative sarcasm, "If you come back, I'll make sure they know."

"Is that right?" and he laughed. " We'll talk about it when I get back." And the door slammed. Eli set about washing the walls ready for painting.

Half an hour later, Hope returned with a box for what they'd retrieved from the wall and went through them herself before placing them carefully inside. She was tender, touching and holding each precious thing, each paper, with a thoughtfulness that should not be interrupted.

It didn't take long to paint the first coat of the primrose yellow that Hope had chosen, and he offered to repair the plaster and do a second coat in the next few days. She had to go and pick up the twins from school. He offered to walk with her. It would be nice to see them. She didn't think it was a good idea right now. She just needed to clear her head.

"Is everything OK Hope? It's a difficult time. If I can - "

"No! It's fine Eli. It was just a girl's diary. Girls' secrets." And then she grasped his arm, "but you could come to the hospital with me. He'll be gone for a long while now – work – and they said it might help to hear people who made her happy." He was glad she'd said that, because Eunice had suggested the same.

Chapter 35

I'm lying in the bath with my head under the water. Mum's talking to me – no – she's with someone else. Wah wang woo. Bee bop boo. Crash bang trays, ting cling clang in the cutlery trays in the dinner hall. My skin squeaks on the side as I turn – mi mi mi – then the water growls like fart bubbles breaking through the surface of water. She's going to tell me off. I mustn't do farting in the bath. Beep. Beep. It sounds like space. Beep Beep. On the Radio. Like with Genesis on Christmas Eve. In the beginning was the word, and the word was … An introduction to a story. I think she's watching a film. She's watching a film. Cowboys. Dun duh duh dun da - a shadow of warm rests into my shoulder. "How long do they think before she wakes up?" And an ache I didn't know, the bath water explodes and sizzles and spits off the iron fire grate. It's Eli. It's Eli.

It's Eli. I am awake Eli. It's me. I'm here Eli. My tongue clicks, breaks away from the roof of my mouth, crashes noisy on my bones. I reach for his sound in the tanglement. The picture of him. And his hand rests on me. I can't move. I imagine I'm a magnet. To him. Sticking to him. "They don't know," says Mum, "They just don't know. Could be anytime. They don't know. Maybe it's never. I've heard stories."

"Was it an accident? How would she not know?"

"Know what?" I say as loud as I can, but no one hears. Maybe I fell off the moon. I am reaching, but my hand is stuck in a porridge of cold sticky stars. Mum begins to cry like in real misery.

"Oh Hope." he says. And I hear her coat rustle and crush as he hugs her. She cries even more. "It's going to be okay," he says. And I feel my nail scratch against something, feel the slow rumble over my stomach. The princess slept for a hundred years. Mum cracks a corona bottle on the edge of the bin and turns with a handful of jagged knives. A hundred years. There's a rumbling. A roll of land comes up over the horizon. As it slowly squashes and gather the hills and trees to itself, it gets high as the sun and darkens the way across the meadow. The old tin Tabernacle holds it back, but you can hear the strain of it stretching the walls. Wailing. Wailing until I fall into the dark.

After that, Eli comes here with Mum more times. I hear his feet stick squeak like the teacher in the school corridor, following mum's click stick heels - and then he shuffles ahead and stops as he opens a door into here and waits for mum to walk through, and he closes it. He sits by her side near me, and they talk. Sometimes their voices just disappear. Like when you turn the on and off knob on the radio. It's silent. Like space. With the beep of the rocket, measuring space. But then there's a jumble of voices. They are still there. Back now. The stone I gave Eli – he keeps in his pocket. He says there wasn't an inch of room on the rocket. He said to Mum, even if they'd asked him for it, he would have said no. It was precious to him. From my hand it was the heart of the moon. Treasure in the Kingdom of Ends. The nurse came in. Stable. Mission Control we have lift off. Are you receiving me?

She said talking is a good idea. Talk about happy memories. When I was happy. The mind was a mystery. Talk like I am awake and in a chat. Mum said it's hard to put words in my mouth. I do answer, but they don't hear. And I forget the words that come from their mouths. But it is love. Sometimes when they are talking it is like the sound of rain, pit pat pit pat pit pit pata. And then me and Eli are on the track. It's been raining and we are splashing through the skyroads, running Splish to Splash down to the docks and back again. Oh Eli, we are flying with the dragons and ships, our coats like sails across the clouds.

One day I hear his feet along the corridor, stick squeak stick squeak stick squeak. But instead of Mum, click stick click stick click stick, it's slower stick ripping stick ripping stick ripping, tearing the ground away. And as the door opens, whoosh, the perfume of flowers. It's Miss Fisher. Eli gets her a chair, the same, and she says, "Thank you Elijah." Eli, it's not Elijah. How can she call him that. I never heard him say that. Not ever. I feel her cold fingers on my head making a cross. "God. Almighty God. Do not forsake your children. Open the doors to your Kingdom." Her voice was trembly and important.

"Eunice. Stop. We don't know -"

"I have my faith. It's all I have to give."

"Faith is good, but it's just an aspect of you."

"Your father used to say that. Look at you now Elijah. A testimony to my faith." And I feel it. Them looking at each other. And now I know. Miss Fisher is Eli's mum. Miss Fisher!

I swoosh back into space. Beep Beep. Through the clouds I zoom into Sunday School. My dress. Miss Fisher holding her elbow to stroke her neck. I can see her, my talk about the moon. Talking about my friend Eli. She's Eli's mum. He got sacrificed for God.

And he came to find her, and she didn't even let him come to her house and he had to stay with us. And I never heard him say about God, but just about all the ideas about thinking, and the moon, and space. And Miss Fisher doesn't like it about space because it gets in God's world, and he wasn't in the pictures. And I look round in space now. It is peaceful. Just beep - beep - beep - beep. And I lie still on top of a cloud and watch a star far, far away.

A warm hand is holding mine, and it takes it to their other hand. It moves the tips of my fingers to touch their fingers, a finger, down from the nail, over the a bony knuckle to a big square front with little ridges – and I know! It's a ring. "I hope you don't mind April." It's Katy. "I had to put in on. Make the club official. I've brought yours too." And she slips it over my finger. It's too big. She pinches it to fit around my finger. "Now. I'll make sure the nurse knows, not to lose it." She begins to cry, "Oh my dear, we thought we were going to lose you. It's so hard to believe what they are saying... that Harold ... played ... any part. I pray for understanding, every day."

I can feel the sun hard on my face. I want to turn away, open my eyes and see what is in the day. In this place. My body won't do it. I can feel my mind tell my body no. Not now. I don't know why. Right down to my guts, my toes, all my hair says no. Something is too big. Like a rock. Holds me there.

The Doctors came in with a nurse to check my notes. "All functions are good." Like a rocket. "The signs are good in the vitals and blood." Take off. "We can't be sure until she is awake. Test her skills and reflexes." Landing we have landing. "Before we allow interviews, test for memory and Mental defectiveness, given family history." One small step for man. "In the light of events – Police have asked that we do a more thorough examination for their report... requested by family representatives. An easier task at this stage. Nurse, if you could prepare a speculum for one of the doctors here?" One Giant leap for mankind. A speculate. What is a speculate? Gold mines in Cowboy land. What are they going to do? I want to ask the nurse when they've gone. My mouth, my eyes, my hands and feet, none of them will do what I say. I can feel her wiping my face, cooling my face from the sun. Squeezing water into my lips. My tongue is flooded. I feel the dribbles run to the back of my neck. I feel her arm under my knees, pull them up, and push apart. Beep – beep. Beep – beep. My heart is wretching. Beep – beep. One giant leap and here I am, on the edge of the crater, watching all the stars crickle-crackle with the Toffee Man. Crickle crackle crickle crackle. Sleepy.

Tick tock.
Tick tock.
Tick tock.

"Rev – Ezekiel. You're a man of God. You've seen repentance of the dying. To leave everything you own to your victim, a child. It is atonement!" He's nearly shouting. I can feel the spit of Sally's dad on my arms.

"I see that Jasper. There was much gossip about that man, but nothing that pointed to anything like - this. She showed no fear of him."

"Fear can hide in the subconscious, where only God can see. She took all those pills Ezekiel. Her father saved her."

"She's not saved yet Jasper. We can only pray." And I hear the scrape of a chair by my side, and a warm breath of a sigh across my arm as he sits. Jasper walks away, and I hear the squeal of his shoes as he turns.

"We have to account for her nature Ezekiel. The alcohol – Hope … Remember this 'child' readily befriended your guest… who was drawn to return across the Atlantic. I'm just saying -"

"Enough! I know exactly what you're 'saying', Jasper." It was silence. Like after a gunshot from the Sherrif.

"You see the best in us all." Sally's dad sounds small. I feel a brush of wind carrying sounds from the distance. "Give me a moment Ezekiel. I just need to check the paperwork for the report with the hospital, and I'll join you." And it's silent again. Just Reverend Fisher's breathing.

I feel it. He is trying to hear me. He is trying to breath like me. To be like me. To be in my mind. He lays his fingers on my wrist. Like the nurse. He is feeling my heart. I listen for him. His breath. And I think of his breath. To breathe like him. In the silence I hear his heart. And we make it the same. It's like speaking together in our minds. And I say in my heart you are right. You are right. He was my friend. He came to be with me on the moon when there was no one else there. He brought his friend. He sat with me and watched until I could come home. I can't get in. "T… T… T…" I feel it soft on my teeth – I hear a sound in my head. I'm making a feeling in my face. "T – T – T – T -"

"T – T – T … April? I can hear you. If you can hear me, repeat it." And I can't stop. It's slow. But it keeps coming. "April. I'm going to call the nurse. Don't stop." I hear him walk and pull the door, and he calls, "Nurse. Could somebody come please?" And I hear the quick march of the nurse."

"Listen," he says. "Listen." And I feel the warmth of them leaning towards me.

"Don't raise your hopes. They often have these involuntary responses. I think she's thirsty." And she squeezes the wet sponge to my mouth again.

When Jasper comes back, the nurse is writing about the beeps. She is telling Reverend Fisher about how my breathing and heart are normal. Not to worry. And then she leaves, and they pray for me. Reverend Fisher isn't listening.

They pray for God to look after my soul and bring me safely home.

Chapter 36

Hope watched as April sought out and dead headed the flowers of summer. It would bring more flowers April said. She didn't say much nowadays. Give her time they said. It reminded her of her own mother. She'd always thought it was the most boring thing ever and had almost disliked her mother for finding some pleasure in it. She had enjoyed the random drifts of thistles, nettles on the meadows and banks that blossomed with absolutely no thought or work at all. That was nature. What grew and survived. When her mother had caught the train down for a few days, Reverend Fisher had picked her up from the station and arrived to find the ordered garden. Hope knew that her mother saw all that she hoped for, as she watched April and her mother work silently in the garden with a sense of sorrow. The shadow of that dislike was still there, streaked through with both pride, and jealousy. She was glad to see her go.

She'd had to tell April that she'd found her notebook, and her pictures, that she knew the truth about The Toffee Man. She'd put the picture of him in the box too. She'd been keeping it, trying to think of some ritual that would ensure relentless torment in hell. She didn't tell her that. She told her she'd told Andy, and she'd told him he could never come back. Believe her. He was never coming back. But she hadn't been quite so honest with April about the legacy. She'd said it had been left to the family. Jasper had advised them that it might be the best way to manage it until she became of age. There'd been more than enough money to modernise the place, put in some electricity and heating, to make it into the home they all needed. Once they had completed the attic conversion, everyone would have a room of their own. As one of the trustees this was something that Jasper felt would be valuable to enable her parents to provide the benefits that Harold Gardner had bequeathed April. Of course, Jasper didn't know the truth. So, it was difficult when he intimated that it might be damaging for April to feel that her home was the wages of sin rather than recompense for her whole family that had suffered the consequence. He was aware of the strain that had been put upon the marriage. Oh, was he?

She watched April come through the door and was reminded how tall she'd become over this year. Still a child though. She asked less questions nowadays. Watched more. She was more childlike in some ways; ready to cling on to her for too long, talk about her times here with the Toffee Man. She rambled about books, about people and places that didn't exist, with problems that never happened. It sometimes came as a relief when she just read. And now, as she came in to grab her coat and reminded her that she was going to go to the cinema with Eli, she felt she could breathe. Liz had taken her mother back to the train station yesterday afternoon, and the boys were at the church hall club. It was a relief to close the door and be left alone without the weight of expectation these new circumstances had put on her. She was tired now.

When she hears the footsteps up the path, she moves out of sight of the window, waiting for a knock that will give up and go away. But a key turns in the lock. Her heart pounds. Who would have a key? She hears a bag slump in the hall. She draws herself back into the space at the side of the shelves.

"Anyone home?" comes the voice. A voice she knows all too well. Andy.

"What you doing here? How did you get in?"

"The key darlin. It's my home too."

"It's not your home. I told you. Where did you get that key?"

"Jasper. Kept it for me, while I've been working. We needed a break – right!"

"It doesn't change what happened. She'll tell them."

"Will she? You need help. My boys have a right to a father."

"Don't bloody try me. You know what I'll do."

"Oh yeah. The notes, the stories. I think they'll see the disturbed mind of a child, overdosing as she copes with her mother's drinking."

"It's different now."

"Is it? Jasper says Liz is keeping an eye on you."

"She's a friend. And Jasper's looking out for us on all the legal stuff. I'll tell him." Andy laughs right at her.

"A friend? He's a paid friend. Oh, and that reminds me –I'm a trustee of this. He was bound to consult me first, legally, as the man of the house," he waves his hand across the room, and takes her hand and pulls her to an armchair, "looking after April's and my family's interests. His reputation too." He cups her face firmly in his hands and pulls her close. She feels no tenderness, but the ache for familiarity releases tensions that flood her body and mind. She falls into a warmth of him, to a time when they were just beginning. "Now, I want us to work together to make this family work, Live up to this reputation I've made. Be a good father to my boys. You can't take them from me Hope. Put the past behind us. Can you do that Hope?" And now he's reminded her, there is a past. She sits back from him, making space, to see all that had happened in the last months. How is she here? It had seemed so simple. It had been wrong. So wrong. She pulls herself up. Tries to be calm. Not shout. Make the tea.

"It's not just me though, is it? I've only just got her back Andy. She needs me."

"I know. And that's why she'll understand." And he stood up again now and walked towards her.

'Understand?' She couldn't tell. He was smiling. Took her hand and led her back to a chair at the table and sat down beside her. He pressed her hands to the table.

"How difficult things could be if we don't pull together on this. You know what people can be like. She'll want to make things easy for you."

"Do you honestly think after what you did I'll even want to make things easy for you? Who do you think I am?"

"You're a realist. Don't think she was all innocence. She didn't make it difficult. She played her part. You told me how you used to flirt at her age."

"That didn't mean -"   He got up, looming beside her.

"Oh, come off it." He was pacing back and forth behind her now, and she could feel the air in her lungs growing thick and hot with fear.

"And she hasn't done so badly. Look, it was a difficult time for us. Difficult years. But we've got a chance now. A chance to put things right."

"It couldn't carry on though."

"It won't. It was a mistake Hope. A stupid mistake. I just saw you when you were well." And when he pulls her up and kisses her, her arms hang limply by her side, she can't push away. "We're going to make it all right." And then she held him to her.

"So, let's get rid of all those notes and 'letters to God'. We can't leave them lying around." And she didn't say. She didn't say that April had hidden them all carefully, in order in a bundle and hid them in the house. In some secret place under a floorboard or panel. Hope hadn't asked. April said it wasn't all about the bad stuff, some of it were about the good things she didn't want to forget. It was all mixed up.

"Oh, you know what she's like. She burnt them all. You don't need to worry about that." It was the least she could do she thought, the best thing to protect April, and herself. She followed as he pulled her into the hall, and up the stairs.

"We need to try out our new room." And he laughed.

Chapter 37

We will go to the cinema. After. I wasn't lying. But first, me and Eli are going to the Tabernacle, The Kingdom of Ends. I brought my secret letters with me. I want to put them somewhere safe in there. Mum said it would be better for us if I didn't show anyone else. It would make things complicated. I didn't know what to say. I had to trust her. Dad's never coming back. She promised. She knows The Toffee Man was a good man. And that's what matters. She will keep me safe. We have to make the most of what we got. Our lives were turned around now. That's what he wanted.

It's good being on the bus with Eli. People think he's my Dad. It felt like he was when he touched my back to balance me as I walked up the steps onto the bus with my box, but when we are talking, he's my friend, or my big brother, or if Mum had a brother. We sat right at the back, so we had more time to look behind as we passed down the hill and along the valley. I think about when we came up this road when it was cold and snowy, and I didn't know this world yet, and I didn't know if I would see Eli again. Now Eli says he's going to see if he can get a job in our country and live here.

When we get off at the bus stop, I can see the bridge across the river by our old field. It looks tiny. Like my giant foot will just fit into the walls on each side. From here it's a patchwork spread of greens. But as we walk down it's like we get swallowed into it and we become small. From the bridge, the hedges along the track are so high that you can only see into to our field over the top of the gate that has a no trespassing sign in red. I run across just to stick my head over. The grass is tall and beautiful except for the bare patches of the hardstands. And so many of the dying trees along the paths have been cut down now. It's strange to see the empty space where we lived, and the toilet block is still there like a little house now.

I turn to look at the Kingdom of Ends, and Eli is already trying to clear the fence by the vestry. I watch as he rips away the white trumpets of the bindweed. I learned in the village they are weeds, and they are not good to have in gardens, but they belong here. I hear them sing into the shadows. I run and take Eli's hand, and I say we can walk to the old port and walk along the river path. We can get in that way. And I must be crying because he looks at me and wipes my face.

On the buildings, there are noticeboards everywhere that say 'Danger' 'Private' 'Trespassers will be Prosecuted'. Once we are on the river path, we can see across the meadow again, all the way along to the vestry door. It's locked, but Eli finds the key just where he left it. We stood in the door when Eli opened it, and he just looked and squeezed my shoulder. 'Not a soul has been here since I left by the looks of it,' and he ducks the cobwebs as he walks over to the desk and pulls out the chair to sit down. I go to the door in the other corner, that opens into my place.

And as I walk in it is light, and light and light. And it feels like my heart will float away through all the coloured shapes of the big window like a rainbow, fingers of colour crossing with colours from the side window. The sun must be shining over the corner now. The holes in the roof are still fixed from Eli when we were here, and the smell isn't damp or rotten – it's the smell of old paper. As I climb through the piles the dust clouds rise from my feet, up through the fingers of blue and green. And my cubby is still there, and my books. And the numbers for Kant's Crater is still on the hymn board. "April." It's Eli calling me, "Can I come up?" He's looking at the Wilson's map of the moon on the wall. I nod, and he comes to sit on the step of my cubby, next to where I put the box down, and he pokes his head in. "How you doing in there?" And it feels like the biggest question I was ever asked, because he really wants to know. He sits on the step of the opening. "You don't need to talk to me about anything you don't want to. You must have been so afraid. The Reverend said you'd given him the hand of friendship. He wasn't well April." He meant The Toffee Man.

"I thought Mum told you. He was a good man Eli. He didn't do nothing. I thought Mum said to you." And he was trying not to be surprised at what I said.

"I know you cared about him April. That's difficult."

"Trust me Eli. He didn't do nothing. He was my friend. Like you." And I reached out and got my box. I got the picture out and showed him. Harold and Joe when they were young. And Eli looked at it for a long time. He handed it back to me. "She knows? Hope knows?" I don't want him to think less of Mum for not telling him.

"Mum said I didn't have to talk about it until I wanted too. She said our secrets are ours to tell." And I know he knows that is true, because he has a secret with his mum as well. I won't tell him I know. I can feel he is simply sad. I go red.

So, we sit in the silence on the step of my old den. Thinking. Across from us, above the big door is the sign I made 'The Kingdom of Ends'. Until Eli says, "You remember when we talked about how The Kingdom of Ends was like a place where everybody mattered, each person had to be treated with respect – and everyone had to return that? Not to use them just to get what you want."

"I think so. I don't think I really knew what it meant."

"Well it's also about sharing the truth when you need to. When someone has to make an important decision that affects their lives, or the lives of those they care about."

"But what if you promised?" And I am thinking about how bad it is that someone who didn't even know the Toffee Man thinks that he is a bad man, even now he is dead. And everyone will believe it.

"It's more complicated as you get older April. A promise cuts both ways. You make that promise because they told you certain things they said and promised were true? If you find out they lied, it will make you sad, it might make them sad they let you down, and they might have made a difficult choice, but it means that what made you happy to share that promise is broken. It's important we make decisions when we know what is true. Listen to me. I sound like my Dad.''

"So, in the Kingdom of Ends, everyone must say what is true so things can work out? Like in books." I have to make it so people in the future know the truth. Like in the Secret Garden. Only now I've promised Mum. I made the decision. "Eli, I have to hide this box here. And it says about the real person. But I promised Mum. It's our secret. But if anything changes. I will think about a new promise. But you have to promise me that you won't come and open this box before that unless I come with you, or I disappear? I want to make the Kingdom of Ends. I just made a promise."

"April. Sometimes people get you to make promises to keep them out of trouble. Not because they are thinking of you, or anyone else."

"You have to promise me. Trust me Eli. I think it is to look after me and other people." Eli let out a big puff of air, and I know he doesn't think I've got it right.

"You said it's complicated. What about you? You never said about your mum yet?" And I didn't want to say that. And it came out all wrong.

"Well – I don't think it affects anyone's life who my mum is."

"You don't know that!" And I shouted, although I didn't mean to and it went right up to the roof and around the walls. He stopped. He took off his glasses and was cleaning them with his shirt, while he was concentrating. He looked round like he was looking for holes to fix.

"You're right. You're right about that. But you're still … young, April. This world doesn't allow you the rights you need to protect yourself… if … if those that need to can't."

"If you say anything to anyone Eli, unless I say it's OK, I'll say you got it wrong. If the promise gets broken – I will tell you or Reverend Fisher who it is." And Eli came close to look at my face, and he put his hands on my ears, and he hugged me to him. I heard his heart beating.

"April. You don't know how hard this is." And I look back up at him and a tear from him falls on my cheek. "OK. I won't speak about this again until you tell me to. Anytime. But, how about you give it to me. You go out. I hide it. And I don't go back to it unless you tell me and we go together, and you get the Fishers to call me if I'm not here. That way, I can protect you, a little." So, I do it. I believe him, and I give the box to him. I go outside and stand between the fence and the wall, and I wait in the song of the grass. And I think of the days of being here. When the valley was our Kingdom.

"Well. It's hidden away. I guess we need to get to that cinema. I'm looking forward to that."

"First, I want to do something. See if I can remember the whole thing. I learned it after you went." I take his hand, and lead him into the Kingdom of Ends, right next to my old moon map. Then I climb to the top, where I used to stand and say my words, 'In the beginning God created the heaven and the earth …" and I say it like I'm in space with The Toffee Man, watching the earth. Only now I feel my veins rushing with blood. My heart full of this room, and the moon and space. And I remember the night, and I feel the stars in my body and I dance the words, and all the words that went up into the sky. I remember Eli and Mum laughing and smoking, and the beautiful castles in the air. And I know that Eli keeps my stone in his pocket. It is the key to the castle in the Kingdom of Ends.

www.ingramcontent.com/pod-product-compliance
Ingram Content Group UK Ltd.
Pitfield, Milton Keynes, MK11 3LW, UK
UKHW040732090325
455944UK00004B/172